ALSO BY ADRIANA TRIGIANI

*Big Stone Gap*
*Big Cherry Holler*

# MILK
## GLASS
### MOON

# MILK GLASS MOON

### A BIG STONE GAP NOVEL

## Adriana Trigiani

RANDOM HOUSE

NEW YORK

RANDOM HOUSE and colophon are registered trademarks of Random House, Inc.

Library of Congress Cataloging-in-Publication Data
Trigiani, Adriana.
Milk glass moon: a novel / Adriana Trigiani.
p.   cm.
ISBN 0-375-50618-7
1. Big Stone Gap (Va.)—Fiction. 2. Mothers and daughters—Fiction.
3. Mountain life—Fiction. I. Title.
PS3570.R459 M55 2002
813'.54—dc21    2002017945

Printed in the United States of America on acid-free paper

Random House website address: www.atrandom.com

9 8 7 6 5 4 3 2

First Edition

*Book design by Victoria Wong*

*For my father,*
*Anthony J. Trigiani*

# MILK GLASS MOON

*T*he Wise County Fair is my daughter's favorite event of the year, and I think it's safe to say that includes Christmas. Etta has been on her best behavior for the past two weeks, so perfect down to the smallest detail (including unassigned chores like making *my* bed and weeding *my* garden) that I'm worried.

We have the window flaps of the Jeep down, and the warm August air whipping through is sweet with honeysuckle. Still, it is no match for Iva Lou's perfume, which wafts up to the front seat whenever we peel around a curve. Etta looks out the window for road signs, searching for proof that we're almost there. I've taken the quicker route, the valley road out of Big Stone Gap up to Norton. As we ascend the mountains in twilight, we pass Coeburn nestled in the valley below, where the cluster of lights twinkles like a scoop of emeralds. Etta smoothes her braids and settles back in her seat.

"Here's the plan. First we eat," Iva Lou announces as she unfolds the special to the newspaper. "I myself am having a jumbo caramel apple with nuts, and if I have to go see Doc Guest for a bridge on Monday, then so be it. Them caramel apples are worth a molar."

"I want the blue cotton candy," Etta decides.

"I want a chili dog with onions," I reply.

"I have a lot of money," Etta says proudly as she sifts through her change purse.

"Ask Dad to spring for dinner. That will leave you more money for the games of chance."

Etta smiles and carefully counts her money without lifting it out of the purse. I see a five-dollar bill folded neatly into a small square (some lucky clay-pigeon operator is about to score a windfall).

"What if we can't find him?" she asks.

"We'll find him."

"Just go straight to the outdoor the-a-ter. He's up there with all them men checking out the rehearsal for Miss Lonesome Pine."

"He built the stage," I remind Iva Lou in a tone that says, *Don't start with that again.*

"That's as good a reason as any, then." Iva Lou meets my eye in the rearview mirror and winks.

We find a parking spot under a tree overlooking the fairgrounds and climb out of the Jeep. Iva Lou checks her hair in the driver's side mirror and then smiles at us, ready to go. She's wearing a pair of dark blue denim pedal pushers and a red bandanna-print blouse tied at the waist. Her Diamonelle hoop earrings peek out from under her platinum bob like giant waterwheels. Iva Lou is ageless; you would never know she is fifty-something. Her look, however, is best viewed from a distance, like a fine painting. You don't want to get so close that you get lost in the details.

Etta looks at the fairgrounds with a clinical eye, surveying the faded striped tents surrounded by torches like birthday candles. She smiles when she spots the Ferris wheel. "Ma, will you go on the rides with me?"

"Sure." But Etta knows that at the last second in line, when we're ready to go up the metal plank, I'll send her father with her instead.

"Do we have to go to the beauty pageant?" she asks.

"I thought you liked it."

"I like the dresses all right. The talent's always terrible." Etta shrugs. She's right. Last year, leggy blond Ellen Tierney, representing Big Stone Gap, did a dance routine to "Happy to Keep Your Dinner Warm"; her tap shoe flew off when she did a high kick, clocked a man in the first row, and knocked him out. The victim was rushed to the hospital and revived, but he may have the imprint of the metal tap on his forehead for life. "And I hate the physical-fitness part when they come out and jump around in bathing suits. Anybody can do that stuff."

"Etta, hon, it don't take a lot of talent to look good in a bathing suit. That you're born with." Iva Lou breathes deeply and straightens her shoulders. "I ought to know."

"I'm never gonna be in a beauty pageant," Etta announces.

"Me neither." I give my daughter a quick hug.

The benches in the outdoor theater are filling up fast. The aisles are covered in Astroturf runners; the stage is banked in garlands of red paper roses; the backdrop is a cutout of a giant pine tree with MISS LONESOME PINE written in gold leaf.

School starts in a few weeks. I can't believe Etta is twelve years old and going into the seventh grade. My mother would have been sixty-six this year. I feel oddly lost between them: not old yet, not young anymore. I thought motherhood was a job with security, but it's not. It's the least permanent job in the world, the only job in which your skills become obsolete overnight. It was that way from the beginning. When I finally got a handle on breast-feeding, it was time for solid food. I worried that Etta wasn't turning over in the crib on her own, but soon she was crawling, and then, before I knew it, walking. When she went to school, I thought she'd need me more, but all of a sudden she had a life apart from me and was just fine. And now, after we've established a routine as a family, in which Etta has responsibilities, she's developed a newfound independence and her own opinions. This is, of course, the point of all of it—preparing your children to leave you—yet I'm so afraid to let go. I don't know how I'll handle it when she's eighteen and leaves for college. How did my mother do it? I wish she were here to lead me through these changes.

"Dad!" Etta waves to Jack, who waves back to her from a platform at the side of the stage. He finishes helping the spot operator set the light levels, then climbs down the ladder to join us. My husband is still agile; his strong arms hook down the ladder rhythmically. His jeans are faded to dusty blue, and his white T-shirt frames his gray hair beautifully. Sometimes, when I see him in the distance, I forget he's mine and think, What a fine-looking man. He still makes my heart race—quite a feat after all these years. His straight nose and lips are surrounded not by wrinkles but by expression lines. He's damn cute, my husband. I try not to hate him for aging so well.

Otto Olinger approaches, wiping his face with a bandanna. "We barely got that stage up in time. Ain't that right, Worley?" Otto turns to his son, whose white hair makes him look around the same age as his father.

"It was rough," Worley agrees.

" 'Cause you ain't got your minds on your work. Too busy ogling the girls," Iva Lou tells them.

"We did us some looking." Worley smiles.

Otto shrugs. "Can't hardly help it, they's so purty. Of course, I ain't never seen me no ugly women, just some that's purtier than others."

Jack gives me a kiss and takes Etta's hand. "You want to watch from up there?" he asks her.

"Yeah!"

"We've got a couple of seats down front for you."

I turn to Iva Lou. "Do you want to stay?"

"What do you want to do?"

"I'd rather wander around."

"Let's wander, then." Iva Lou turns to go up the ramp.

"Okay, we'll catch up with you later." Jack Mac takes Etta to the ladder and helps her to the top. She kneels on the platform as her father explains something about the equipment. She listens and nods. I can't believe she's my kid and not afraid of heights. In fact, she's fearless about everything—picking up stray animals, speaking in public, boys. Etta cares about how things work; in that way, she is just like her father. She is all MacChesney, and that's not always easy for me to accept.

"What are we gonna do?" Iva Lou asks.

"We're going to see Sister Claire."

"Who the hell is that? A Catholic?"

"No. She's a fortune-teller."

"No voodoo for me, girlfriend."

"Come on. After she makes you drink a cocktail of eye of newt and puts a spell on you, it's all uphill."

Sister Claire has a small dark green tent by the edge of the grounds. Two folding chairs are set up outside the flap. I'm surprised there isn't a line of people waiting. Sister Claire is well known in these parts; she's from the mountains of North Carolina near Greensboro. A pharmaceutical salesman out of Raleigh who traveled through Big Stone encouraged me to see Sister if she was ever in the area. He told me that she was the genuine article, a true mystic. I'm surprised when a small, gentle woman of sixty, with a heart-shaped face and skin the color of strong tea, emerges from the tent to greet us.

"Are you here to see me?" she asks. "I'm Sister Claire."

Iva Lou turns away and grabs my arm to return to the hub of the fair, where no one knows the future, not even the judges of the Miss Lonesome Pine Contest.

"Yes ma'am. We are." Iva Lou shoots me a look, so I correct myself. "I am," I say earnestly, not knowing exactly how to address a psychic.

"Welcome."

"I think most of the people are at the beauty pageant," I tell her, apologizing for her lack of clientele.

Sister Claire turns to Iva Lou and looks her straight in the eye. "I understand if the idea of a reading makes you uncomfortable. I don't like to have my cards read."

"Really?" Iva Lou squeaks.

"Really. It's a commitment to believe. It takes blind faith. Sometimes not even I have that."

"Well, it's not that I'm scared, and I certainly believe in the comings and goings of the spirit world. It's just that I, well, I live my life a certain way, and I don't want to know where it's all going."

"I understand."

"Wait here, then. Okay?" I give Iva Lou a wink and follow Sister Claire inside. The tent is sparsely furnished with two folding chairs and a small red lacquer table between them. An electric cord attached to a small generator runs up the side of the tent to a low-wattage bulb, which dangles in a protective metal sleeve overhead. Sister Claire motions for me to sit, then pours us each a glass of water. She sits down at the table and rests one hand on a deck of large tarot cards.

"I hear you're a Native American," I say as she shuffles the cards.

"Cherokee. Descendant of the great Chief Doublehead. 'Course, all of us that's Cherokee claim that." She smiles.

"Mother and father both?"

"Yes. But I'm mixed. I also had a grandmother who was African-American and a grandfather who was Irish."

"The green eyes give you away."

"Every time."

"How did you discover your talent for this?"

"It's not so much a talent as a way of being. It tends to run in families. My mother read cards and had visions, and so do I." She stops shuffling the cards and asks me to pick one. "How can I help you?"

I was prepared with an answer—I have lots of questions about the future—but suddenly I can't speak. "I'm sorry."

"Don't be sorry. Let's look at you." Sister Claire shuffles again and places twelve cards on the table, creating a sunburst pattern.

"What is your name?"

"Ave Maria."

"That's unusual."

"Especially in these parts."

"That's the name of the Blessed Mother. You can tell a lot by a person's name."

"What does my name tell you?"

"You're named after a strong woman, some would say a goddess. You've been surrounded by strong women since the day you were born. You're very lucky. You are loved and protected, and I see many women around you, almost making a fence. Your mother passed?"

"Yes."

"She did and she didn't. She's with you always." Sister Claire sits back in the chair and closes her eyes. "She's wearing purple."

"My mother?"

"Yes."

"I buried my mother in a purple suit. She made it herself out of crepe silk she bought on one of her husband Fred Mulligan's buying trips to New York. She told me that, for the longest time, she didn't want to make anything out of the fabric because it was so beautiful she couldn't bear to cut it into pieces."

"Fred Mulligan was not your father."

"No ma'am."

"And it caused you great pain when you learned the truth."

"It did. But in a way, it was also the great blessing of my life. I found my real father in Italy, and my whole family."

Sister Claire leans back and closes her eyes. "Your mother is showing me a house with many rooms. She is hanging curtains in the windows."

"She used to make curtains."

"There's a boy in the room. He just walked in. He has brown eyes and curly brown hair. Who is he?"

"My son."

"He passed?" she asks me quietly.

"Yes ma'am."

"Very young?"

"He was four years old."

Sister Claire laughs. "He's funny. He's happy with her. She is looking out for him." She opens her eyes and looks at me.

Sister Claire goes on to tell me lots of things—about my job, about Jack, about Etta. She sees us traveling together, and she sees Etta taking a new path, which validates my feeling that my daughter is going where she wants to go, with or without my blessing.

"Sister, how does the afterlife work?"

"What do you mean?"

"Will my son always be four years old and my mother the age she was when she died? And when I die . . ."

"What do you think?"

"I thought that they were in a holding pattern, waiting for Judgment Day."

Sister Claire laughs, though I wasn't trying to be funny. "That's a possibility, and it all depends. Your mother and son wanted you to know they're okay, so they came to me in a way you would recognize them. This doesn't happen every time."

"So they are . . . somewhere, right?"

"I like to think the *idea* of them is somewhere, but that their energy is eternal and that it's very possible they'll return to life as different people to learn new things."

"So they could be here?"

"Anywhere."

"Should I be looking for them?"

"You won't have to look for them; they'll find you." Sister Claire shuffles the cards and this time lines them up in a single row. She asks me to pick another from the deck. "Now for your future."

I take a deep breath. "I'm ready."

"You've set many goals for yourself in your lifetime. And you've met most of them. But what I see here is that you have to begin anew. You have to decide where your life is going; you must redream."

"Redream?"

"You have to reinvent your life. You have to think about what you want to accomplish in the second half of your life. Do you understand?"

I nod that I do, but I don't really, or maybe I'm not ready to think about the rest of my life. My present path is so clear—I want to raise my daughter, nurture my husband, and keep working. I don't think much beyond that, though I know it is dangerous not to. "Sister Claire? I never think about what I want anymore, or about what the future holds. I barely have time to get everything done in the present. How do I redream?"

"There are two times a day when the soul is open to new ideas. The first is when you rise, in the stillness of morning. The second is at night, when you're in that hazy place between being awake and going to sleep. At those times, ask your inner voice to guide you. Your intuition will lead to the answers you're looking for."

"My mother used to say that all the answers were inside me."

"She was right. The problem is, we don't trust our inner voice. But that voice will guide us in the right direction every time. It really is the key to happiness: just listen." Sister Claire slides the cards into a single deck once more.

I pay her and quickly review all she said to me. There's so much to think about. I am a little stunned that my mother and son could be looking for me but I might not know them. What good will that do? The smell of Iva Lou's cigarette brings me back. She's sitting on one of the folding chairs outside the tent, puffing away. "All set," I tell her.

"Well, honey-o, since we're here, maybe I'll get a reading too." Iva Lou turns to Sister Claire and points with her pinkie finger. "But I'm warnin' you, Sis, don't tell me when I'm gonna die, even if you know. Okay, I amend that. You can tell me when I'm gonna die if it's at a hundred and one with all my faculties intact and a young man up in the bed next to me who thinks I'm better than pepper jelly."

Sister Claire laughs. "You got a deal."

They go inside the tent, and I can hear the quiet muttering between them. I sit down, stretching my legs and leaning back in the chair. From this angle, I can see the spotlight at the beauty pageant make a tunnel of silver light against the black mountain. It is a smoky beam, barely visible as it competes with the Ferris wheel spinning streaks of pink glitter. The mountains funnel the sound of the applause and the wolf whistles up into the night sky; the way the sound carries in these hills, the pageant could be a thousand miles from here. How easy it is to get lost in the noise of this world, to find yourself leading a life of acceptance and resignation. When will I find the time to question my life again? Is there anything new ahead of me, or is this it? Being a wife, a mother, a pharmacist? What does Sister Claire mean when she tells me I have to invent myself all over again? To be what? And how?

After what seems like a much longer time than my reading took, Iva Lou emerges from the tent, fishing in her purse for another cigarette.

"So?"

"Oh, honey, I've never heard such good news. Sister Claire was chock-full of all kinds of information. I just hope I can remember it all so I can write it down. She said I'm an eagle."

"Is that a good thing?"

"Absolutely. I'm regal and self-possessed and all that. But of course, tell me something I didn't already know for fifteen bucks. How about you?"

"Mama and Joe came to me."

"What did they say?"

"They didn't say anything. But it's okay. They showed up; that's all I needed."

Iva Lou puts her arm around me as we head back into the lights and the noise, but I don't see them or hear it. My mind is in that house with many rooms.

After helping Etta scrub the last of the blue veil of cotton candy off her face, I tuck her into bed. She wants to read one more chapter of *Harriet the Spy*, but she's exhausted, so I convince her to go to sleep. Etta is fascinated with the story of Harriet, an eleven-year-old girl who doesn't play with dolls but has a notebook and goes around the elegant Upper East Side of Manhattan spying on her neighbors and recording their activities. Etta checks it out of the library so often, I wonder if anyone else in her class has read it.

"Mama, someday can we go to New York City?"

"Sure." I look down at my daughter, who is still a girl but is starting to look like a young woman in subtle ways. As I tuck the blanket around her, I know that soon this ritual will end, and that fills me with sadness.

"I think I'd like it."

"The big city? All that noise and confusion?" I kiss Etta and walk to the door.

"It would be fun and different, Ma," she says, rolling onto her side.

I turn the light out. I'm already in the hallway when I hear her voice softly call out to me. "Mama?"

"Yes?" I turn back and lean against the doorframe.

"Am I pretty?"

"Yes, you are."

"How do they decide who's pretty?"

"Who?"

"People. You know, it's like the group knows who's pretty, and then they treat that person like they're the prettiest, and that person always knows it."

"I don't know, Etta. I've never figured it out."

"I mean, sometimes I can see it. But sometimes I don't think the prettiest girl is the pretty one."

"You're pretty," I tell her plainly and sincerely.

"Okay." Etta says this in a tone that says, *You've got to be kidding.* I wait for her to say something else, but she doesn't, so I head downstairs.

Jack is in the kitchen making coffee to have with the cherry pie we bought at the fair.

"That was weird," I say.

"What?"

"Etta asked me if I thought she was pretty. Doesn't she know I think she's pretty?"

"Maybe not."

"Don't I tell her?"

"You tell her she's smart and a good reader, and capable and all that, but you don't heap a lot of compliments on her in other ways," Jack says matter-of-factly.

"God, isn't it more important to be smart?"

"Sure. But she's a girl, Ave."

"I'm well aware she's a girl."

"Well, I've been married to one for thirteen years, and been raising one about that long, and it seems to me that girls can't hear they're pretty often enough, even when they have other things going for them." Jack smiles.

"I'll compliment her more often." I can tell I sound defensive.

"I don't think you're doing anything wrong. I just think Etta's entering a new phase. She's going to be a teenager. Misty Lassiter told them all about sex tonight."

"*What?*"

"Yeah. She decided to drop the bomb."

"Oh God. Where did Misty get her information?"

"She's two years ahead of Etta in school, and you know, she's like *her* mother. Let's say she's slightly advanced."

Misty Lassiter is the daughter of Tayloe Slagle Lassiter, Big Stone Gap's most beautiful homegrown girl. I see Misty when I pick up Etta at school. She's the Willowy One, taller than her classmates, the leader, with blond hair in perfect yellow ropes tied with ribbons that look sophisticated, not cutesy. Back when I directed the Outdoor Drama, I cast Tayloe in the lead when she was just fifteen. She wasn't a great actress, but it didn't matter; you wanted to watch her, her delicate features, long limbs, and those eyes, so clear, blue, and heavy-lidded. She was so beautiful, you thought she knew the secret to something, some ancient truth born in her and obvious in her every movement. Tayloe has taught her daughter well. Misty is every bit as popular and perfect as she was. Quite a feat when you live in a small town, particularly if Bo Lassiter (of the low-forehead Lassiters of East Stone Gap) is your daddy.

"Etta's got so much more going for her than Misty. What did Misty say about sex?"

"Everything." Jack pours our coffee. He sits down and slices the pie with his fork.

"Well, what exactly is everything?"

Jack does his best to do an impression of Misty giving the girls the goods. " 'Now, first, there's a man. And the man has a different part from the woman.' "

"Oh no." I don't want to hear this, but I indicate to Jack that he should continue.

" 'And the man takes his part and lets the woman know he has one. Then she decides if she wants his part or not. Now, if she does, it's called sex. If she doesn't want no part of it, she's a virgin.' "

"Great." I rest my head, which feels like it weighs a hundred pounds, on my hands.

"I thought it was funny."

"Etta told you this?"

"I overheard them when they were waiting for their cotton candy. The line was long."

I wish I had been there. Why was Jack with her when she heard the facts of life the first time, and I was off in a tent getting my cards read? That is not how I planned this. "I am going to talk to Tayloe."

"What for?"

"She needs to tell her daughter not to be scaring the kids."

"Etta's not scared."

"What do you mean she's not scared? Who isn't scared of sex—" I stop myself. Jack looks at me. I open my mouth wide and yet no words come out. Jack is well aware of my so-late-I-almost-missed-it bloom-ing. I honestly thought it didn't matter anymore, but thanks to Misty's sex talk, those old feelings of separation and alienation just went from a trickle to a roaring river within me. Once the town spinster, always the town spinster. "No wonder." I cut another piece of pie.

"No wonder what?"

"She doesn't talk to me about it. She can tell I don't want to talk about it."

"You got that right." My husband looks at me and smiles.

"She should be able to come to me about anything. I just didn't see the signs. She's still coloring with crayons, for Godsakes. This is hap-pening too fast."

"Well, fix it."

"What do you mean?"

"Talk to her." Jack shrugs like it's as simple as teaching her how to play checkers.

I take a long sip of the hot coffee (Jack always puts in just the right amount of cream). Then I slip off my loafers and put my feet in my husband's lap. "I wish she would stay a girl forever."

"That's not an option, honey." Jack squeezes my foot. And he's right. This is like a tire race down Stone Mountain—once you let it loose, it's gone.

———

We're having a sidewalk sale at the Mutual Pharmacy. It isn't a big deal, just a couple of folding tables borrowed from the First Baptist Church and loaded with stuff that hasn't sold—pale orange lipstick, strawberry hand cream, and shoe boxes filled with greeting cards neatly arranged by holiday. We start the sale with everything 50 percent off, but by Friday, we'll be giving the stuff away. Folks know this, so they wait a few days, linger after lunch in the Soda Fountain, and then hit Fleeta up for a freebie. Fleeta, in her smock and tight black leggings, is leaning against the building to light a cigarette. Once it's lit, she stands up straight and lightly touches her blue-black upsweep (she's tried the new Loving Care line that just came in) to make sure it's in place. I wave to her as I pull into my parking spot.

"Pearl's pregnant," Fleeta barks.

Before I can ask her to repeat the news, Pearl comes out to the sidewalk. "Fleeta!"

"I know it's supposed to be a secret, but you know I can't keep one. You shouldn't never have told me," Fleeta says to Pearl, taking a long drag off her cigarette. "Besides, when you upchuck three times in one morning, I ain't gonna be the only one 'round here that's suspicious."

"Is it true?" I ask Pearl, whose smile tells me it is. "How's your husband?"

"Thrilled."

I hug her. "How far along are you?"

"About two months."

"Fantastic."

"I just didn't want to say anything until I knew for sure."

I watch Pearl walk back to the Soda Fountain, and now that I know, I can see the pregnancy. I figured she had put on a couple of pounds, as we all do from time to time, but this is different. Pearl is changing. Her waist is beginning to fill out; she's walking more slowly, feeling the burden of the new weight on her knees. I remember the stages of pregnancy, all right. It's true that the suffering is worth it in the end, but for every moment of those nine months, I felt as though I had rented my body out to a tenant who had no respect for the property. The morning sickness, which is really daylong seasickness, the bloated breasts, swollen ankles, and for me, painful big toes from having to walk in a whole new way—I remember every one of these details as though it were yesterday.

Pearl turns around and says to me, "I'll be counting on you for advice."

"Oh, I have plenty of it."

"What about me?" Fleeta asks. "I done blowed out three babies, and Pavis—he was a back birth—snapped my tailbone like a cracker on his way out. I got me a lot of advice to give, 'specially about the birthing itself."

"I'll need your advice too, Fleets." Pearl goes into the kitchen.

"Pavis really broke your tailbone?"

"Yeah, and that was a goddamn omen. That boy never give me nothin' but trouble and heartache and pain, of both the physical and the mental variety. First he stepped on my tailbone, then on my feet—you know, when he was a-crawlin'—and then when he went to prison, he done stepped on my heart."

"You ever hear from him?" Pavis has been in prison in Kentucky for as long as I can remember.

"When he gets a phone day." Fleeta pulls another box of greeting cards out from under the folding table. "This here sidewalk sale is already a bust," she tells me, sorting through the cards like they're junk.

"You have a bad attitude."

"If it was a good idea, every vendor on the street'd have one. You don't see Mike's Department Store hauling out the Agg-ner leather goods, or Zackie putting out the Wranglers. But we have to make a show peddling crap nobody bought all year." Usually when Fleeta gripes, you can see that she's just having a little fun, but today it sounds entirely serious.

"Is something the matter? You're not your sweet self," I tell her.

"Doc Daugherty told me I have to quit smoking."

"Did he find something?"

"He saw a spot on an X ray, said it weren't nothin' now, but if I didn't quit the smokes, it would turn to the emphysema. And I'm mighty pissed about it."

"Fleeta. It's simple. You have to stop smoking."

"I can't," she says simply and sincerely.

"You have to."

"Don't you understand how bad my mood would be without my smokes? I'd kill three people by breakfast if I couldn't light up."

"You don't know that."

"I don't? Ave, my nerves is so bad that I shake most days. I need 'em, and I told Doc that."

"What did he say?"

"He tole me he understood but he didn't want me gittin' the emphysema neither. He tole me to quit gradual. Keep cuttin' back till I'm down to one a day. One smoke a day. Can you beat that?"

"You can do it. I know you can."

"I'm not gonna be easy to be around," Fleeta promises.

Spec Broadwater, Otto, and Worley are sitting at the counter in the Soda Fountain eating the lunch special: beef stew and biscuits, with a side of fried apples. Spec's cigarette smolders on his saucer. I put out the cigarette on my way to the coffeepot.

"Hey, what'd you do that fer?" Spec bellows. He adjusts the name tag on his pressed khaki shirt. His legs, too long for the stools, are slung to the side like railroad ties. Spec has taken to putting gel in his thick white hair. The sides are so shiny and close to his head that he reminds me of the great George Jones, who is as famous for his coiffure as for his singing.

"You're not supposed to smoke. Remember your bypass?"

"Quintuple. Don't worry, Ave. I'm cutting back."

"While you're cutting back, you need to set an example for Fleeta. She needs to quit."

"Since when is Fleeta Mullins my problem?"

"Since she went to the doctor and he told her to stop smoking."

"Jesus, Ave. I got enough on my plate. Don't make me surgeon general of Wise County on top of everything else." Spec adjusts his glasses and fishes for his pack of cigarettes.

I stop him. "You're in here every day for lunch. She needs your support." I pour myself a cup of coffee and freshen Otto's while I'm at it.

"I can stand up for my own damn self," Fleeta announces from the floor. "I don't need the support of any of y'all."

"Aw, Fleeta, relax."

"Don't tell me what to do, Otto Olinger. Just 'cause you is president of the Where's My Ass Club that convenes up in here every day for lunch don't mean I got to take any bull off of ye."

"What do you mean, Where's My Ass?" Otto asks.

"Look at ye, all y'all. Not a one of ye has an ass. I don't know how your pants stay up."

"It's called a belt, Fleets," Otto says with a chuckle.

"I ain't never gotten a single complaint about my hind end," Spec tells her, sounding hurt.

"Somebody down in Lee County's bein' nice. If old Twyla Johnson was honest . . ."

The mention of Spec's woman on the side down in Lee County sends Otto and Worley into a giggling fit. (I thought Spec had given up his girlfriend, but I guess not.) Fleeta continues, "She'd tell you the truth: it's flat and square. Looks like somebody dropped a TV set down your drawers." Fleeta goes into the kitchen.

"She's on a royal tear," Worley says, shaking his head.

"Jesus, does she have to get personal like 'at?" Spec dumps cream into his coffee.

"It's only gonna get worse, boys," Fleeta bellows from the kitchen.

———

I make a run over to Johnson City to pick up some olive oil Jack ordered. He's become quite the chef, picky about his ingredients and accomplished in his techniques. Sometimes he dreams about opening an Italian restaurant. It never dawns on him that folks around here are not interested in sampling pesto made with fresh basil; they much prefer their own cuisine, biscuits and gravy and name-your-meat chicken-fried. Besides, the Soda Fountain at the Mutual is all the food service I can handle, and it's strictly lunch fare. Pearl and I were surprised when we saw the profit sheets last year. With our local economy struggling as the coal industry dies out mine by mine, it's a good thing Pearl is such a risk taker; the fountain did more business than the pharmacy.

As I cut through Wildcat Holler and head back into Cracker's Neck, I practice my opening to the Sex Talk between Etta and me. There is so much to say on the subject that I wrestle with whether I should begin with the physical and segue into the emotions; or if I should just start out by asking about her feelings and what she knows already; or if I should make it a family meeting and invite her father into the discussion. It bothers me that I want Jack there. This shouldn't be so hard. I want the sort of closeness with my daughter that I had with my mother. She was my protector, and I was her defender. We never talked about sex, but I felt I could surely ask her anything if I wanted to. The truth is, I never felt comfortable asking her about sex, relationships, or intimacy. I knew she was in a less than romantic marriage, and maybe I didn't want to remind her about what she didn't have. I never wanted to make my mother uncomfortable, to say or do anything to cause her pain. Maybe this is the root of my repression—the feelings I could not express. I don't blame my mother for that, though. It was my choice.

As I drive up to our house, negotiating all the pits where the stones have settled on the road, I see Otto and Worley on my roof. Jack used to tackle all home repairs, but the irony of a career in construction is that he no longer has time to fix things around here. (They say, "A shoemaker's child goes barefoot"; well, a construction worker's wife has holes in her roof.) I don't mind it, though. Having Otto and Worley around reminds me of my single days, when they would come to my house down in town and take care of whatever needed fixing without my having to ask. As I jump out of the Jeep, I see a third figure on the roof: my daughter.

"Etta, what are you doing up there?"

"Helping Otto and Worley."

"I want you to go inside."

"Why?"

"Because it's not safe."

"It's safe," Etta says defiantly.

"I got an eye on her, Miss Ave," Worley says without looking up.

"Me too," Otto says to reassure me.

"Go inside anyway, Etta."

Etta looks so small from the ground. As she gingerly crawls across the roof toward the window, it reminds me of when she first learned to crawl, and instead of being thrilled that my baby was learning a new skill, I was terrified that she was beginning to move in the world without me.

"Etta! Watch it!"

The toe of Etta's right shoe gets caught where a shingle has not been bolted. She tries to pry the shoe free, but she is on all fours and cannot. She tries to use her left foot for leverage, but it hits a slick spot and she begins to slide toward the gutter. Otto and Worley drop their tools and crawl over to her, but Etta's weight against the slope of the roof makes her slide even faster.

"Ave, git the ladder! Git the ladder!"

The ladder is propped against the far side of the roof. I'm frozen, thinking I can catch Etta if she falls. But I know this isn't possible. The drop is almost twenty feet, time is passing, and the fabric on her jacket is tearing away as she slides. I heave the ladder from the side of the house to the front gutter, where her feet are dangling dangerously over the edge. Worley has thrown his body sideways across the roof and has grabbed one of Etta's hands, which stops her from falling.

"Come up, Ave. Come up and git her," Worley says, panting. Otto attempts to crawl closer to Etta, but he is afraid to disrupt the precarious balance of their weight on the roof, so he stops. I dig the feet of the ladder into the soft earth and climb up quickly. I feel more confident when I get to Etta's feet and can get a grip on her legs. She feels so small in my arms; I remember what it was like when I could control everything to keep her safe. I carefully pull her to me. Worley lets go when I have a good hold on her. I hold Etta by her waist and slide her onto the first step of the ladder, shielding her with my body.

"Do you think you can climb down?" I ask her. Etta barely whispers a reply, and we descend the ladder one step at a time. I try not to look to the ground, it seems so far away. With each step I take, and each one Etta takes, I breathe a little easier. By the time we reach the ground, Otto and Worley have come through the house and are waiting to help us off the ladder.

"Sorry about that, Miss Ave. We thought she was safe up 'ere with us," Otto says.

"That's okay," I tell him. Then I turn to my daughter, who examines the palms of her hands, streaked with a little blood where the shingles burned them during her downward slide. I wince. I have never been able to stand it when she bleeds.

"Come on, let's wash up." I take Etta into the house and hold back until we are out of Otto and Worley's earshot.

"What in the hell were you thinking, Etta?" She has never heard me yell this loudly, so she backs up several steps. "You are not allowed on the roof. You know that. I don't care who is here doing what, you know the rules. You could've fallen and broken your neck."

"But I didn't!" She turns on me.

"What?"

"I didn't!"

"Because you're lucky. Lucky I was there to catch you!"

"Yeah, I'm lucky you were there," Etta says sarcastically.

"Are you mocking me?"

"What do you care, anyway?"

Etta has never spoken to me in anger, and I don't know how to respond. I don't know whether to admonish her for sassing me or to answer the question.

Etta looks me in the eye. "You don't care about me."

"Where do you get that idea?"

"All the time." Etta storms off and up the stairs.

I follow her. "Stop right there!"

She turns and faces me.

"That's a very cruel thing to say to me. Of course I care about you. But when you do something stupid, something you know you're not supposed to do, you can't turn around and blame me for it. You're the one who's wrong here. Not me."

"That's all that matters to you. Who's right and who's wrong."

"Watch your tone."

"You just don't want me to die like Joe. That's all." Etta slams her bedroom door shut.

For a moment, I think I might honor her privacy, but my anger gets the best of me. I throw the door open. "What is the matter with you?"

Etta is on her bed. My heart breaks, and I go to sit beside her. She pulls away.

"We need to talk about this."

"I don't want to talk to you. I want Daddy."

When I attempt to reach out to her again, she gets up off the bed, goes to the old easy chair with the broken arm, and throws herself into it and away from me. I have never seen this sort of emotion from my daughter, and I am stunned. But I am also so hurt that I don't know what to say. So I rely on my rule about being consistent in my discipline. I'm not going to let her off the hook. "Dad is not going to bail you out of this one. You need to think about what you did this after-noon. And about the way you talked to me."

I leave the room and close the door quietly behind me. I walk down the front stairs and go through the screen door to the porch. I sit down on the steps as I have done so many times at twilight. Otto and Wor-ley pack up their truck without saying a word. They take full respon-sibility for Etta being on the roof, and I don't want to say anything more. They get into their truck and wave somberly as they descend the hill.

I lean back on the stairs and take a deep breath. The mountains, still green at the end of summer, seem to intersect like those in a pop-up book. This old stone house is hidden in their folds like an aban-doned castle, with me its wizened housekeeper, taken for granted and obsolete. I feel myself hitting the wall common to all mothers: the day your daughter turns on you. And it happened on such an ordinary day in Cracker's Neck Holler. Nothing strange or different or particularly dramatic in the weather or the wind. The sky meets the top of the mountains in a ruffle of deep blue. The sun sets in streaks of golden pink as it slips behind Skeens Ridge. I get lost in the quiet, the color, and the breeze, and I'm back in simpler days, the brief time before Jack and I had children, when this house was a place where we made love and ate good food and tended the garden.

The cool air soothes the throbbing in my head. I am making a mess of motherhood. What do I know about children, really? I was an only child. Maybe I baby-sat here and there, but I never had a grand plan that included children. When I found out I was pregnant, I made Iva Lou order me every book on parenthood from the county library. I read each one, choosing concepts that made sense and figuring out how to implement them. When my kids came along, I thought every-thing would fall into place. But my daughter isn't who I expected her to be. I thought she'd be like me, like my side of the family, marooned Eye-talians in Southwest Virginia who made a good life and fit in. But she's pure MacChesney, freckled and fearless. My kid has no dark corners, no Italian temper or Mediterranean largesse. And I know that I have disappointed her too—she needs an outdoorsy, athletic mom, one who encourages her to take risks. I do the opposite; I encourage her to stop and think. My goal is to keep her safe, and she resents that. Sometimes I am filled with dread at what lies ahead. How do I stop fearing the future? No book can tell me that.

The high beams on Jack's pickup truck light up the field as he takes the turn up the holler road. He slows down to check the mailbox, and I see him throw a few envelopes on the front seat. Then he guns the engine again, spitting gravel under his wheels. Soon I hear my daughter's footsteps as she runs down the stairs. The screen door flies open and she jumps down the steps two at a time, ignoring me, and over the path to meet her father as he parks. I hear the muffled start to her version of the Roof Disaster and wish briefly that I weren't the mother but the wizened housekeeper after all, so I wouldn't have to rat her out. But I know that I have to be unwavering so that at some point when she must make hard decisions, she will remember these days, find the wisdom born of experience, and make the right choice (yeah, right). I have to be the bad guy. Jack puts his arm around Etta as they walk up the path. I stand up. Etta passes by in a businesslike huff without looking at me. She bangs the screen door behind her.

"Are you okay?" Jack gives me a kiss.

"My nerves are shot," I tell him with a nice teaspoon of self-pity.

"We're going to have to come up with a doozy of a punishment," he promises.

"Great." My carefully rehearsed Sex Talk is ruined for now, another plan gone awry.

"Kids taking chances, taking risks, it's all a part of life, Ave." Jack sighs.

As we walk up the stairs, I want to tell my husband that I'm scared. It is one thing to parent a helpless infant and then a child, but when that child develops a will, the future becomes clear—I won't be in charge anymore, and I won't be able to protect her. My husband will have to guide us through these rough patches, since parenting seems to come so naturally to him. I have to learn how to calm down and lead my family. And then I have to find a way to love my job as a mother as the requirements change, and I'm going to need Jack to help me do it.

## CHAPTER TWO

*I*t's been three weeks since Etta almost fell off the roof. She survived two weeks of being grounded, which was pretty terrible for her because she missed all the end-of-summer barbecues and the picnic trip with her friends to the Natural Bridge. She moped around for days, and then at the one-week mark, things began to get a little better between us. She made French toast for us on Sunday morning and did her laundry without my asking. Since things are back to normal, Jack has taken her over to Kingsport for their annual father-daughter shopping trip for the first day of school. Etta wants a backpack she saw at Miller and Rhodes.

I go through the house with a laundry basket, loading it up with things that need to be put away. Etta's shoes, comic books, notebooks, pencils, and gear fill the basket. As I go up to her room, Shoo the Cat bounds up the stairs next to me. He charges into Etta's room, and I follow him.

Last summer we let Etta paint her room. She chose periwinkle with white trim. Her iron bed, painted antique beige, is covered with one of her grandma MacChesney's quilts, a pattern called "Drunkard's Path." She has a poster of Black Beauty over her bed (does every preteen girl in America love purple and horses?).

Etta has a map of the world on her far wall. In red she's circled where she's been, and in pencil the places she wants to go someday. (I'm surprised to see locations in India and New Zealand circled in pencil.) I trace my finger from the United States to Italy and find my father's hometown of Schilpario, north of my mother's: the city of Bergamo, high in the Italian Alps. Etta has written the names of her relatives next to the dots that mark the mountain villages. South on the Mediterranean coast she has circled Sestri Levante and written her cousin Chiara's name enclosed in a heart. Since I took Etta to Italy, she and Chiara have been faithful pen pals, and in many ways, Chiara, who is fifteen, is like a big sister to Etta. Chiara wants to come to the States one day. Judging by the length of her letters, she will have a lot to say when she gets here.

Etta's toy chest, only a year ago filled with dolls and stuffed animals, is now filled with equipment. There's a fishing basket, Rollerblades, a basketball, and several small branches (what she uses them for, I have no idea). She should have been a boy, I think as I prick my finger on a fishhook. I gather up some loose pencils from the bottom of the trunk and return them to the cup on her desk.

The top of the desk is covered in butcher paper, on which she has drawn a map of the heavens and written STARS OVER CRACKER'S NECK HOLLER in calligraphy along the top. She has made diagrams of the constellations and labeled each one. This pencil drawing was done with a ruler; it is so precise, I'm surprised it's hers. Granted, there are many places where the paper is worn thin from erasures, but for the most part, her work is sure-handed. Etta loves astronomy—she points out the Milky Way on clear nights, or a planet when she recognizes it sparkling in the sky—but I didn't know she was so passionate about the subject that she would take time to study the night sky in such detail. Evidently, Etta has an inner life that I know very little about.

When I was a girl, I spent a lot of time thinking about why I'd been born in Big Stone Gap, of all the places in the world. I would look up at the sky and wonder where it ended. I had such longing to explore that I couldn't make the connection that my fate was somehow tied to a mountain town in the hills of Southwest Virginia. I thought a girl like me, who loved to read big adventure stories from centuries long ago, should have been from a more exciting place, a magical place. So when I found out that my mother had in fact left Italy pregnant with me and without a husband, I had my exotic point of origin at last. Etta might be very different, but she has my longing for the Big World deep in her bones. These mountains may protect us from the outside world, but they won't hold us. We can see our way through them and over them, something lots of folks around here could never imagine.

At the bottom of the butcher paper is a very detailed drawing of our stone house, square and rustic, with its four chimneys and the front door painted pale blue. Etta has drawn the windows and their filmy lace sheers rustling in the wind. She has penciled in the roof shingle by shingle (now she knows the shingles firsthand), and her bedroom window, which overlooks the roof. Sitting in the window is Etta herself, with huge eyes and caterpillar eyelashes. In her hands, she holds a small telescope through which she gazes up to the stars above. She must have been out on the roof plenty before I caught her.

The phone rings. One of Etta's punishments was the removal of her phone, so I have to run downstairs to answer it. I pick up on the third ring.

"Ave!" When I hear the voice of my closest friend of twenty years, I become the woman I used to be—young and trouble-free. The worst problem I had when I was single, a hole in the roof of my house, seems silly in comparison to my daughter falling off one.

"Theodore! How are you?"

"Moving."

"Finally, you've come to your senses and you're moving back to Big Stone Gap."

Theodore laughs. "Not likely."

"Come on. We got killer majorettes, and our horn section is the best in the county."

"Don't tempt me."

"You're not going far, are you?" I have loved having my best friend so close in Knoxville. Many weekends, I jump in the Jeep and ride down to see his theatrical halftime shows at the University of Tennessee.

"It's a dream move."

"No. You didn't get a job in—"

"Yep. New York City!"

"No!" Theodore used to talk about New York City as though it lay between heaven and Oz, a place of perfection and possibility. Now he'll see for himself.

"I've only wanted this all of my life, and now it's actually happening," Theodore says gratefully.

"What school?"

"Not a school."

"Not a school? Are you switching careers?" I can't imagine Theodore giving up the life of a band director. He's just too brilliant at it.

"No. I'm just going pro. I've been offered the job of associate artistic director at Radio City Music Hall."

"Oh my God! The Rockettes!"

"The Christmas show, the Easter show, the concerts. All of it. I'm going to be working with the great director Joe Layton. He directed *The Lost Colony*, that outdoor drama. Remember when we drove down to North Carolina to see it?"

"One of our better road trips," I remind him.

"Who would have thought playing Preacher Red Fox in your drama would have gotten me in the door?"

"That's hardly what got you the job. You're a theatrical genius, and now everyone will know it. You're going to the big city! New York City!" I hope I'm not yelling, but I'm so excited for him.

"Now all we have to do is figure out when you're coming up."

Etta and Jack get home around suppertime carrying her new backpack, a three-ring binder with Halley's comet on the cover, a hot-pink down vest, and more. I meet them outside to tell them Theodore's news.

"When can we go?" Etta asks excitedly.

"He'd like us to come up for Columbus Day weekend in October."

"Dad's coming too, right?"

"I'm not slick enough for New York City, Etta." Jack winks at me.

"You don't have to be slick. You just need to move fast and cuss and push people out of your way," Etta tells him with great authority.

"Etta knows all about New York. She's read *Harriet the Spy* about seventeen times."

"You and your mama will do fine without me."

I've made Etta's favorite dinner: spaghetti in fresh tomato sauce with meatballs, a big salad, and brownies with vanilla ice cream for dessert. She clears the dishes without a fuss.

"You girls got mail." Jack comes in from the hallway with the familiar blue airmail envelopes. Etta practically dives on her father for her letter. "I forgot about them in my pocket, they're so thin," Jack apologizes.

"It's from Chiara!" Etta shrieks. "Here, Ma. You got one from Grandpop."

"Those two keep the Italian mail service in business." My husband takes the newspaper and goes into the living room.

"No kidding." I rip into my father's letter. It is full of news. Papa and his new wife, Giacomina, are getting along great, but his mother is causing her share of agita. Nonna is having a hard time letting Giacomina take over the household. Papa says the negotiations continue;

I guess Jack isn't the only man in the world who plays referee to two women. Papa has been down to Bergamo quite a bit and over to see my mother's family, the Vilminores, on Via Davide. There's even an update on Stefano Grassi, an orphan my zia Antonietta cared for as though he were her son. After she died, the rest of the Vilminore family began to look out for him. He'd come for dinner and help Zio Pietro in the wood shop, though he continued to live at the nearby orphanage. He is a few years older than Etta, and she developed a big crush on him during our last visit. Evidently, the Barbari family has as well: Papa took Stefano to the opera with Giacomina and has included a picture of the three of them on the steps of Teatro alla Scala in Milan.

"Stefano Grassi sure is cute." I give Etta the picture.

"Ma, he is Major Cute," Etta corrects me. And she's right. He's lanky with a great face, a straight prominent nose, dark eyes, and blond curls that make him look like a Renaissance poet. "Stefano is way more mature than the boys around here."

"He wants to come and work in the States next summer. He's studying building and architecture and wants to apprentice with Dad," I tell her.

"Ma, can he come? Please?" Etta lights up like a Roman candle.

"We'll have to ask your dad. But I don't see why not."

Etta sits down and studies the picture. "That's the famous opera house La Scala," I tell her.

"I like Italy better than Big Stone."

"You do?"

"Maybe not better. I love my friends and my school and everything. But I miss our family over there. Like Grandpop. He's the only grandparent I have."

"We don't have a lot of kin around here anymore, do we?"

"Only Aunt Cecilia. And she's about four hundred years old."

"Well, your dad was an only child, and I'm an only child—"

"I know, I know, and you got married later in life, and therefore you didn't have lots of kids like people that get married when they're young."

"Who says that?"

"You do. All the time." Etta smiles. "Is it okay if I keep the picture?" I tell her it's fine, and she goes up to her room. I suddenly feel like following her and explaining every choice I've ever made, how not every one was designed to deprive her of siblings and cousins, noise and competition and long waits for the bathroom, but rather the result of chance or luck or fate that blew through my life, woke me up, and changed my single path to this married one, and then unexpectedly, delightedly, to motherhood. But I am not going to justify my choices tonight. And I certainly can't explain her brother's death and the fundamental changes it wrought. I don't know how to tell a twelve-year-old there are things that happen in this life that have no explanation. I wonder why I am always defending myself to my daughter. When I figure that one out, perhaps I'll be ready to tackle the big issues with her, including the ones Misty Lassiter has prematurely placed on the front burner of our lives.

The Tuesday lunch special at the Soda Fountain is soup beans and corn bread, so all the regular diehards pile in for the bargain. (We're doubly busy when the first of the month lands on a Tuesday because the black-lung benefit checks arrive.) I'm stuck in the pharmacy filling meds while Fleeta mans the Soda Fountain. It gets crazy.

"Ave Maria Mulligan MacChesney, I'm a-goin' to Florida, and don't try and stop me!" Spec announces from the door.

"You're going on vacation?"

"Yup. Surprised?"

"Very. You've never had one."

"No, only if you count when me and Leola take the kids to the lake. But we ain't never left the state. I figger after forty-seven years, my wife deserves a sandy beach and a mai tai. What do you think?"

"I think it's fantastic. When are you going?"

"Thanksgiving. First off, we're gonna drive down and spend six days at Disney World, then we're gonna hit Sarasota—she got her a cousin down there—and then we'll circle back up the coast of the Sunshine State and come on home."

Fleeta hollers from the Soda Fountain. "Spec, stop jackin' your jaw. I ain't holdin' this seat of yorn no longer, I got me a wait list over here." Spec never misses a lunch special, so he motions to Fleeta that he's on his way.

Iva Lou greets me from the door (I guess everybody in town has a yen for soup beans today). "I had to double-park behind your Jeep, it's so crowded," she says as she places her purse on the counter.

"No problem. I'm not going anywhere."

"Need a hand?"

"You can do labels if you want." I give Iva Lou the labels run off the computer. She adheres them to the prescription bags as I load the sacks.

"I hired Serena Mumpower out of Appalachia to be my assistant at the library. Top of her class at Mountain Empire."

"How's that working out?"

"She's on the phone constantly. Most popular girl in the county, I believe."

"She's pretty."

"Ain't nobody *that* pretty."

"You'll have to have a talk with her."

"I guess. I don't want her to use the Slemp Library as Dial-A-Date."

"Feel like running over to Appalachia later?"

"Sure. What do you need?"

I whisper, "Etta needs a—a bra. I thought we'd go to Dave's."

"I wouldn't miss it. Etta's first bra? Nothing like a bra to define a figger and emphasize a waistline. I can't believe it. Etta is a young woman who needs support! This is my favorite feminine rite of passage. Well, maybe my favorite was hittin' the hair dye for the first time. I was fourteen when I got yeller streaks in my hair, did 'em my-self with peroxide. Big chunky streaks like Tammy Wynette on her greatest-hits album. That's when I discovered that not only do blondes have more fun, they have *all* the fun."

"We're going for utilitarian here, not Wonderbra," I remind Iva Lou.

"Well, if you want plain industrial bras, why don't you just cross the street over to Zackie's and get 'em in a box? Mike's has training bras too, and they're just across the way."

"Etta doesn't want to shop in town. She's a little sensitive about the whole thing. She tried to convince me to go to Kingsport, but I don't have time."

"I'll wear my darkest sunglasses and a Lana Turner scarf so nobody recognizes us."

"Don't laugh. I think Etta would like that."


Iva Lou and I have worked out a routine to make Etta's first bra-shopping expedition casual. Iva Lou is going to buy a pair of boots; I'm going to look at a skirt set that's on sale; and buried in a list of things that Etta needs is her first bra. I called Julia Isaac, who owns the place, ahead of time. She laughed, as she's been down this road with every girl in Appalachia.

Dave's Department Store has been around for years and carries a variety of clothes, from miner's overalls to chiffon mother-of-the-bride dresses that Julia picks up on buying trips to New York. The juniors' section is more hip and, for our area, fairly cutting-edge. Etta skims past the bras on their small plastic hangers and goes to look at shoes. Iva Lou and I look at each other. "I know what to do," Iva Lou whispers.

I watch Iva Lou as she fawns all over a pair of loafers Etta likes. As Etta tries them on, Iva Lou tries on her boots, and then they place both pairs on the checkout counter. Iva Lou leads Etta over to the ac-cessories, showing her a small purse that clips on a belt and matches the loafers. Then Iva Lou stacks several packages of panty hose by her boots. The checkout counter is filling up. Iva Lou stops and admires a lace bra on her way to the juniors' section and makes Etta look at it. It's too mature for Etta, but I don't interrupt; I'm hoping Etta will choose a more appropriate style. She does. She takes a sporty bra off the rack and shows Iva Lou, who guesses Etta's size and hands her several in that range. Then Iva Lou takes the lacy one to try on herself; Etta goes behind one changing curtain, Iva Lou behind another. Lord love her, Iva Lou is making this fun. My friend is the most natural mother in the world and has never raised a child.

"Ma, I'm done," Etta hollers to me from the checkout desk.

"Where's Aunt Iva Lou?"

"She's still trying things on."

I look down at Etta's stack of items as Julia rings them up. Three tasteful cotton bras with a piqué trim are hiding under the T-shirts Etta wanted.

"Iva Lou?" I say through the curtain of the dressing area. She doesn't answer. "Are you in there?" She still does not respond. I look around the store. It's empty, near closing time. "Iva?" I ask again. I peek through the curtain. Iva Lou is inside, sitting on the bench with her head in her hands.

"What's wrong?" I ask her.

"I'm just draggin', honey-o." Iva Lou looks up at me. Under the fluorescent lights, I see through her makeup that she is exhausted.

"I'm sorry. Did Etta wear you out?"

"No, it's not the shopping. I'm tarred all the time."

"What do you mean, all the time?"

"Around five o'clock every day, I just need to set down and rest."

"Have you been to the doctor?"

"Doc Daugherty said it's gettin' older. That I need to slow down. The usual BS."

"Oh, please."

"What else could it be?"

"A million things." I sit down on the floor next to her. "You may have an insulin problem."

"I don't have the sugar."

"Could be you're vitamin-deficient."

"That could be, 'cause I never do take no pills."

"We can get you over to Holston Valley Hospital for them to do a complete workup on you."

Iva Lou stands. She doesn't argue, which tells me that she's hurting.

"We'll get to the bottom of this, okay?" I reassure her. She pats me on the shoulder, then breathes deeply, peels back the curtain, and walks to the checkout.

"You girls can do some shopping." Jack looks up from watching the news.

"We needed everything we bought. Right, Etta?"

"Yep." Etta takes her shopping bags and goes upstairs.

"I'll bet," Jack says, going back to his program. The phone rings. Jack doesn't make a move for it (he never does), so I pick up in the hallway.

"Ave?"

The familiar voice sends a surge through me. "Pete?"

"How are you?" he says in a tone that makes me feel like I need to sit down.

"I'm doing fine," I tell him. Pete Rutledge has gone from my Italian Summer Crush (okay, old crush, it's been five years since I romped with him in a field of bluebells above Schilpario in the Italian Alps) to family friend.

"Me too. How's Etta?"

"Growing up fast."

"Uh-oh."

"Yeah, she'll be thirteen next April."

"I'm sure you can handle the changes."

"I'm trying."

"Is Jack around?"

"Sure, let me get him."

I call Jack, who smiles and comes to the phone when he hears that it's Pete. When I first met Pete, he was in Italy looking for marble; he's an importer from New Jersey. Actually, he recently added guest professor at NYU to his résumé—there aren't many marble experts in the world. In the time since that tumultuous summer, he's become friendly with my father and Giacomina and still visits them every time he goes to Italy on buying trips. Jack often uses marble on his jobs now, so he buys it from Pete. Their business relationship eventually turned into a friendship, which gave me the creeps at first but now is completely natural. I never realized until I got married how hard it is for men to make good male friends. Most men just have a pleasant, jocular relationship with one another; they don't get emotional or seek advice, something that comes so naturally to me and my women friends. So, even though sharing Pete Rutledge with Jack Mac is strange, I'm actually happy that my husband has made a friend.

I hear Jack hang up the phone. He comes into the kitchen and puts his arms around me as I bread chicken cutlets at the stove.

"What'd Pete want?"

"We're redoing the foyer at the Black Diamond Savings Bank up in Norton, so I need some marble. He said you should be sure to call him when you and Etta go to New York."

Jack goes and washes up for dinner, and I break into a sweat. Nothing happened with Pete, I remind myself, except that I was tempted. And, of course, I always offset my temptation with the fact that Jack was back here getting chummy with Karen Bell, a lumber-supply saleswoman from Coeburn. (Jack buys his lumber locally now. It's a little unspoken agreement we have.) These trials didn't sink us—in fact, they helped our marriage. We looked hard at our relationship and began to resolve our differences. If Karen Bell and Pete Rutledge hadn't come along, I don't think Jack and I would still be together.

Don't get me wrong, I don't want to send Karen Bell a thank-you note for her trouble, but in retrospect, I see that she did me a favor.

"Ma?" Etta interrupts my thoughts.

"Yeah?"

"Thanks for the clothes." Etta sees the table isn't set, so she goes about gathering plates and silverware.

"That was fun."

"Yeah, it was fun," Etta agrees.

I turn around and look at her. "Did you try it on?"

"I have it on," Etta says, adjusting her bra strap through her T-shirt. "What do you think?"

Etta shrugs. "A bra's a bra, Ma."

I laugh. This is so typical of Etta. I go out of my way to make things easy for her, and she doesn't need me to! She is just like her father, who tackles a problem, finds the solution, and doesn't dwell on it further. Of course, this makes me look like the great overreactor of all time, since I'm asking for a follow-up report on the shopping trip I planned like a CIA run.

"Come on, Ave. They's at Zackie's already. Shake a leg!" Fleeta calls to me from the front doors of the Pharmacy, swinging the doors back and forth to make noise with the chimes in case the hollering didn't get my attention.

"I'm on my way."

"Hell's bells! I hear the snares! Hurry it up!" Fleeta bolts out the door into the street.

A good-size crowd has gathered on Main Street for the Powell Valley High School marching band practice parade and mini-concert on the post office steps, a pre-football-season fall ritual. The kids are fresh from band camp and anxious to show us what they've learned.

Leading the parade is Big Stone Gap's state-of-the-art fire truck, driven by Captain Spec Broadwater (also captain of the Rescue Squad). The wax job on the fire truck is so shiny, it's hard to look directly at. As Spec goes through the first stoplight, he hits the switch to activate the truck's flashing red light, which is the band's cue to pivot right and create a formation on the library steps. Spec has a look of such seriousness on his face, you'd think he was heading into a meeting with General Patton about how to split Berlin. There's plenty of decoration on top of the truck, though—the cheerleaders are draped on the ladders like fan dancers in a Busby Berkley musical. They wave their Carolina-blue pom-poms, which match the afternoon sky. Spec slows the truck to a full stop, leaving the light flashing for dramatic effect. He lights a cigarette and scans the crowd. When he makes eye contact with shopkeeper Zackie Wakin, he nods solemnly instead of waving. Not far behind, the band, marching to a snare-drum cadence, continues to drain off Main Street in perfect rows that stretch from the post office all the way back to the Dollar General Store.

The band is not in uniform; they are wearing jeans and crisp white T-shirts. The majorettes are in red short shorts and tank tops; evidently there was some coordination between them and the cheerleaders, who are wearing white short shorts and red tank tops. My Etta is one of two banner carriers selected by Kate Benton, the new band director. The banner carriers are always middle-school-age; it encourages the younger kids to see their peers march with the big kids, and it certainly encourages them to try out for the marching band when they reach high school. I have never seen such a focused band. Theodore would be so proud. Of course, on weekends Miss Benton is a sergeant in the National Guard, so she knows her stuff.

Etta's posture is perfect. She nods to the other banner carrier, little Jean Williams, whose braids are laced with red ribbons and look glamorous against her rich brown skin. Jean nods back solemnly. I resist the urge to wave to them (I don't want to embarrass them in their official capacity as parade leaders).

As the band falls into formation on the post office steps, the crowd pushes in to watch. The director hands each of the girls a red cellophane hat (the bowler type they give out on New Year's Eve) while the woodwinds pipe the opening bars of "Puttin' on the Ritz." The majorettes use their batons as canes in a Charlie Chaplin dance, but the woodwinds are suddenly drowned out by the fire whistle, which rings long and loud from across town. The drum major doesn't know what to do, so he continues to direct the music.

Spec leans his head out of the fire truck. "Everybody off!" he bellows. The cheerleaders look at one another in confusion (nothing like a pack of panicking cheerleaders).

"I said *off!*" Now the crowd gets into the act, extending arms to help the girls disembark.

"Girls, get off my goddamn truck!" Spec bangs the door with his fist, scaring everyone.

"Calm down, Spec!" Fleeta hollers from the sidewalk. "You'll give yourself a heart attack!"

The girls climb down off the truck quickly, putting their feet in places they shouldn't, making sounds that are less than ladylike, yanking at the hardware, grunting as they shimmy over spikes and notches on their way to the ground. Kelly Gembach, the most agile and petite, rappels down the back using the hose as a rope. The rest of the girls hit the ground like a spray of Red Hots. Only solidly built Kerry Necessary, the captain and the base for most of their gymnastic stunts (she also placed first in the all-county girls' division shot put last year), takes her time sliding down the windshield, creating a big red eclipse for Spec and his buddy Don Wax, who rode shotgun for fun (I'll bet he's sorry). Kerry's sweaty hands leave streaks all over the spotless glass. When she finally comes to a stop, she is on her belly and eye to eye with Spec. The look on his face scares her so badly, she tucks and rolls off the engine to the curb. Her fellow cheerleaders gather around and dust off her shorts.

"Clear the urr-ree-uh!" Spec turns on the siren. The onlookers recoil at the blast, covering their ears, then push back to let Spec through, and he speeds off down the street toward Frog Level, where something is burning.

"That's a bad omen. Gonna be a shit football season, you'll see," Fleeta says under her breath. The drum major cues the band, but the woodwinds, still paralyzed from Spec's rant, barely have the breath to blow out the opening bars. I look over at Etta, who sees me and shakes her head slowly. This wasn't the grand start to her band career that we were hoping for.

With Etta back in school, Iva Lou and I are determined not to let anything interfere with our once-a-week lunches. We've devised a system where we rotate our lunches between the library (pack your own), Stringer's (serve yourself, all you can eat), and Bessie's Diner (the classic burger joint in Appalachia).

"You'd better set down." Iva Lou rises out of her seat at Bessie's to make room for me in the booth. She has ordered for me, my usual sloppy joe and Diet Coke, and has already picked at her macaroni and cheese.

"I'm sorry I'm late. What's wrong? Did your tests come back?" Iva Lou had a full-service physical at Holston Valley—blood, stress test, the works.

"Hell, they told me I was fine over there. I just have to go back for a couple more things, but so far, I'm as healthy as a horse."

"Good."

"No, honey, this is about Etta. I'd rather you hear it from a friend."

"What?"

"It's a beaut. I gotta say, at least your daughter sticks to the tried and true."

My mind races, but I can't imagine what could be wrong. Etta has been an angel since the Roof Incident. She went to the band festival in Bristol, which Jack and I chaperoned. Her first report card of the year was all A's. She doesn't talk on the phone too much and isn't boy crazy. In a week, she and I are going to New York City to see Theodore, just the two of us. I can't imagine what Iva Lou is talking about.

"It's gonna be all over town, and you need to know first."

"Know what?" I say in a measured tone.

"Etta pulled a prank."

"A prank?" This is a word a mother hates to hear.

"Well, here's what happened. Ole Kate Benton made the kids run laps after a bad band rehearsal. Evidently, the kids were really slacking off, and of course, she made everyone run the laps, from the flag girls to the banner carriers."

"So?"

"The kids thought this was unfair, and they rebelled."

"How?"

"Etta and a few other kids ordered a ton of coal to be delivered to Miss Benton's house over on Wyandotte Avenue."

"Oh, no."

"Yep, and she has gas heat."

"No." Delivering coal to someone with a gas furnace is one of the classic pranks that local kids pull, and it surfaces every ten years or so. Basically, some kid calls the coal-delivery service and asks to have a ton of coal delivered for the winter. In these parts, everything, including coal delivery, is done on an honor system; no deposit, they bill you after they deliver. The customer sets the date (usually sometime in November), and the truck shows up and dumps a mountain of coal in the yard. The customer is responsible for shoveling it down into the basement. You can tell how much of the winter season is left as these mountains of coal diminish in backyards all over town.

"I don't believe it."

"It's true." Iva Lou laughs.

"It's not funny. It's against the law."

"Oh, loosen up. I remember when I was girl, we called the Roy A. Green Funeral Home over in Appalachia, and we told them our principal died of a heart attack and to come fetch him. So old Roy got in his black Buick and drove over to the principal's house. His wife came to the door, and Roy looked at her with them sad bug eyes and said,

'Ma'am, we've come for the body.' She fainted dead away. Now, that was a good un."

"Hilarious," I tell Iva Lou. But I'm not laughing.

I call Jack, who heard the news from the principal, who is first cousin to Jack's business partner, Rick Harmon, and is about to head up to the school. He's furious and tells me that he will handle it.

As I drive back to town, I take a turn toward Wyandotte Avenue to assess the damage for myself. I'm not sure which house the band director lives in, but then I remind myself, don't be stupid, just look for the two-story pile of coal in the backyard.

I find her house, and it's even worse than I imagined. The mountain of shiny black lumps glistens in the afternoon sun like the diamonds they would be someday if left in the earth. The ranch house actually looks smaller than the pile of coal, but that's probably due to my fury and perspective. There's a car in the driveway (it too looks miniature compared to the coal pile), so I pull up and park. I see Spec's Rescue Squad wagon parked near the coal. He makes his way around the side of the house and joins me, shaking his head. "It's a humdinger."

"Hey, Spec. What are you doing here?"

"Miss Benton didn't know who else to call, so I told her I'd come and make the arrangements."

"I can't believe my kid did this."

"She had her some help."

"Don't defend her, Spec," I tell him gently.

"Oh, I ain't. I ain't. But you know how them kids is, they git that group-think goin', and here's the result of it."

"It just makes me sick."

"I talked to Delmer Wilson over to the coal company, and he's ready to send a truck over whenever y'all figger out who's going to pay for the labor."

"I'd like to send Etta to a military academy."

"Now, Ave." Whenever Spec says this, it means fatherly advice is to follow. "You need to keep a cool head in a hot 'tater of a situation. Overreactin' is as bad as no response. Remember what I taught you about responding to emergencies? Stay in charge and remain calm. Okay?"

Spec walks me to the front sidewalk, pats me on the back, and heads back to his wagon. My legs are weak as I take the steps up to the front door; I am so full of dread, you'd think I had pulled this prank myself.

Miss Benton comes to the door. She is wearing a windbreaker and white sweatpants and has a whistle around her neck. She has an aristocratic face—a fine nose and the high forehead of a leader. Her sharp jawline is softened by her auburn curls, pulled into a loose ponytail. She might be forty, but she is tall and lean with square broad shoulders, so she's in that ageless category.

"Hi. I'm so sorry, Miss Benton."

"It's a mess," she says quietly.

"We will punish Etta."

"I just put sod in the backyard so it could take before the winter. Now it's ruined."

"We'll replace it."

"Well."

"I'm really sorry." I don't know what else to say. She doesn't invite me in, but then why should she? My daughter has ruined her property. Suddenly she turns away.

"Miss Benton, are you all right?"

She turns to face me, her eyes full of tears. "It's just so . . . shitty." She takes a deep breath. "You know I moved here from Richmond, the big city, and I thought, well, Big Stone Gap, in the mountains, it's a small town. It'll be fun, a new adventure. All my friends warned me, it's a dead end to move to a place where there's no life outside of school. But I love what I do, and on weekends I have the National Guard, so

I thought I'd give it a shot. But this is just, well, it's too much. I don't mind not being liked, but I don't want to be hated."

"They don't hate you!"

"Oh, okay. This is something that kids who like you would do," she snaps.

I am standing face-to-face with a woman whose shoes I've been in, whose frustrations I shared for most of my adult life, and I want to tell her that I understand what it means to be single in a small town, to be alone, to have to take care of a house, from leaks in the roof to kinks in the furnace to mowing the lawn, to deal with bad news from family far away and hear good news from the same and have no one to share it with. To long for connection, to want to be a part of the bigger picture and yet to love your solitude, to have time to think and silence to read with no one to answer to or tend to. To hoard privacy, the greatest luxury, knowing that though it's the very thing that keeps you separate from people, it's so meaningful and delicious that you don't care. I know about working hard all week and being so busy that weekends aren't weekends, just two extra days to be useful. I know what she is feeling, and I want her to know that.

"I understand. I was alone in this town for a long time," I tell her.

"Then you know."

"Yes ma'am, I do."

Kate puts her hand on the door, signaling that she is done opening up to me. I turn to go down the steps. She stops me.

"What's a ferriner?" she asks quietly.

"Someone who moves to these parts from the outside. A foreigner. Why do you ask?" But I have a sick feeling I know the answer.

"I was just wondering. One of the kids called me that."

"We'll get the coal cleaned up and the sod replaced," I promise her. She closes the screen door.

I feel so bad for Kate Benton. She might feel like a ferriner, but now she knows that is exactly how she is perceived. Every time we attract talented people to this area, we end up driving them away when they dare to do things differently or take a firm stand with our children. Ferriners are outsiders, but we make them outcasts. Why should she stay here? What is here for her? At least I had Theodore to share things with, to go places, to have a life outside my work. We loved all the same things—good books, good food, and the theater. I hardly noticed time passing in the ten years that Theodore lived here, I was so happy to have a like-minded friend. We'd go and climb around caves and see movies in Kingsport and go to the mall. When one of us needed an escort to some party or event, we'd always go together. Kate Benton doesn't have a Theodore. I don't know how long she'll last around here without one.

Fleeta is locking up when I stop by the Pharmacy on my way home.

"How bad was it?" she asks as she sorts through the keys on a large brass ring.

"It's terrible."

"Yeah, Misty confessed the whole thing to her mama, who told Iva Lou at the li-berry." Fleeta pauses, waiting for me to respond. When I don't, she continues, "Yeah, it's a bad thing them kids did. But at least Etta made the group confess to the principal. That ought to make you feel better." Fleeta lights up one of the two cigarettes she's smoking per day now.

It should make me feel better, but it doesn't. "I don't want to talk about it, Fleeta."

"All youngins git into messes one time or another. You know what I went through with Pavis." Fleeta exhales so deeply, it's as if she blows out an additional pocket of old smoke from deep within her lungs.

How could I forget Pavis? When he was in high school, I had to advance Fleeta her paycheck several times so she could bail him out of the town jail for infractions that varied from public drunkenness to selling illegal fireworks to minors.

"Poor pitiful Pavis," Fleeta says as though it's his given name. She continues, "When the police picked him up the first time, they come by my house to let me know they had him. And I don't even remember the charges, I just remember I took a fit of cryin'. I said to the cop, 'Why? Why do I have two normal youngins who act right and one Pavis who's forever in a mess? How could one child turn out so badly?' And he said, 'Ma'am, there's an old saw, and it's true: You plant corn, you git corn.' " Fleeta sighs and goes to lock up the Soda Fountain.

My hands begin to shake on the steering wheel as I make the turn up Cracker's Neck Road. I try to remember what Spec told me, try to stay calm, but my body has other ideas. When I told Jack I would meet them at home, we were both furious, but I think he was still a bit taken aback by my tone of voice. And now that I've seen the pile of coal, my mood is even worse. I park my Jeep and take a moment to sit and breathe before going inside.

"Etta. Come down here. Now."

Jack stands back from the stairs, signaling that he wants to have a private talk with me. I raise my hand to stop him. I don't even put my purse down. Etta appears at the top of the stairs and grips the banister in fear.

"I just came from Miss Benton's house."

"I'm sorry, Mom."

"Really."

"I really am."

"Have you told Miss Benton?"

"The principal called us into the office before band practice, and Miss Benton came, and we all told her that we were sorry."

"So it's all better now?"

Etta shrugs.

"Answer me."

"No."

"No, what?"

"No ma'am."

"Come downstairs."

Etta gingerly makes her way down the stairs. I go into the living room. Jack and Etta follow me. I motion for her to sit. "How did this happen?"

"Me and Misty—"

"Misty and I."

"Misty and I were in the library, and she told me that when her dad was in high school, he called Westmoreland Coal and had a ton sent to Mr. Bates, his biology teacher. And we thought it was funny."

"Oh, it's funny. Did you see what you did?"

Etta shakes her head.

"Do you know that Miss Benton just moved here and she's all alone? Can you imagine how she feels?"

Etta looks at me. Clearly, she hasn't thought about Miss Benton.

"First of all, you're going to clean up the mess. You and your pals."

"She knows that." Jack looks at her sternly.

"And you're not going to New York."

Etta looks up at me. "What?"

Jack almost says something, but I don't give him a chance. "You heard me. You're not going to New York."

"But it was a joke!"

"I hope you had a good laugh, because that's all you're getting out of it. Go to your room."

Etta gets up slowly and walks to the doorway. I can tell she wants to say something, but she thinks better of it and climbs the stairs to her room.

I collapse onto the couch. Jack sits down next to me.

"How could this happen?" I ask him.

"They're kids."

"That's no excuse. I'm really worried about her."

"Why?"

"She runs with all these older kids. That's not good."

"You mean Misty?"

"Misty, the kids in the band."

"She carries the banner."

"Still."

"She's really sorry."

"Too bad."

"No, she really means it. She cried at the principal's office."

"What is it, Jack? Do you think I'm overreacting?" Jack doesn't answer me. "I went to see Kate Benton, and she was devastated. I bet she moves out of town over this."

"Why?"

"God, Jack, don't you get it? She's all alone over there. She moved here on a lark, thought it would be interesting to live in a small town, and look at this. She's a joke to those kids. How would you feel?"

"I'd take control of the situation. You have to when you work with kids." Jack leans back and puts his feet on the coffee table. This nonchalant movement infuriates me further. I want to shake my husband, wake him up to what this *is*, show him that it's not just about a cruel prank, it's deeper than that. It's about Us and Them, Ferriners and Natives. How do I explain that I've been a ferriner all of my life, and that I relate to Kate Benton? My daughter will never have the experience of being an outsider. With her MacChesney name and her lineage, she is one of Them. I can't get into this with my husband. He is one of Them too. He doesn't see it, doesn't think it's important. So instead, I blast him for his indifference.

"You know what? *You're* not taking control of this situation."

"She said she's sorry."

"Maybe that's my problem. I don't believe her. She's old enough to know this was a terrible thing to do. Where's her conscience? Her compassion? Don't you worry that she's not sensitive to other people's feelings?"

"Like you're sensitive to mine?" Jack asks softly.

"What?"

"When did we talk about a punishment? You just sort of sprung the New York thing on her and me. I want to back you up, but you need to at least let me know what you're going to do."

"I don't believe it! You're turning this into something *I'm* doing wrong."

"If you want me to help, you have to let me make the decisions with you. That's all I'm saying." Jack's tone is even and calm, as though we've had this argument before. (We have.)

"I'm sorry. This incident hit a nerve."

"I see that." Jack puts his arm around me. I sink into him like a spoon in cake batter.

"All the books say to get a grip on your emotions before you discipline your child. Haven't I done that in the past? I usually have a grip, don't I?"

"Yes, you do. Most of the time."

"But this time I saw myself in it. I was like Miss Benton for a lot of years. It's like Etta did something personal to the person I used to be."

Jack holds me for a long time, and I don't say a word. No matter how many years go by, I'm never very far from who I was, the ferriner, the unmarried one, the lone Eye-talian. And no matter how many years go by, I carry her inside me. Somehow I know that I always will.

Etta has left for school early. She has the Girls' Athletic Association preschool basketball game, but I'm sure she wants to avoid me. Jack is off to work already, so the house is quiet. As I pull a mug from the kitchen cabinet, I see a letter addressed to me propped on the windowsill. With the end of a teaspoon, I open the letter and unfold it, then I pour myself a cup of coffee.

Dear Mom,

I know you hate me right now but I wanted you to hear my side of things. I did do the wrong thing. I did call the coal company and place the order on a Friday when we knew they were rushing to get out of there and wouldn't check. I don't hate Miss Benton, except for the laps she makes us run, she's been a pretty good band director. We thought it would be funny to see a pile of coal in her yard. I didn't think about how we would get it out of there. I am very sorry. I am sorry I hurt Miss Benton and sorry I can't go to New York where I've always wanted to go. I won't order a coal dump in anyone's yard anymore.

Etta

I grab some paper and a pen and write Etta a note back.

Dear Etta,

    I don't hate you. I don't like what you did, there's a difference. I believe you are sorry for the coal dump and that you won't do it again. But next time you think of doing something for the sport of it, would you please consider the person's feelings? How would you like someone to do that to you?

Love,<br>Mom

I leave the letter on Etta's bed, noting that her room has never been so neat. She's not a bad kid, I remind myself as I pack up for work. She didn't try to weasel out of her punishment or blame anyone else for the prank. Maybe she even learned something. But it's uncanny to me, how my kid can zero in on my sensitivities. She knows I'm protective of new folks who move to town. And she knows equally well what is required for me to set myself on the path of forgiveness.

Life in Cracker's Neck Holler has been so quiet since the coal dump a month ago, you'd think this old house was a monastery. I chose not to back down on my punishment. Etta will not be going to New York City with me (this time), and Jack agreed. It is so hard to follow through with this decision, because one of my dreams for my daughter is to travel, to expose her to the outside world, to museums, plays, culture. A couple of days ago, I almost buckled, but Jack reined me in. It won't be Etta's last chance to visit New York City, he reminded me. And both Jack and I feel it's more important to stand by the punishment than to let her think we can be softened up with a few nicely made beds. I keep a picture of Pavis Mullins in my head at all times to remind myself that once children think they can get away with something, they'll continue to try.

Iva Lou volunteered to chauffeur me to the airport—I got a great fare, and I'll be in New York City by suppertime. Etta has a football game, where Jack is working the Band Boosters' refreshment stand; Conley Barker, who runs the taxi service, is unavailable because he also announces home games for the radio, so Iva Lou generously volunteered, even though she loves Powell Valley football and hates to miss a game. I apologize for putting her out.

"It is no problem. So, you gonna see that hunk from New Jersey when you're up there?" Iva Lou adjusts the rearview mirror and looks at me. The road to the Tri-Cities airport is hilly, and I get butterflies as Iva Lou sails over the bumps.

"Who?" I play dumb.

"Pete Rutledge." Iva Lou draws his name out slowly.

"I don't know." I'm lying, of course. I would like to see Pete, my what-if fantasy. What married woman doesn't have a Plan B? You know, the handsome man from the past who, if the circumstances were different, would be the Man of the Present. Pete was very romantic and very interested four summers ago in Italy, but of course, I was married. So I safely placed him on a back burner, to lift the lid on *that* pot only when I was mad at Jack or bored with my life or stressed by my daughter. Pete Rutledge is like a good old movie that I return to in my mind's eye when I need a lift. In those moments I tell myself that if anything ever happens to Jack, there is always Pete. I do feel guilty about it, but I consider it Practical Fantasizing: when I'm being taken for granted or I get bogged down by drudgery, I can return to that field of bluebells and imagine what might have been.

"I thought New York and New Jersey were as close as Coeburn and Norton."

"They are."

"So he's right *there*, and you're right there. Did you pack your high heels?"

"What for?"

"So you can walk all over him."

"Don't you think I have enough to worry about?"

"Yeah, you do, honey, I'm just messin' with you." Iva Lou laughs.

"We're talking about me, not you. I'm not a flirt."

"Hmm. So you been thinkin' about how to get away with something."

"Absolutely not. I have a good husband, and I don't need any excitement."

"Oh, honey-o, excitement is the only thing worth livin' for." Iva Lou stops at the light outside Gate City. "But I'll make sure that things are as dull as dirt in the Gap. I'll keep an eye on your husband while you're off *not* gettin' excited."

"Not necessary."

"I'll be the judge of that. We just hired him to build us some storage units at the library, should keep him busy about a week." Iva Lou winks at me.

"Isn't that funny—the exact amount of time I'll be gone."

"Uh-huh. We murried gals got to stick together and form a shield around our men," Iva Lou says with a resolve I haven't heard since she went before the county to request a new Bookmobile (she got it).

As I board the plane, I look back and wave good-bye to Iva Lou. I have no problem leaving my life in her hands, none whatsoever.

## CHAPTER THREE

*T*he first rule about living in New York City (according to Theodore Tipton) is that no one ever picks up a guest at the airport.
Never. Apparently, La Guardia Airport is a zoo, and it's up to the guest
to get in the taxicab line (I'm not taking the bus; Theodore's instructions were too confusing), tell the driver your address, and sit back
and hope he doesn't take you on a hayride to Connecticut or beyond.

I went digging into my mom's trunks for my wardrobe for this trip.
I found a vintage cropped jacket in a navy blue velvet and embroidered pants, the wide-legged, high-waisted style from the early 1940s.
Theodore said the weather had turned cold early and to dress warmly,
so I figured the velvet would be perfect. I want to dazzle Theodore's
friends, so I even threw in some of Mama's jewelry. She made a
brooch of jet beads, which I'll wear to a night out at the theater. My
only wardrobe worry is shoes—mine are woefully not up to snuff, so
I'll splurge on some new ones in Greenwich Village (Theodore calls
Eighth Street, near his apartment, Shoe Town). I'm wearing a black
turtleneck and black jeans; I figure that's a standard New York look, so
I won't look like I have "tourist" tattooed on my forehead.

It's surprising how self-reliant I become when I'm alone. Part of being married is getting lazy; when I'm home I leave all the logistics (directions to Biltmore House and Gardens for a school field trip) and icky weird chores (cleaning the furnace, trapping mice) to my husband. It's empowering for me to negotiate my way through one of the busiest airports in the world. I pass under the entry portal, where LA GUARDIA pulses overhead in giant red letters; how thrilling, a fellow Eye-talian and former mayor of New York City with an airport named after him!

As I wait for my luggage, it seems like thousands of people are milling about, no two of them alike. New York really is the capital of the world, and I'm as intrigued by the wide-eyed Indian woman in her turquoise sari with strips of gold lamé on the hem as I am by the tall Russian in a bad mood who yanks his oversize duffel bags off the carousel and loads them onto a cart. I reach my hands up over my head, embracing the whole scene, and have a good stretch, thrilled to be here, so happy to be a part of something so exciting and new (to me, anyway).

"Your first trip?" a voice says behind me (I guess my look of wonder and appreciation has given me away). I drop my arms and turn.

"I went through JFK once on my way to Italy." Do I sound like a defensive tourist or what?

"Hmm. You Italian?"

"I am." In New York, you're an American second and where you immigrated from first.

"Me too." The man is around sixty, with a shock of salt-and-pepper hair. He is small and trim, and has a long nose with a very fine bridge (according to the ancient art of Chinese face reading, he may well live to be a hundred years old).

"Where are your people from?" I ask.

"Napoli."

"You're southern."

"And you?"

"North. The Alps."

"They're pieces of work up there." The man laughs.

"How do you know?"

"I married one." The man doesn't take his eyes off the baggage carousel as it rotates. "Once my wife and me, we were in Atlantic City and went to a show, and they had a comedian there—you know, the warm-up guy. Anyway, he came over to our table and said, 'You two married?' and we said that we were, and he said, 'Ladies and gentlemen, these two agree about *nothing*.' And everybody laughed, and so did we, 'cause it's true. Northern Italians and southern Italians might as well be from two different planets, you know what I mean?"

I nod that I do. I can't believe how fast people talk here. That same observation would have taken someone in Big Stone Gap about three hours to relate. Of course, back home we *have* the three hours to spare. Here everyone is in a hurry.

My cabdriver is Pakistani, and he is happy to tell me all about his homeland. I am having more interesting conversations in five minutes in New York than I do in a year in Big Stone Gap. We turn off the Grand Central Parkway and onto the road that leads to the Queens end of the Fifty-ninth Street Bridge. The driver waves his hand over the Manhattan skyline as though presenting a box of jewels. At any moment I expect Fred Astaire and Ginger Rogers to spin across the sky; I see the clouds as her marabou cape and the stars, the heels of his black patent-leather wing tips, their glittering shoes barely touching down on the emerald-cut horizon as they dance. What could top the magnificence of this picture? Theodore is so lucky, and I am so lucky that my best friend now *lives* under these lights and inside this fabulous madness. I feel a pang of guilt, though. Etta should be here.

"You okay, lady?" The driver looks at me in the rearview mirror.

"I wish my daughter were here," I tell him.

"New York City is not going anywhere. It will always be here," he says, and smiles. And, oddly enough, that makes me feel much better.

A doorman in a navy blue uniform with gold epaulets greets me in the small but ornate rococo lobby of Theodore's building on the corner of Fifth Avenue and Ninth Street in Greenwich Village. After I got out of the cab, I must have spent five minutes looking down to the arch at Washington Square Park, a four-story pale blue horseshoe that conjures the Champs-Élysées in Paris. "I just want to take one more look," I tell the doorman as he buzzes Theodore. I go back outside and look up Fifth Avenue to where the yellow stripes in the center of the street become one giant arrow that disappears into the darkness of uptown.

"Hey, the reunion's inside!" Theodore says, stepping out of the elevator. "You made it!" He looks handsome. His red hair is sandy with gray. He is in great shape, as though auditioning for the dance corps at Radio City instead of directing it. He looks younger somehow. The worry creases between his eyes are gone, and it seems like the whole of him has relaxed (no small feat for a perfectionist).

Every detail of Theodore's new home interests me: the elevator with the shiny brass buttons; the walnut panels inlaid with 1930s Chinese foil wallpaper in the hallways; the carpet, a black and gray wool harlequin pattern (very deco). Any moment I expect Carole Lombard to peek out one of the doors looking for William Powell. We reach the door to Theodore's apartment. The small name tag over the doorbell that reads TIPTON proves that this whole trip is not a dream.

"What do you think?" Theodore stands in the middle of his living room, tastefully done in simple grays and off-white, very spare and neat. There are three large windows that overlook Fifth Avenue. I walk over to take in the scene below. The traffic streams toward Washington Square like a loose string of pop beads.

"Sure beats your log cabin in Powell Valley."

"I wish I had the closets I had in Big Stone Gap. But the only people with big closets in this city own the buildings." I follow Theodore down a small hallway with track lighting. "Check out the bedrooms.

This one is yours." He drops my bags in a room so small, there is only a single bed, a nightstand, and a straight-back chair. He has decorated it simply with an antique quilt made by my mother-in-law (a gift from me when he got the job at the University of Tennessee). "And this is mine." Theodore pushes open the door to his bedroom. It looks sleek, with a platform bed and a gray slipper chair in the corner. It's almost the size of the living room, except it overlooks Washington Square Park.

"Oh my God" is all I can say.

"I know, I know. Every night before I go to bed, I think of Henry James."

"That's the actual spot where Dr. Sloper lived, isn't it?" I point to a row of brownstones that faces the park.

"Could be."

"Remember when we used to read *The Heiress* aloud?"

"Yep. Your interpretation of Catherine Sloper will never be topped. Even though I am the only person in the world who heard you read it." Theodore laughs.

"Let's just say I could relate to the story." And boy, did I. The story of an oppressed daughter of a cruel father rang true to me. "Who would have ever thought you would be living in Henry James country?"

Theodore hasn't changed so much as evolved. He is comfortable in his skin, in this apartment, in his life. There is an ease to him that was never there before. "You look better than you've ever looked. I'm not kidding."

"That's what happens when you find the place where you fit."

"Weren't you nervous to move here?"

"Oh, God no. I couldn't wait. I'm just glad I finally made it." Theodore looks at me and smiles. "You look good."

"Oh, come on."

"No, you do."

I follow Theodore into the kitchen. A bar counter separates the kitchen from the living room, and he's set the small dining table and chairs in front of the counter with white china and a white tablecloth. Then we hear a buzzer.

"Dinner's on."

"Dinner?"

"I can't possibly top Charlie Mom's Chinese. Wait till you taste the honey spareribs. Sit here so you have the view."

Theodore answers the door. A cute Chinese kid delivers two brown bags. Imagine. Dinner delivered hot to your door. How I wish I had this sort of setup in Big Stone Gap! Theodore unloads the bags, filling the table with small white boxes. "Tell me why you didn't bring Etta."

I tell Theodore every detail of the coal prank. He listens without interruption.

"What was the punishment?"

"We made the kids shovel the coal back onto the truck and resod her yard."

"They got off easy. I would've made them shovel the coal into wheelbarrows and walk it back to Appalachia." Theodore loads my plate with all sorts of delicacies—tiny shrimp, fluffy rice, chopped vegetables. "Etta organized five other kids to pull this off?"

"Yes. I couldn't believe it. She was in charge, but she had Misty Lassiter egging her on."

"Tayloe's daughter?"

"Yeah. She's got all of Tayloe's beauty and talent plus a cunning criminal mind, which really adds to her allure."

Theodore smiles. "That bad, huh?"

"Well, I'm a little put out by the whole thing." I stab a sparerib. "I feel like I can't trust Etta now, and I hate that. If she's not climbing on our roof, she's pulling pranks. I don't want to monitor her every move. I don't want to hover. But she doesn't leave me a choice."

"You need to keep her busy."

"She's in the band; she plays basketball before school; she works with her dad on weekends. How busy can I keep her? I don't know what else to do, short of sending her to convent school."

"There's a good one right across the river in Jersey."

"Don't tempt me."

"Back when I was teaching kids, I noticed patterns—"

"What kind of patterns?" I blurt nervously. As usual, my mind leaps to the worst-case scenario.

"Relax. It's just that the smartest kids were the ones who pulled stuff. Now, I'm not talking about the suck-up brainiacs, I'm talking about the kids who, no matter how many clubs and activities you put them in, still have time to cut up. Etta sounds like she's bored. She's hanging out with older kids, she's got time on her hands during the school day. These are all the classic signs of a troublemaker. You have to help her find a way to engage her mind."

"I'd like to find a way to engage her heart," I tell Theodore plainly.

"What do you mean?"

"I'd like her to think of other people and their feelings. Don't get me wrong. I know it could be worse and I know she has a good heart, but she's more headstrong than loving."

"She sounds like Mrs. Mac." Theodore leans back and laughs, remembering my mother-in-law. "That was one tough lady. She had that cane. She didn't carry it around because she needed the support, she used it to intimidate people. She was always banging it on the floor or catching a closing door with it. I remember I was in the post office once, going out, and she was coming in. I was in a rush, so I sort of sprinted out of there. She stopped me and said, 'Mr. Tipton?' And then she whacked me on the butt and said, 'Youth! Always in a hurry!' "

"How about when she came into the Pharmacy and asked me why I didn't accept her son's proposal? I was humiliated."

"She wound up getting her way, didn't she?" Theodore laughs and refills our wineglasses.

"How *are* you and Jack doing?"

"We're in a good place."

"No distractions?"

"You mean Karen Bell?" If there are even rumors about your husband straying, it becomes the touchstone of every conversation you'll have about your marriage. But I don't mind, because this is Theodore. "Well, I haven't found any notes, and there haven't been any phone calls, and Iva Lou says that Karen found a serious boyfriend up in Honaker, and Fleeta says she hasn't heard tell of her in Norton, so I guess she's out of the picture entirely."

"Well, that's good. It's funny about affairs, though, isn't it? They're so—I don't know, *urgent* when they're happening, uncontrollable almost, and then once they're over, it's hard to remember why the passion consumed you in the first place."

This is why Theodore and I remain so close after all these years. He can look at my life and see it clearly, in ways that I cannot. He reads my heart like a passage from a play, with emotional understanding of the moment but with one eye always on the bigger picture. Wherever he is, I feel at home with him, even in New York City, a place that once lived only in my imagination.

The guest bathroom is loaded up with all sorts of bubble baths and soaps in a basket. I take full advantage of a faceted bottle marked CALM, pouring the opulent lavender milk into the hottest water I can stand. The stress of my trip and all the anxiety leading up to it float up and out the transom in the steam. I let it go and breathe deeply.

Theodore knows how to treat a guest. The candles, nestled in a series of crystal cups, are scented like sugar cookies and throw shadows of snowflakes onto the wall. There's a stack of fluffy white towels in a wrought-iron antique stand; they're monogrammed not with initials but with the word RELAX. There's even a shower radio, and I turn on some music while I soak. (It's set on a country station, which makes me laugh.) Theodore thinks of everything; maybe that's why Radio City Music Hall snapped him up—great art is in the details.

Theodore gets me up early with a large paper cup of coffee and a giant cinnamon and raisin bagel in a brown paper bag (does everything to eat in this city come in a sack?). He wants me up and dressed so we're ready to hit the day running. Theodore has to be in the office, and he has mapped out places around Radio City that I can visit while he's working. He has a whole itinerary worked out; we'll see shows, sightsee, and even watch the Columbus Day Parade down Fifth Avenue on Monday. "You'll really get your fill of Eye-talians," Theodore promises.

The offices at Radio City aren't really offices at all. They're small beige cubicles, sort of like a giant egg carton. The walls overflow with charts and calendars and swatches of fabric, braids and trims for costumes, watercolors of set designs, and shoes (you'd be surprised how many kinds of tap shoes there are). The phones never stop ringing. Everyone is young, and everyone seems rushed. They barely look up when Theodore introduces me; they aren't rude, just busy. When he walks to the center of the maze, he is besieged by everyone from the dance captain to the receptionist. Of course, this is their busiest time of year; they're in preproduction for the Christmas extravaganza. As a small group gathers around Theodore, I reach into his jacket pocket and pull out the list of places for me to check out on my own and indicate that I'll be back for lunch.

There must be a hundred makeup kiosks on the main floor of Saks Fifth Avenue. I think of Fleeta, who complains about having to load two measly spin racks at the Mutual's; I wonder what she'd do if she had to help stock this operation.

I am spritzed with four different perfumes on my way through (they asked politely and I couldn't say no) and invited to have my makeup done, French look, high-fashion look, the natural look, or any look I want—these salesgirls are wide open to the possibilities of the paints they're peddling.

There is a girl around Etta's age sitting on one of the high-backed chairs in front of a mirror at the Clinique counter. Standing next to her is her mother (obvious from the analytical expression she wears while studying her daughter). As the makeup consultant dabs a little concealer on the girl's face, the mother leans in.

"Too much."

"Mom."

"Amy, don't argue with me."

"Use a light touch and it won't even seem like she's wearing it," the consultant says, reassuring the mother.

The girl examines her face in the mirror. "It hardly looks like I have anything on."

"I don't want it to look like you have makeup on."

"I need it," Amy responds in an all-knowing tone my daughter uses on a regular basis.

"Makeup doesn't make you pretty, it's what's inside that counts," Amy's mother reminds her.

"If you're a nun," Amy says flatly.

"There's nothing wrong with nuns. They serve humanity. Plus, you'll get much further in life focusing on your brain." Now she's gone too far; she sounds like the Universal Mother whose generic wisdom can be cracked in two and read aloud like advice in a fortune cookie.

As I take the escalator up to the next floor, I look down on Amy and her mother, who become smaller and smaller as the stairs lift away. Suddenly I don't see them, I see Etta and me. That's just the sort of conversation we have, where we disagree and haggle back and forth about the most insignificant things. After we finish one of these sessions, Etta feels misunderstood and I feel like I can't say anything right. I wonder why it is so hard for mothers to remember that daughters are just learning about being women and that this time in their lives will never come again.

"How was your day?" Theodore asks as I hang on to the strap in the back of a particularly speedy cab on our way to dinner.

"Busy. I went to Saint Patrick's. Rockefeller Center. Saks. Then I walked up to Central Park. As I was walking around, I saw a stray cat, but when I looked more closely, it was a rat. Once I realized it was a rat, it was too late to scream, and he went behind a rock anyway. And then I went to the carousel, and I just sat there for a long time and watched people. Women really know how to dress in New York."

The doors to Blue Pearl are painted bright blue with gold tassels drawn on them trompe l'oeil style. Theodore opens the door for me. "Ignore the decor. It's over the top," he whispers as we enter.

I like the decor. We're inside a blue cave, with booths lit by low-hanging fixtures. The tables are small squares, perfect for two, with blue rose petals sprinkled in the center. Even the mirrored walls are smoky blue, reminding me of a 1920s speakeasy. The maître d' leads us through the crowded restaurant to a corner table, handing each of us a menu.

"How did you pick this place?" I ask Theodore.

"I know the chef. He's a special friend of mine."

The way he says this makes me think that the someone special is *his* someone special. "You have a boyfriend?" I say too loudly. Theodore nods. "Why didn't you tell me?"

"Wouldn't you rather just meet him?"

I follow Theodore to the kitchen doors. He points through the porthole window. The kitchen is small but neat. There is a long silver prep table, and behind it, an open grill with two deep overhead ovens. Theodore takes my hand and we go through the doors; we wedge into a corner observing the action, but we're in the way in this tight space. There's a phone with rows of blinking lights that look like they need to be answered, and quickly. Theodore points to the phone. "Told you the place was hot."

"Torch the brûlée!" The chef, his back to us, bellows through the din, and an assistant obeys him instantly.

"That's Max." Theodore points to the baritone in the tall white hat. Max has a stocky build (mostly muscle), and big forearms and hands. His hair is black and cut close to his large head (which, in face reading, means he will always make a good living). His black eyes don't miss a trick; he scans the pots, rearranging them as the food simmers. Finally he senses invaders and looks up. He smiles and wipes his hands on a dish towel looped through his belt as he joins us.

"This must be Ave Maria." Max takes my hand.

"This is Max Berkowitz," Theodore says proudly.

"I'm so happy to meet you," I say. Max has a great smile and deep dimples (though I don't think his staff sees them very often).

"I hope you're hungry."

"I am."

"Go sit and relax, and get ready. I'm gonna dazzle you." Max winks at Theodore.

The feast brought to our table begins with a lobster bisque so light and buttery that I want a second bowl, but I'm too ashamed to ask. It's a good thing too, because what follows is so scrumptious, I would have been sorry to miss it. Max makes us baby lamb chops on a bed of sweet-potato puree, followed by a salad of spinach, pears, walnuts, and curls of fresh Parmesan cheese—it's the dressing that kills me; it's made with raspberries and balsamic vinegar.

"I wish Jack were here. Max would have an apprentice. Jack still talks about opening a restaurant."

"You're lucky you have a man who cooks."

"So are you. How did you meet?"

"One of those introduce-the-new-guy-to-town parties."

"You met and that was it?"

"Sort of. It grew slowly. Thought he'd be a good friend. He was so interesting, I never met anyone like him. He's so expressive and pas-sionate."

"And talented!" I add.

"Definitely. And I haven't changed much: it's still hard for me to get close to anyone. So Max has to spend a lot of time pulling my feel-ings out of me. And I have to say, I like it."

"You deserve someone who understands you completely."

"I think Max is The Guy."

"You *think* I'm the guy?" Max pulls up a chair next to me. "Hardly sounds like an endorsement. Table six is having risotto, I got two sec-onds to kill. Ready for dessert?" The waiter brings two small dishes filled with some sort of custard. "Lavender flan," Max announces. "Sounds like a weird combination, but it just works." Max smiles at Theodore and goes back to the kitchen.

"Was he talking about your relationship or the flan?" I ask Theo-dore.

"Both."

Theodore and I are full, so we walk the twenty blocks or so from the restaurant to his apartment. I love the twisty Greenwich Village streets lit by lamps and old sconces in the doorways. The brownstones stacked close together, walls touching, remind me of my favorite thing, a shelf of books. And they are not unlike great books, full of characters and their stories. How I wish I could live in a place like this, maybe not forever but just long enough to hear their secrets.

Theodore turns on the lights in his apartment, dropping his keys with one hand while hitting the answering machine with the other. He takes my coat and hangs it in the closet.

"Uh, Theodore Tipton? This is Pete Rutledge," the familiar voice on the machine begins. "I understand you have a houseguest. I've been tipped off by her husband. Ask Ave Maria Mulligan if she can give me a shout at my office at NYU. Two-four-three, five-four-one-zero. Thanks."

"Mulligan? I haven't heard that in fifteen years. Does he think you're still single?"

"Oh, please." I say this casually as I throw myself down on Theodore's easy chair. I would never admit that I'm secretly thrilled Pete called. Why should I tell Theodore that Pete is my escape-hatch fantasy?

"What are you thinking about?" Theodore asks suspiciously.

"Nothing." My voice goes up an octave.

"You went off somewhere. Somewhere dangerous," Theodore observes.

"I was thinking about Jack and Pete. You know."

"No, I don't."

"I'm not going to do anything with Pete on this visit, don't worry."

"Who said anything about you doing anything with Pete Rutledge?"

"That's what you meant, isn't it?"

"No, it's what *you* meant." Theodore looks at me as though I'm up to something, and I kind of like it. At my age, I like to look into the eye of danger—okay, maybe take a peek, because *that's* as much of a thrill as I can handle.

I sleep peacefully and wake up feeling so refreshed, I believe anything is possible. I had a flying dream. It's my favorite kind of dream, where I'm walking along (in this particular dream it was Schilpario in winter, high in the Italian Alps with snow coming down like powdered sugar out of a sifter), and I'm with my father on an alpine path, chatting about nothing in particular, and then the breeze abruptly kicks up, and I hold out my arms and the wind lifts me off the ground and into the sky. I rise, higher and higher toward the stars, until the world below loses all detail, and any movement looks like coffee grounds scattered across a countertop. I can't hear anything, the sky is perfectly quiet, and even the sound of the wind stops. And for what seems like hours, I am flying, dipping, and sailing, so lightly I could disappear into the clouds I float through.

Theodore has already left for work, leaving me another sack breakfast; this time a large cappuccino and an oversize cinnamon bun. I'm going to gain ten pounds on this trip, but I don't care—I'm on vacation. I feel so good, I pick up the phone and dial Pete Rutledge's number. A secretary answers the phone and asks if I am attending Pete's lecture to the graduate students in architecture that night. I ask her if visitors can attend, and she says I'm welcome, so I tell her sure, put me on the list, since I know Theodore is working late. I tell the woman that Pete doesn't have to call me back, I'll see him after the lecture. When I hang up, I instantly regret that I agreed to attend. What if Pete acts distant or doesn't have time to see me or doesn't look good? (How shallow of me!) It will take the rosy glow off my favorite Italian daydream. Okay, if it does, I'll live with it. But I am going down in style. I'm going to look good tonight, and I will start with my feet. I set out for Eighth Street in search of the perfect shoe (it worked for Cinderella).

What am I going to say to Pete when I see him? After all, it's been a long time. We've spoken on the phone quite a bit, Christmas cards and all that, but I haven't *seen* him. Have I changed in four years? I'm sure he hasn't—men barely skip a beat between forty and fifty. He's probably as desirable as ever. He's probably met thousands of women on his travels, thousands of women with whom he hikes the Italian Alps, wades in natural hot springs, and rolls around in fields of bluebells. Do I think I'm the only one? I know I'm not. And maybe it's this knowledge that convinces me to go to this thing tonight; after all, we're Just Friends.

The Casa Italiana Zerilli-Marimo building is only a couple of blocks away from Theodore's apartment, and I'm grateful for the cold night air and the walk. I had put on Mama's pants and jacket but decided the pants made the whole thing too dressy, so I kept the jacket but changed to jeans instead. Then I put on my new black suede New York boots, which took me half the day to find and all of my shoe budget to purchase. I feel I look my best, and it's always a good idea to look your best when you're half of an unplanned reunion.

The lobby is crowded with students and assorted professional types. I follow the crowd into a large lecture hall and take an aisle seat toward the back. When the room is full, a studious-looking professor comes from the back of the room and stands in front of the lectern. Her opening remarks are dry until she mentions Pete Rutledge, and then a wave of excitement seems to peel through her body, forcing her to rise onto her tiptoes and hold the position for a second until she realizes she is punctuating her introduction with a bit too much enthusiasm. She rolls back down onto her heels and explains that Pete is a marble expert and guest professor in their architecture department. The next thing I hear is applause. Pete has emerged from a door halfway up the aisle and is making his way to the podium, carrying a bottle of water.

The women in the audience sit up in their seats. They study Pete the same way I did the first time I saw him. All the things that made my heart stop at that outdoor disco are still there: his height, the chiseled features (he looks even more like Rock Hudson now), the perfect lips and smile, and those eyes, slate blue and bright. He is wearing jeans and a brown tweed jacket, and the look is sexy. Why does he have to look so good?

Pete puts down the water bottle and scans the crowd as though he's looking for someone. I want to dive under the seats in front of me, but I don't, and I'm glad when I see the look of total surprise on his face as our eyes meet.

Pete lectures extensively about the marble mines in Italy—his favorites are located in Bari, near the Adriatic Sea—and describes the mining process in detail. After the talk is over and the enthusiastic applause has subsided, a group of students gathers around the podium. Pete listens to their questions, but he keeps looking up at me, as if to make sure I'm still there. I indicate that I'll wait for him in the lobby. After a minute or two of nervous pacing in the lobby, I am tempted to bolt, to run back to Theodore's; okay, I've seen Pete Rutledge, he's the same, still gives me butterflies and that's all I wanted to know, now I can go back and let this infatuation or whatever it is go. I decide to slip out. He won't miss me a bit; he's got a roomful of fans. Just as I'm turning toward the door, I feel a hand on my shoulder.

"Where are you going?" Pete stands in the doorway, folding his speech into a tube, which he bangs against his thigh.

"I was just going to get some air."

"No, you were leaving." Pete takes my hand and kisses me on the cheek. "You look beautiful."

"Great lecture."

"Glad you could make it."

"I'm interested in indigenous Italian marble."

"Really."

"Yeah. I was particularly enlightened by your description of the new mining techniques."

"You were."

"I was."

"Are you hungry?"

"Very," I blurt. I should have lied. I certainly didn't intend to have dinner with him. I just wanted to say hello and get back to Theodore.

"I want the whole story. What you're doing here, how long you're staying, especially how long you're staying." He smiles *that* smile, and I think I'm going to pass out (maybe it isn't him, maybe I'm really hungry). I casually put my hand on the frame of an enormous painting by the door and lean against it. The security guy shoots me a look. I pull my hand away.

"Professor Rutledge?" A beautiful girl in her early twenties approaches us. She has gorgeous red curls that spiral out in every direction, a sprinkle of freckles on her nose, and a body that, well, I'll never see the likes of in *my* mirror.

"I'm Sharon Hall. I'm in the architecture school here."

"Congratulations."

"Thank you. I'd like to interview you for our newsletter."

"Sure."

"Where can I reach you?"

"Um, you know what? Call the office and leave me a message, and I'll get back to you."

"Great. Great. Sorry I interrupted." She smiles at me warmly. "And thank you so much." She smiles demurely at him (redheads always have great teeth).

"I didn't know architects looked like that," I say after she's walked away.

"They don't generally," Pete says, laughing.

As Pete and I walk through the Village, I tell him why I'm here and what I've been doing since I landed. Every time I try to get him to talk about what's going on in his life, he somehow eases the conversation back to me. When we reach the public library on the corner of Sixth Avenue and West Tenth Street, Pete finds a small X carved into the sidewalk cement and makes me stand on it.

"Now look up. See the owl?"

"I see a clock." In a bell tower, there is a beautiful clock with four faces, each pointing in a different direction.

"Look again." Pete stands behind me and casually puts his arms around me; as I look up a shiver runs through me.

"I see it!" The two clock faces form the eyes, and the roof the head, of the owl. "Etta would love that."

"Show her next time." Pete rattles the wrought-iron gate on Patchin

Place, a series of small brownstones painted in yellow and white separated by a small cobblestone street. "This is where e. e. cummings lived."

"The Patchin Place poems!"

"That's right. Greenwich Village has been home to a lot of great writers. Bret Harte lived up the street; Eugene O'Neill down a ways. This is the biggest advantage of working at NYU. I'm in the middle of literary history. It's romantic, isn't it?"

It's bad enough that I'm thinking romance, worse that he's pointing it out to me, but that's Pete: a perfect man in a romantic setting (I wonder, does he *plan* these settings?).

"Here we go." Pete takes my hand and leads me up a small staircase into a quiet bistro filled with mahogany antiques, odd chairs with needlepoint seats, and benches along the wall. The only light is coming from a refrigerator case that holds some of the most ornate pastries I've ever seen: tortes layered with frosting, éclairs festooned with tiny pink roses on their chocolate sleeves, a strawberry napoleon with stripes of custard and jam nestled between paper-thin crust.

"They have real food too."

"This *is* real food!" I insist.

"Let's go in the back." Pete takes me to the garden room and points to a booth in the farthest corner. We sit down, and though the wood is old and mottled, it's comfortable.

"You like this place?"

"I love it." The waiter places a basket of bread and butter on the table. "And I love fresh bread!" I tear off a piece of bread.

"You're an easy woman to make happy. So, how's Etta? How's Jack?"

"She's fine. He's fine."

"I like him, you know."

"I know. But hey, he's a great guy. Why wouldn't you like him?" I rush to promote and support my husband like the good soldier I am.

"I usually don't like the competition."

I ignore his flirting and bite into the bread, so Pete redirects the conversation (thank God). "I saw your dad last time I was in Italy."

"He told me. It was so nice of you to visit."

"He's an interesting man. There he is living in a mountain village, but there's nothing about him that's small-town. He reads, and he's interested in the bigger universe. He wants the place to grow yet maintain its charm. He'd be a kick-ass urban planner if he lived in the States."

"Sometimes I wish he did."

"Do you ever want to move over there?"

"I couldn't. Jack's construction business is going really well, and I have the Pharmacy, and Etta's in school—"

"I'd like to drop everything and move there tomorrow," Pete says convincingly.

"Why don't you?"

"Complicated." He smiles when he says this, and it makes me laugh.

"How so?"

"I'm getting married."

Now, I'm a bad actress and I know it, so I smile supportively even though his news is the last thing I expected to hear. "Oh," I say instead of "Congratulations."

He doesn't wait for me to thaw, just tells me his love story in technical steps, as if he's describing how to dig a quarry. "You know, I've lived with a couple of women, and it never seemed right. And then I met Gina about a year ago. She's divorced, has a thirteen-year-old son. At first I wasn't interested at all. She's not my type. She's small and blond and analytical. But we hit it off. She's smart, and she's caring. And she's into commitment. She wants a family structure for her son, and I can't blame her. It's important."

"When's the big day?" I must have said this too loudly, because a man at the next table looks over at me.

"We don't know."

"Oh."

"Well, what do you think?"

"I'm thinking what took you so long?"

Pete throws his head back and laughs. "Well, there was just one thing holding me back."

God, do I need to hear this? Do I need to hear how hard it will be for him to give up women, as various and delectable as the French pastries in the display case? "What's that?" I ask, knowing the answer.

"You." He reaches across the table and takes my hand.

"Me?" I pull my hand away, not just to defuse the tension but also to support my head before it hits the table like a slab of marble.

"Yeah. But I can't have you. So what can I do?" He picks up the menu and begins to read it.

"Pete?" The tone of my voice makes him put down the menu and look at me. "Did you ever see *The Ghost and Mrs. Muir?*"

"Gene Tierney."

"Yeah. And Rex Harrison."

"What about it?"

"Sort of like you and me. You're like the sea captain."

"Wasn't he dead?"

"He was the ghost who lived in the cottage Gene Tierney rented from his estate. And he didn't want anybody living in the house, so he haunted the tenants. But Gene Tierney fell in love with him, even though he wasn't real. He was unavailable to her just like you're un-available to me and I am to you."

"But I'm real."

"I know. But I'm already married, and I love my husband. So, truthfully, you might as well be a ghost. You know, we get one life-time, and we make choices. And we can't have everything we want. Gina sounds wonderful. And you care about her. And you shouldn't think about what you're going to miss out on, but what you *have.*"

"You make a lot of sense." Pete looks away for a moment.

Now, what I can't tell him is that I liked the idea that he was an eternal bachelor, an Unattached International Bon Vivant tied to no woman, no vows, and no country. I liked knowing he was out there traveling the world, collecting rock samples, and occasionally thinking of me. Ciao to my Plan B. As we eat, I make him laugh with stories of home. We talk about poetry and architecture and Italy. We have many things to cover (this was always the case), so we zigzag from subject to subject, feeding the hunger we have for each other's conversation, knowing that we may never visit alone like this again.

As Pete walks me back to Theodore's, we don't say much, which is weird because there's still plenty we haven't covered. When we arrive at the building, we stand under the awning and look at each other. It isn't normal gazing, it's as if we're studying each other, wondering what this means, what we mean to each other. I get very still inside myself, so still I can feel my breathing. I take my hands and place them on Pete's chest. Why I'm doing this, I don't know, but in the quiet, I feel his heart beating, and it reassures me.

"I've got to go." Pete looks down Fifth Avenue as though he's seen something in the distance that is calling him. He starts to say something else and stops.

"What?" I ask.

"If someone had told me that this would be the story of my romantic life, I would've laughed," he says with a smile.

"I'm sorry." For some reason, in this instant, I feel that it's all my fault.

"It's all right. It's timing." Pete puts his hands in his pockets.

"Can I tell you something?"

"Sure."

"When I'm sad, I think of you."

Pete looks at me carefully. "Why?"

"Because." I close my eyes as though the words I need are written on the front page of my mind. "Because you see the girl in me." It's true. Nobody remembers her anymore. She got lost on the road of responsibility and within the natural process of aging (ick). When

Pete Rutledge tells me I'm beautiful, I believe him. And boy, do I need to hear it. I need to *know* it. When I'm with him, I'm not taken for granted, I'm not just a pharmacist or a wife or a mother, I'm me, the real me. I'm celebrated. It's something that even the best husband can't deliver; it must come from the unfamiliar, or the new, or memory itself. That's the trade-off we all make in the security of commitment: excitement for comfort.

"Good night, Ave."

"Bye, Pete."

I watch him as he walks down the street. He turns. "Ave?"

"Yeah?"

"Tell Jack I'll send the samples this week, okay?"

"Okay."

Pete turns the corner and is gone. But just like Gene Tierney, I have a funny feeling that this is not the end of this fantasy. This is not the end of Pete Rutledge.

## CHAPTER FOUR

"Don't ask. Let me get into my pajamas," I tell Theodore, who perches on the couch like a cat waiting to be fed. "I can't believe you stayed up this late. Are you that curious about Pete Rutledge?"

"What can I say? I love a soap opera. I'll get the wine." Theodore jumps up and goes into the kitchen.

"I could've gotten into Big Trouble," I tell Theodore on my way to the bedroom. "But I didn't." As I change, Theodore hollers from the kitchen, "Boy, are you lucky. You had the 'my best friend the gay guy is waiting for me upstairs' excuse."

I take a glass of wine from Theodore and gulp it down.

"Now, give me all the details."

"Where's Max?"

"Never mind him. He's home. Exhausted. Come on. What happened?"

"Well, I went to the lecture, and then we walked around, and then we went to the Caffe dell'Artista on Greenwich Avenue."

"The cannoli there are as good as foreplay."

"No kidding."

"Go on."

"And he told me that he was going to get married."

"No."

"To a nice woman named Gina with a son."

"He didn't hit on you at all?"

"Yes, he did. Sort of. A little. And I was very happy about it, okay?"

"Don't get mad at me. I'm only asking the questions. Does he love the Gina woman?"

"He didn't say that. He said Gina wanted a commitment, and that her son needed him, you know, it was like a Red Cross deal. He's saving them or something."

"Uh-oh."

"And then he told me that—"

"Let me guess. He loves you but he can't have you."

"Yes! That's it! That's exactly what he said!"

"This is too good."

"It's terrible."

"It's perfect."

"How is it perfect?" I pour myself another glass of wine.

"You know that there's a great guy out there who adores you, and you never have to clean up after him or feed him or wonder if he's out catting around, or any of the bad stuff. You get only the good stuff. Who said fantasy is better than reality?"

"Everybody says that."

"Because it's true. Once you fall in love, and you're *in* love, the magic gets used up. That's not to say that the day-in and day-out routine of love isn't totally reassuring, of course it is. But it's flannel sheets instead of satin."

"Jack and I are definitely flannel. But it's more complicated than that. Pete helped me get over Joe's death. And because that bond was so strong, I had to decide if I was going to stay married to Jack. In my marriage, there's the world before Joe died, and then there's the world after. And sometimes at night, when it's just Jack and me, we talk about how everything changed after Joe, which we could never do until I went away that summer with Etta and met Pete. He helped me see where I was in my life. In a way, he even helped me to see that Jack was the right man for me."

Theodore doesn't say anything. What can he say? I just admitted that Pete Rutledge was, in a very real way, responsible for my ultimate happiness because he made me look honestly at myself and decide where I belonged. I chose Jack MacChesney, and maybe I'll always wonder what might have been. But who doesn't?

I cry all the way through the Columbus Day Parade. When the float made of red paper roses carrying Miss Italy drifts by, I see youth and beauty and possibility and feel at odds with myself. When the cornet band of old Italian men with handlebar mustaches marches by play-ing "Oh Marie," I think of my mother and her Louis Prima records, and how she never got the man she wanted the most. I wonder if there is some old village curse on the women in my line. I hope Etta avoids it. Somehow I think she will, as she has the MacChesney feistiness. I don't think an evil-eye curse would get my daughter down.

When I was growing up, my mother and I were the only Eye-talians in Big Stone Gap. I thought we were the only ones in the world, be-cause we were so removed from life beyond the Blue Ridge Moun-tains. But I was wrong. There were lots of us out there, and today I'm surrounded by them. I feel at home among the strong features, the prominent noses, the thick hair, the posture, the pride, all the char-acteristics I think of when I think of my father in Schilpario, or my mother. Sometimes her face flashes before me. I see her by the sink, or in the garden, or kneeling before me as she pins up a hem. I re-member her smile and how she made me feel safe. I see her in these young women, in the strength of their dark eyes.

I want to run into the middle of the parade and tell everyone, "I am one of you! I belong here!" My dream since childhood, to belong, to be part of a bigger family, a family that looked like me and felt the things I did. And here they are, thousands of them, on the sidewalks cheering and marching down the street. Finally, I fit in the world, and yet I'm still alone. I look around, and I'm the only person crying.

When the plane takes that first dip out of the clouds and into the clear, I see the Blue Ridge Mountains roll out before me in full autumn. The trees have turned bright yellow topaz; there won't be much orange or red tint to the leaves this year because of the Indian summer. I am happy to see these mountains again, to be home, where my husband and daughter wait for me. Southwest Virginia is an uncomplicated place for a complex person, and I miss it whenever I go.

I bought Etta lots of little things, not to make up for the punishment but to let her know that she was in my thoughts the whole time. I have a goal this fall: I want to get on good footing with my daughter. I want to understand her. I want her to understand me and why I parent the way I do. I hope she learned that when she does wrong, there are consequences. Now we need to work on her compassion. I know it's in there, I just have to help her find it.

"Yoo-hoo. Girl! Over here!" Iva Lou waves to me from beyond the checkpoint. I don't hide how thrilled I am that she came to pick me up. "How was it?" she asks as she gives me a big hug.

"Theodore is so happy. He's in his groove."

"I want to hear all about it." She lifts an eyebrow, and I know her next question is about Pete Rutledge. "So?" she says, dragging out the "o" until I answer.

"He's getting married."

"I knew you'd see him!"

"I saw him."

"Are you sad?"

"No."

"How did he look?"

"Better than ever," I tell her.

"Of course he does. That's how they keep us hooked. The rats."

As we wait for my luggage, I notice that Iva Lou is fidgeting nervously. And she seems to be chatting loud and fast as she gives me the Gap update since I've been away—the manic chitchat is not her style.

"Are you okay?"

"Uh-huh."

"No. Something is not right."

"Oh, Ave." Iva Lou exhales deeply and buries her hands in her jeans pockets.

Immediately I think of Iva Lou's husband. "What is it? Lyle?"

"No, no. He's okay. It's me, hon, and it's probably nothing."

"What, then?"

"You know how I've been draggin'. Not myself."

"So you went to the doctor. And you did your tests, right?"

"Yeah." Iva Lou takes a deep breath. "They found something."

"What did they find? And where?" I know in moments like these, it's best to collect the facts and not show any panic. Iva Lou needs reassuring; her eyes are filling with tears.

"On my breast. A lump. It's about the size of a pea. But it was hard, so they did a biopsy."

"Okay. What did it show?" I know all about this stuff, as I went through it with Mama.

"It was malignant."

"God."

"Malignant. Can you imagine?" Iva Lou taps her foot.

"First of all, don't panic."

"That's what my doctor said."

"They can get you better."

"He said that too. I went to that new wing at Holston Valley. They have a comprehensive breast center. They're very up-to-date over there, so if anybody can help me, they can."

"What's the next step?"

"They told me they caught it early, but I still have to move quickly."

"That's good news." By the time they found my mother's breast cancer, it was too late. It's as if Iva Lou reads my mind.

"I been thinkin' about your mama a lot."

"Yeah, but that was a long time ago, Iva Lou. And Mama didn't want to be aggressive in her treatment. She didn't want chemotherapy or any of that. She felt it best to let nature take its course, and that was a huge mistake. There was so much they could've done, and she might still be here if she had listened to the doctors."

"Well, I'm determined not to die."

"Good."

"I mean, I feel fine otherwise. I'm just so ding-dang tarred all the time. It just drains you, and maybe it's the mental part of it, but I ain't myself. I git home around seven, and I'm in bed by eight. It's crazy. I've always been a night owl, and now I'm acting like a shut-in senior citizen. That ain't like me!"

"It sure isn't." I put my arm around my old friend. "I'll be with you every step of the way."

"I know you will. Now, tell me about that Radio City. Did you get me an application to be a Rockette like I asked ya?"

I don't answer her. After all, what is a trip compared to what she's going through? We stand there a long time and finally look up and realize that all the other passengers have left. We're alone, and my luggage is circling around the carousel waiting for me to claim it.

"Let's go home," I tell Iva Lou.


Iva Lou and I ride most of the way home talking gossip and funny stories. Iva Lou isn't one to dwell on her problems, so we make light of things. I give her a big hug and tell her everything is going to be fine as she lets me out in front of my house. She's anxious to get home to Lyle, and I'm happy to be back in Cracker's Neck, surrounded by these old mountains, whose every ridge I know and every path I've followed. It's so peaceful here, I think as I stand on the front steps and look out over the dark field that leads to the lower road into town.

New York is magical, but I missed the sound of the wind and the low rustle it makes through the trees before the leaves fall.

"Hello, beautiful," my husband says to me as I drop my bags in the front hall.

"I'm going away more often," I tell Jack as he takes me in his arms and kisses me.

"Nope. Not without me. I wanted to fetch you, but Iva Lou insisted—"

"No problem." Iva Lou asked me to keep her problems confidential, and though I'd like to tell Jack, I'll keep my word.

"Where's Etta?"

"Upstairs. She has a slumber party tonight."

"That's right. It's Tara Kilgore's birthday."

Shoo comes down the stairs. I stoop to pet him, but he sniffs and walks away. "Not everybody around here missed me."

"She did," Jack says and points up the stairs.

"Seriously?"

"We did a lot of talking while you were gone. You may see a little difference."

The door to Etta's room is open. She is packing her overnight bag, taking the neat pile from her bed and stuffing it into the duffel.

"Hey, Etta!" I stand in the doorway. She smiles at me (good sign). I go to her, and she hugs me (even better).

"How was New York City?" she asks, then continues packing.

"It was great. I made a list of all the places I'm going to take you when we go back. And Uncle Theodore sends his love. Now, tell me, what's new?"

"Let's see. While you were gone, I got an A on my geography test. I was the only one in class that knew all of Asia Minor. And we had to take Shoo to the vet. He had a respiratory problem. He stayed out all night when it rained."

"He seems fine now."

"He is. We gave him drops. And Dad made polenta."

"How was it?"

"Hard. But you know how he is about his cooking, so I ate it anyway."

I smile. Maybe there is more compassion in Etta than I realize.

"You know, Ma, Miss Benton ain't so mad anymore." Etta corrects herself. "Isn't so mad."

"She isn't?"

"No, she was sort of laughing about it at school on Friday. We were complaining that we had an extra practice, and she said after the coal incident, she was adding in seven more practices a week. After we got the coal picked up, Dad went and put down new sod. I helped."

"Good. I'm glad she's feeling better."

"You ain't mad at me anymore, are you?" Etta asks without looking at me.

"Only when you use 'ain't.'" I sit down on the bed. "Is Tara having a big party?"

"Six of us. Her mom asked Ethel Bartee to come over and teach us how to do manicures. Mrs. Bartee is not real patient, though. She did our hair for the band photo and went so fast it hurt when she teased it. I'm sure she's gonna get over there and try to show us stuff and then just give up and give us the nail polish to do it ourselves."

Etta zips her bag and sits down next to me. She doesn't say anything, but it isn't awkward. Our conversations are funny to me. Often she answers a question in one word or a quick sentence, but I always feel that she wants to say more. Sometimes she even takes a breath like she's going to and then stops herself.

"I got you a present in New York." I give Etta a preteen makeup kit I got at Saks. There's nothing conspicuous in it: sheer lip gloss, a facial cleanser, and a perfume that smells like vanilla.

"Cool!" Etta digs through the kit. "Thank you!"

"And, most important, this." I give Etta a hardcover copy of *Harriet the Spy.*

"My own book! Now I don't have to check it out all the time."

"Give the other kids a turn to read it, right?"

"Thanks, Mom." Etta gives me another hug, and it's worth everything we've been through. As I hold her, I wish for a second that I had another lifetime just to be her friend instead of her mother.

When I get home from dropping off Etta at the slumber party, Jack is waiting for me on the front steps with a picnic basket.

"What's that?"

"I'm taking you out to dinner."

"You are?"

"Yeah. I found this chef. He's ornery, but he makes real good fried chicken, and his biscuits are almost too good to eat, they're so fluffy. And he recommends this Tuscan wine, a robust red, and he swears it puts his wife in the mood."

"Really. And where did you find this chef?"

"He lives around here."

"Hmm." I play along. "In an old stone house in Cracker's Neck that needs a new road, a new water heater, and a sump pump in the spring because the basement fills with rain?"

"You know what? That sounds familiar." He smiles. "So, you want to go out with me?"

"Sure."

We take Jack's truck and go down the mountain, turning onto the valley road that will take us up to Big Cherry Holler. I slide over to the middle of the seat and put my arms around my husband just like the kids do when they borrow their daddy's truck and head for the Strawberry Patch, Big Stone's number one make-out perch, for a date.

"You missed me?" I ask my husband, knowing the answer.

"Yes, I did."

"Why?"

"It's no fun around here without you."

"Come on."

"No, you don't appreciate what a constant source of amusement you are to Etta and me." My husband pats my leg.

"Thanks." I remove his hand from my leg and put it back on the steering wheel, but I stay snuggled against him.

A full moon the color of sandpaper floats over Big Cherry Lake like the face of an old clock. Jack is loaded down with a duffel bag, a picnic basket, and a flashlight. He shines the beam down the narrow path covered with pine needles. When we get to the water's edge, he pulls a camping lantern from the basket and lights it. The glow makes a pale golden mist on the water's edge.

I laugh as he unpacks his parcels. "You're a regular Sherpa."

"That's what I was going for. As a rule, those Sherpas are pretty sexy, right?" He winks at me.

"I don't know. You're the first one I ever met."

Jack lays an old quilt on the ground. I sit down next to him. "Are you hungry?" he asks.

"Not yet." I climb into my husband's lap and take his face in my hands. I do love him, I'm thinking to myself as I study his hazel eyes and the bridge of his perfect nose. I kiss him over and over and hold him close. "You don't change," I tell my husband.

"Good thing or bad thing?"

"Good thing."

"Do you know what tonight is?"

"The night my husband surprised me with a picnic?"

"You're worse than a guy. You don't remember."

"Remember what?"

"October fourteenth. It's the night I proposed to you the first time."

"Apple Butter Night!"

"Whatever you want to call it, darlin'. I call it the Night You Turned Me Down Flat."

I can't believe he remembers the date. Jack used two jars of his mother's fresh apple butter as an excuse to visit; he blew into my house and started chatting, and pretty soon he was talking marriage out of the blue. It was the worst marriage proposal of all time. He compared me to a fully loaded pickup truck and implied that neither one of us had enough time left to be choosy. I said no, and not too politely, but I am not going to remind him of any of that. I say, "I'm glad I came around, honey."

"Me too. Are you happy now?" he asks.

"Very."

Over breakfast this morning, Theodore told me that I should use my attraction for Pete on my husband. I thought this was strange, although I realize you can love your husband and still be attracted to other men. To use Theodore's metaphor, Pete "stirred me up," but I've come home to let Jack finish "cooking the dish." I kiss Jack again, this time like I really mean it.

"You *did* miss me." Jack laughs.

"Shh." I try not to laugh as I hear our echo across the lake. In the event that some mountaineer is out here hunting grubs, I don't want him to find us. Jack reaches across the quilt and turns off the lantern. Now all the light we have is from the moon glistening off the reservoir. As Jack kisses my neck and rolls over onto me, I look up at the moon, and now I see the hands of the clock speeding around. I close my eyes. For the first time in my life, I feel time passing quickly, and I want to stop it. I feel full and whole and loved and wanted, and there isn't a place inside of me that is lonely or disconnected. Each kiss my husband gives me tells me that he is here to stay and I am the only woman for him. The ground is cold beneath me as I hold on to him. Tonight I choose him all over again, and I know that every time I do, it's the best decision I make.

The prescriptions are so backed up at the Pharmacy, you'd think I was gone a year instead of a week. As I count out Nancy Toney's sinus medication, I get a whiff of Jade East cologne, and there's only one man left in Big Stone Gap who wears it.

"What's up, Spec?"

He stands at the door, sorting change from his pocket. "I need to talk to you. In private."

"There's nobody here but me."

"I heard about Iva Lou."

"How?"

"I was dropping off Arline Sharpe over to the heart center, she's fine by the way, and ran into Beth Hagan, Lyle Makin's sister-in-law, and she told me the bad news."

"Iva Lou doesn't want anybody to know."

"I don't know why she wouldn't. Get them Methodists and Prez-bees and Freewill Baptists all competing with their prayer circles, and by God, she'll be cured PDQ."

"For now she wants it kept quiet." I make a mental note to stop by and tell Beth about Iva Lou's wishes.

"It ain't right." Spec fishes for his cigarettes.

"I know, people talk too much." Of course, what did I expect? Iva Lou should have just gone ahead and run an ad in the paper announcing her illness.

"No. No. I mean about Iva Lou and her . . . Well, she's got the best figger in Wise County, including those gals half her age. Truthfully, she could win Miss Lonesome Pine tomorrow if she wanted to."

I want to shake Spec, or yell at him, but he doesn't mean it like it sounds. "Spec, when it's your health, you really don't care about appearances. It's more about life and death."

"I know. I know. I'm just saying, as a man, I think it's a helluva thing for her, of all people, to git *that*. Iva Lou Wade Makin's assets are like the Natural Bridge, or the Roaring Branch, or Huff Rock. They're a thing of beauty, God-given, and by God, we should be God-grateful. That shape of hers is landmark status."

"There's more to Iva Lou than her great body."

"I know. I'm just saying." Spec breathes out impatiently. "I'm runnin' down to Pennington. You need anything?"

"No, thanks anyway," I tell him.

Fleeta pushes through the doors juggling two Tupperware cake domes. "Jesus, Spec, you live here?" Spec holds the door for her on his way out. "Git yourself a home or something, would ja?" She coughs, then says to me, "Ave, you heard about ole Iva?"

I shoot Fleeta a look. "Where did *you* hear it?"

"Supermarket. I ran out of eggs."

"God forbid anybody around here wants to keep things private."

"God forbid anybody'd tell me anything around here before I hear it thirdhand out in the street. What are you gittin' mad at me fer? Cripes a-mighty on a mountain, I'll stay home if I'm gonna git my head bit off." Fleeta heads back to the Soda Fountain to open up.

Pearl pulls up in front of the Pharmacy. As I watch her get out of her car, I can really see that she's pregnant now.

"How was your trip?" she asks. "How was Theodore?"

"He's having the time of his life. He sends his best to you. How are you feeling?"

"I have morning sickness all day."

"It's rough. Have you tried Sea-Bands?" When I was pregnant with Joe, I wore the elastic pressure bracelets they give you on cruises to keep down the nausea. They worked.

"I got 'em up my arms like gypsy bangles. Cleared the stock of the Norton store." Pearl smiles.

"Got the baby something on my trip," I say.

Pearl opens the package from Saks Fifth Avenue and shrieks with delight when she lifts out a tiny yellow sweater with a taxicab design. "I love it. Thank you!"

"You tell Pearl about Iva Lou?" Fleeta wants to know.

"No, I didn't."

"Iva Lou's got the breast cancer," Fleeta announces.

"No!"

"Yeah, but they think they got it in time."

"I'm surprised you're not passing around copies of the X rays," I tell

Fleeta. She grunts at me and heads for the supply room. "Iva Lou wanted it kept confidential," I explain to Pearl.

"Well, this is confidential, Big Stone–style. People know everything about you in this town, including your underwear size."

"For the record, I wear a six," Fleeta calls from the supply room.

"She's going to be all right, isn't she?"

"It's very early, so yeah, we're hoping," I reassure Pearl, but I'm not so sure about anything anymore. I can't believe that two of the most important women in my life have gotten breast cancer. And I don't ever forget my aunt Alice Lambert, who let it go untreated until it went to her bones. Pearl looks worried, so I tell her what I keep telling myself, that treatments and technology have improved vastly, and there is real hope for Iva Lou.

"It's not just Iva Lou." Pearl sighs.

"Is something wrong?"

"Ave, I've been thinking about closing the store down in Lee County. We're not doing well there at all. They have a Rite Aid now, and it's more like a department store. And there isn't enough of a population to justify two pharmacies. I hate to do it, but we're losing money."

"Hasn't the prison brought in more business?" We were all so excited when the government decided to build a federal prison in Big Stone Gap. Our people were hurting from the coal-industry bust, and the new jobs created by the prison seemed like the answer.

"It helped. But we need more industry here."

As I watch Pearl go into the office, it's hard to believe that she's the same mountain girl who used to stock my shelves when she was in high school. Pearl is a rare person. She hasn't forgotten what she came from, or the folks who helped her get where she is today. I was afraid she'd be too kindhearted for business, that people would take advantage of her, but she has natural street smarts—I'm sure she could show the hard-boiled businesspeople in New York City a thing or two.

———

Part of my plan to cheer up Iva Lou (she acts like she doesn't need it, but of course she does) is to fuss over her, so on Saturday I take her for a girls' night over in historic Abingdon. We have a delicious dinner at the Martha Washington Inn, an old, sprawling colonial landmark that looks like something out of a storybook, with gas lanterns and a grove of pink dogwood trees, perfect for strolling. I bought tickets to the Barter Theatre show for after supper, so we're really making a night of it.

The theater is across the road from the inn, so we decide to walk. It's early November, and the breeze is changing. Folks are using their fireplaces already; we inhale the smell of smoky applewood, my favorite sign that fall is here.

"Look, Ave," Iva Lou says, pulling me behind a tree.

"What's the matter?"

"Look in the carriage." Iva Lou urgently points to the inn's horse and carriage, moving up a stately circular driveway.

The horse clops the carriage past us. Sitting in the backseat with a blanket over their knees are Fleeta and Otto, dressed in their Sunday best. We stay behind the tree so they don't see us.

"Are they on a date?" I ask, mystified.

"They ain't collecting buckeyes. Did you know about this?" Iva Lou asks me.

"I had no idea!"

"How could this happen and none of us would know about it?" Iva Lou wonders.

"Maybe it's a new development."

"They don't look like it's a new development. Otto had that 'I'm pitchin' woo on a Saturday night' face, and Fleeta seemed pretty durn happy to be on the receiving end of his attentions."

"What do we do?"

"We go to the show and act like we didn't see 'em." Iva Lou smiles. "I always thought old Otto had the fish eye for Fleets."

"You're kidding, aren't you? She's always so mean to him. One time she told him he didn't have an ass. I heard her say it."

"What'd he say to her?" Iva Lou wants to know.

"He laughed."

"See there, he likes her. She was flirting with him. I've yet to meet the person on the face of this earth who doesn't need a little sex."

"I haven't noticed that it's helped Fleeta's mood any."

"Well, there are those people, few and far between, who indulge in sexual relations, and instead of calming them down, it serves as an agitator. Fleeta might fall into that category." Iva Lou shrugs.

Iva Lou and I have been coming to the Barter for years. It's been the state theater of Virginia since the Great Depression, but it is most famous for being the oldest regional theater in the United States and the launchpad of many great actors, including Ernest Borgnine. We always enjoy the opening-night speeches by the artistic director, Robert Porterfield, and the prize drawings in which the winner gets a Virginia ham. In its early days, lots of folks couldn't afford tickets, so they bartered goods or services instead (hence the theater's name). There is a long history here, inside the pristine white walls with wedding-cake trim around the ceiling, a grand crystal chandelier, and a balcony that swoops over the orchestra seats and wraps around to the downstage area. The seats are ruby-red velvet, and Iva Lou thinks they look like roses when they're not filled.

"You want something?" Iva Lou asks as we stand in line at the refreshment counter during intermission. "I'm having myself a white wine. Stop looking around. They're not here. Fleeta doesn't like plays, only wrestling shows."

"You're right." I don't think Otto and Fleeta are theater people. "How do you like the play?"

"It's about time they put Lee Smith's words to music. 'Fair and Tender Ladies.' That about describes us, doesn't it?" Iva Lou laughs.

"On a good night."

"Well, Ave, I done made my mind up." Iva Lou gives me a glass of white wine.

"About what?"

"I saw Dr. Phillips over at the hospital."

"What did he say?"

"He laid out all of my options, and he recommended a lumpectomy—that's where they take part of the breast—and then chemotherapy and radiation. He said there was a bit of a spread to the lymph nodes, but not to worry, the radiation would zap it. Now some of them nodes is on the other breast but he said he could git them too."

"So when do they operate?"

"Soon. But I'm not going with that plan exactly."

My heart sinks. I went through this with my mother. She had her own ideas about how to deal with her cancer, and no doctor was going to tell her how to handle it. "Oh, Iva Lou, listen to the doctors, they know best. If he tells you this will work, it will work."

"You're probably right. But I'm a hundred-percent girl."

"What does that mean?"

"I want a one-hundred-percent guarantee that I am cured. I want to come out of this thing knowing that I won't git it again. I don't want to go through all this and then five, seven years down the line find out I have to go through it all over again. And with maybe even less chance of success. I want it done with."

"So what do you want to do?"

"I told him to take them."

"Take them?"

"Both. I want a double mastectomy."

"Iva Lou, why don't you think about this a while longer? This has happened so fast. There's so much research going on, and the drugs are better, and chemotherapy gets results—"

She cuts me off. "No, I decided. And I sat down with Lyle, and he's with me on this. My doctor said to get a second opinion. He understands how I feel, but he thinks he can help me with the other line of treatment, and I'm sure he could. But he cannot guarantee that I'm cured. Remission, yes, but not a cure. I want a cure."

"Oh God. I don't know, Iva Lou. In a strange way, I understand. You know, I learned a lot from my mother. I learned that every person handles this sort of thing in her own way. I might even do what you're doing in the same situation. I don't know. Now, Mama, she was ready to go. She had done her job raising me, and I don't think she saw a bright future for herself. But you're different. You want to live, and live a long time."

"That's right!" Iva Lou looks so relieved. For the first time in weeks, that little crease between her eyes is gone. She is done thinking about it. "Look, this ain't easy. I love my breasts. I have loved them and celebrated them from one end of Wise County to the other for most of my life. I was always so proud of my figure. I had it all. Honey, I worked it, I knew I had something special, and I'm, well, I'm the age I am now, and I've had a nice amount of years to enjoy them. And now they gotta go, because they have ceased to serve their purpose, and now they're just gonna cause me problems. I am grateful that I had 'em. It's been tremendously fun. But now I want something more. I want a guarantee that I'm gonna wake up every morning and live."

I can't argue with Iva Lou. She is going to do this, second, third, fourth opinions notwithstanding. She has made up her mind.

"What's the matter with you?" Iva Lou gives me a poke. I must be frowning.

"I just wish you didn't have to go through this at all."

"Honey, that ain't on the list of options. There's so much I want to do with my life. I'm not gonna let this get me down. I got plans. I think of all the places in this world that I want to see, and how happy I'll be when I get there. I've never looked at my life like it would end. But now I have proof that the clock is ticking. And by God, I'm not leavin' until I've seen and done everything I've always wanted to do."

Iva Lou's words tumble out of her. She's resolute and relieved, has made her decision, and is clearly at peace with it.

Iva Lou and I go back to our seats, and as beautiful as the music and words are, I don't hear them. I'm thinking about my friend the "one-hundred-percent" girl.

The doctors weren't kidding when they told Iva Lou they were going to schedule her surgery quickly. They wanted to get her in before Thanksgiving, and they have. I worked today, but it was a blur, knowing that Iva Lou would be operated on tonight. I picked up Etta after school, came home, and took a long, hot bath, and now I'm getting ready to drive over to Kingsport. Iva Lou didn't want a crowd there, just Lyle and me. I'm putting on my makeup in the bathroom. Etta comes in and sits on the edge of the tub.

"Ma, can I go to the skate rink with Tara?"

"Is Dad going?" I ask, applying lipstick.

"He said he would."

"Then you can go."

Etta stays and watches me, as she has done so many times since she was little. I remember when I used to do the very same thing with my mother. I was fascinated by the way she powdered her perfect skin and drew her lips red with precision. She used to run a little water on her hands and then smooth her hair down. I imagine Etta with a daughter someday enacting the same rituals. I put on my perfume and then give Etta a quick dab (our little addition to Mama's routine).

"Is Aunt Iva Lou gonna die?" Etta asks quietly.

"I don't think so."

"But your mama died from cancer, didn't she?"

"Yes, she did."

"Were you scared?"

I sit down on the tub ledge next to Etta. "Terrified."

"How did it feel when she died?"

Most people focus on the grief that follows a death, or the process that comes before it, but no one, until now, has ever asked me about the day she died. "I thought it was the worst day of my life. And it was, until your brother died. But I could sort of understand when my mother passed away; she was sick a long time, and toward the end I begged God to take her. She was so thin, and she was in a lot of pain. They always tell you that they can give you something for the pain, but they really can't. I don't think it's just physical pain either, it's the sadness at leaving the world and the people you love."

"Were you with her when she died?"

"No." I breathe deeply.

"Why?"

"I went to work. Mama insisted. She felt okay, and I had been home for a few days tending to her. She was never bedridden. She could always walk around and do a few things, and then she would just get weak and tired and have to sit in her chair. I didn't want to argue with her, so I went to work. I remember Nellie Goodloe brought me a sack of Red Delicious apples that day, and I knew Mama would love a baked apple, so I was looking forward to getting home and making her one." We sit quietly for a few moments. I would like to end the story here, but Etta wants to know more.

"Then what happened?"

"I got home and I went into the house, and I called to her, and she didn't answer. It was so quiet, it scared me. I dropped the apples, and they scattered across the floor. It seemed to happen in slow motion, with no sound. I knew something was terribly wrong, but I couldn't seem to move my feet to go to her. Then I sort of came to and ran into her bedroom, and she was in her chair. She was gone."

"Do you think when I die that your mama will recognize me?" Etta wonders aloud.

"Oh, yeah."

"And Joe, will he know us?"

"I hope so."

"He was so little, maybe he wouldn't," Etta says quietly.

I don't know how to answer Etta. No matter how long you've been a mother, sometimes your children ask you things for which there are no answers. The pat descriptions of an eternal life, of pearly gates and angels on clouds and God in a white beard, seem as removed from reality as Santa Claus at the North Pole. Etta is too big for the pretty stories, because she's asking the deeper questions.

"I hope he'll know us." I sit down next to her.

"You're not sure, are you, Ma?"

"No, I'm not." Maybe I shouldn't be honest; I should reassure her. "I know it helps me a lot to think that I will see my mother and Joe again."

"Then you will." Etta smiles and gets up. "Might as well believe in something, Ma. It can't hurt."

Holston Valley Hospital sits above Kingsport, Tennessee, like a castle. As I pull into the parking lot, the sun disappears behind the brown mountain in streaks of orange and gold like a tiger's-eye agate. I'm not afraid as I walk into the hospital, I'm confident for Iva Lou. I don't know where this optimism is coming from, but it feels real.

"Now, Lyle Emmett Makin, don't talk Ave's ear off." Iva Lou is lying on a gurney in the preop hallway with an unattractive paper shower cap on her head. The nurse tucks a blanket around her. Even without makeup, Iva Lou looks luminous. She has the unlined face of a woman at peace with her decision. Judging from the look in her husband's eyes, he is thinking the same thing. Lyle kisses his wife's forehead as she is wheeled into the elevator for her surgery. I blow her a kiss, and she smiles as the doors close. "I'm gonna git a face-lift while I'm in here, y'all!" she shouts from behind the doors. I hear the nurse laugh as the elevator pulls up and away.

"How about coffee, Lyle?"

"Thank you, ma'am."

Lyle Makin has been Iva Lou's husband for thirteen years, and I can honestly say I know him as well today as the first day I met him. He never says a lot (though he's mannerly), and I haven't heard much about his past (he's from Roseville, down in Lee County) or his work (he repairs heavy mining equipment), but I never needed to—he's Iva Lou's husband, and I love him because she does.

Lyle is over six feet tall. He, like Iva Lou, has kept his shape trim over their years together. His salt-and-pepper hair has turned to white, and he's grown a beard now, so he looks like one of the old guitar pickers at the Carter Fold. He has deep-set dark blue eyes (sign of a private person; boy, is that accurate) and a tawny complexion. I wouldn't be surprised if he was part Melungeon. Melungeons, our local mountain folk, once scorned, have become popular lately, and their exotic looks have been celebrated in books and plays. Lyle has their bronze coloring, which indicates a mix of Cherokee, Turkish, French, African, and English.

"How you holding up, Lyle?"

"I'm all right. How about you?"

"I'm okay."

We walk the long hallway in silence, and when we get in the line in the cafeteria, I'm surprised to see Lyle load up a tray. He has baked cod, a side of creamed spinach, two dinner rolls, black coffee, a small container of orange juice, and a slice of coconut cream pie. "Iva told me to eat," he says, and shrugs.

"She told me you've been very supportive."

Lyle doesn't say anything for a minute, then takes a deep breath. "She's my girl."

"I know."

"I was in Vietnam. Did you know that?"

"I didn't."

"Yep. I volunteered late. I'd served in the Korean conflict, and then when Vietnam came around, I felt I needed to go. So I volunteered."

"There weren't many people who felt that way."

"The army was the best thing that ever happened to me. I dropped out of high school in 1951, and they took me, so I felt like I owed 'em something." Lyle shakes his container of orange juice before he opens it. "I was in active duty over there, and it was a sight. I lost a few of my buddies, saw several more of 'em injured bad, and one night, we was settin' around and I told 'em that if I ever got wounded and was paralyzed that I wanted one of 'em to promise he'd finish me off right there. I told 'em I didn't want to live like 'at. So one of my buddies, a guy named Bill Kelly out of Lansing, Michigan, promised me that he'd carry out my wishes should the time come. 'Bout a month later, I got hit. I told Bill, 'Scratch what I told you, buddy. I want to live.' And he looked at my leg and said, 'It's a good thing. They just got your thighbone. But I'm gonna shoot you anyway, 'cause you said I could have your watch.' We had us a good laugh, and he carried me out of there and got me to the doctor, and sure enough, it wasn't the end of my road, and they saved my leg. I tole Iva Lou this story last night, hoping it would make her feel better; like I understood, as much as a man can, what she was goin' through. And she looked at me the way she does, and she said, 'For Godsakes, Lyle, I can't walk on my boobs.'" Lyle laughs. "She missed the point." He stirs his coffee and looks at me. "You know, she's all I got." He pushes the tray away without having touched his food. "My kin is gone."

"She's gonna be fine, Lyle."

"You think so?"

"I know it. She could whup anything or anybody that comes in her path."

"That's for true."

I'm sure this is the longest conversation I will ever have with Lyle Makin, but it certainly gave me insight into why Iva Lou gave up years of Happy Swinglehood for him. Lyle loves her in that everlasting way, and Iva Lou sensed that somewhere down the line this would be exactly what she needed.

## CHAPTER FIVE

The ride home from the hospital flies by (it helps that I'm going eighty miles an hour and that there are no trucks on the road between Gate City and Big Stone Gap). The doctors met with us after Iva Lou's surgery and told us they thought they "got it all." Iva Lou was still under anesthesia when I left; the doctors hoped she would sleep until morning. The staff was nice enough to provide Lyle with a cot so he could sleep in the room with his wife.

By the time I get home, Jack and Etta have had dinner, and he's now in our room watching TV. I give him a report on Iva Lou, then go upstairs and check on Etta, whose bed is covered with open schoolbooks, notebooks, and pencils.

"Looks like you got a lot of work ahead of you."

"I do. How's Aunt Iva Lou?"

"She's okay. She's gonna be fine."

"When can I go see her?"

"Saturday," I tell her.

"Good. Dad left you some pizza in the kitchen."

Etta goes back to her homework. Instead of heading into the kitchen, I go out the front door and sit on the steps. I'm not hungry, I need air, lots of air. I roll my head in circles slowly, as Theodore taught me to do years ago, in order to relieve an oncoming headache. It works. I can hear my neck bones crack at first, and then, after a few rotations, nothing. I walk around the house to the backyard. I think about going into the woods but decide I'm too tired, so I lie down on the ground and cross my arms under my head. I feel spent. I've been worried about Iva Lou and burying it, afraid to show my feelings to her or my family, and now it's all catching up with me. I feel a cold teardrop at the corner of my eye.

The sky is a strange color tonight, gunmetal gray, and the texture of the clouds makes it look like a skein of old wool. It reminds me of storms in adventure movies where all is calm but the sky, which churns overhead in anticipation. Maybe that's why it's warm; any minute the sky, like a ceiling soaked through by a broken pipe, will come crashing down and with it the cold rains of winter.

"Here, Mama." Etta joins me and gives me my jacket. "Don't get up." She lies down on the ground next to me and looks up. "Those clouds are creepy."

"Aren't they?"

"Have you ever seen them that color before?" she asks.

"I don't think so."

"Isn't it weird that it's not cold? It's almost Thanksgiving, and it hasn't been cold yet."

"It's very weird," I agree.

We lie there for a while until Etta asks, "If you got cancer, what would you do?"

"I guess I'd find the best doctors. Then I'd listen to what they had to say. After that, I'd come home and talk to you and Daddy. Why do you ask?"

Etta does not answer. The sound of the old coil on the screen door interrupts us. Jack stands on the porch. "What are my girls doing out here?"

"Talkin'." Etta shrugs.

"No moon tonight," Jack says, and sits down next to me.

"Oh, it's there," Etta promises.

"Where?" her father wants to know.

"Northeast." Etta points.

"How do you know?" I ask her.

"Well, at the end of the week, we'll have a rising crescent moon, which is a bright moon because it's lit by the sun. Plus, it gets a dose of earthshine, which is sunlight reflected off of the earth and onto the moon."

"Where did you learn that?" I sit up and look at my daughter with newfound respect.

"In books. Plus, Mr. Zander lets me stay after school and study his maps. 'Course, he told me that I could study the constellations for the rest of my life and not even make a dent in understanding what's out there."

"You used to stand in your crib to look out the window at night. I could never figure out what you were looking at. Now I know." I nudge Etta, and she laughs.

"I like the constellations because they're fixed. Like tonight. You can't see any stars because of the clouds. And when the moon is full and there's a lot of light, it overpowers the sparkle of the stars, so you think they're gone. But they're there. In science, the only concept you can prove is that things always change. But the truth is, they also stay the same."

"Now, that's a philosophy," Jack says as he looks up at the sky.

"It means that, like the stars, we have a fixed place. A destiny. There are facts and then there is fate, which is out of our control."

The clouds shift overhead, and in the exact spot Etta pointed to, the moon emerges, a white half-smile covered by a filmy veil of clouds.

"All right, my little scientist," Jack begins. "What do you call that moon?"

Etta looks up. "A quarter-moon?"

"Nope, although that's probably the right measurement. My grandpap called it a milk glass moon, because the clouds give it a smoky haze like milk in a glass after you've drunk it. And he said that meant it would rain the next day."

"That's nice, Dad, but I don't think it's very scientific."

Jack and I laugh; this is the best moment to be a parent, when you see that your child is going to surpass you, that her curiosity will take her places and teach her things you never even thought about. As for Etta's idea that the stories of our lives have already been written, well, this is one I'll have to think about. It makes me feel better to think the things in this world that have no explanation or cause pain (like Iva Lou's cancer) are part of a bigger picture; it makes them seem manageable and less overwhelming. But it's hard for me to accept that notion and cling tightly to everything I love. When the clouds come, I'm not so sure the stars are behind them.

Fleeta, Pearl, and I decide to drive over to Kingsport to see Iva Lou after visiting hours at the hospital. Between the staff of the county library, Iva Lou's old Bookmobile customers, and a round of old boyfriends, she has not lacked for company. I checked in three times today by phone, and each time she told me of another floral tribute delivered to her room. "It's a shame I ain't dyin'," she told me, "'cause these flowers would fill the sacristy at Freewill Baptist." The most stunning flowers come from Theodore Tipton, who ordered a spray of yellow roses edged in gold glitter. Iva Lou calls them her "Viva Las Vegas" bouquet.

On the drive there, Pearl sits in the back so she can put her feet up (a must for pregnant women) while Fleeta fidgets in the front seat. She keeps pressing the nicotine patch on her arm like it's a call button. "Fleeta, it's not like a morphine drip. Pressing it won't send more nicotine into your bloodstream," I inform her.

"To hell it don't. I press on this thang every few minutes, and it gives me a jolt."

"I think that's in your imagination."

"I guess the fact that I got the shakes twenty-four-seven is imaginary too."

"You're doing great," I tell her. And she is, she's down to one ciga-rette a day.

"Fleeta, have you been keeping a secret from us?" Pearl wants to know.

"What sort of a secret?" Fleeta hacks.

"A boyfriend secret," Pearl says softly.

"Hell noooo." Fleeta looks out the window.

"I heard you're dating Otto Olinger." I can't believe Pearl came out with it, just like that!

"Where'd you hear that?" Fleeta coughs.

"Folks have seen you around. Arby's in Kingsport. The Galley up in Norton. You know, around." Pearl shrugs nonchalantly.

"I saw you in a horse and buggy over in Abingdon," I chime in.

"When?"

"Awhile back."

"Why didn't you say hello?"

"You and Otto looked like you wanted your privacy."

"You were right about that. So let's drop it." Fleeta smoothes the creases on her new jeans.

We ride in silence for a few moments. Finally, Pearl says, "I think it's nice."

Fleeta turns to face Pearl. "Now, don't make a big deal out of it. It's a vurry vurry casual thing. I resisted as long as I could. Menfolk are nothin' but a brand of rash—they have this way of gittin' under yer skin and makin' it itch. Now, I know for a fact that April Zirkle had the hots fer Otto fer quite a spell. Her husband's been gone about three year', 'course he ain't dead, just missin', but still. And I told him that ole April would love to go with him and she's still got all her breath, she don't git winded like me goin' from here to there, she's a nonsmoker, I think. So I tole him call her up and take *her* out."

"But he likes *you*!" I interject.

"I know that. I'm not an idiot. Otto Olinger's been chasin' my tarred ass since we lowered Portly into the ground over at Glencoe Cemetery." Fleeta settles back into her seat and folds her arms across her chest like a little girl.

"That long? No way!" Pearl leans forward in her seat.

"Yes ma'am. And I done tried everything to deter him. But he likes what he sees." Fleeta inhales deeply through her nose and sticks out her chest. "But I don't need it."

"You're not attracted to him?"

"Now, Ave. Honestly."

"It's okay if you are."

"If I'm gonna make a move, I don't want me an old man. I know, you look at me and you say, Fleets, you're old yourself. I know I am. But I never liked me old men, not when I was young and not now. I don't like lookin' at stick legs and a saggy bottom in my bedroom. I'm sorry. I see a Pierce Brosnan or somebody like 'at in my mind's eye when I let my mind's eye roll in that direction. I certainly don't see some ole hilljack with a beer gut, a flat ass, and a set of fake choppers from Doc Polly."

"You've always been particular, Fleeta," I tell her.

"I'm glad you noticed." Fleeta sniffs.

"It's very sweet," Pearl says softly.

"You're so gullible. You'd believe anything a man told you, wouldn't you?"

"If I respected him, I would."

"You can respect a man and he'll still tell you a pack o' lies. Trust me on that one."

I can't hold it any longer, and I begin to laugh. Soon Pearl joins me, and we laugh so hard, we cry. Finally, Fleeta joins us, and as we pull into the lot at Holston Valley Hospital, you'd think we were going to the circus.

Hospitals are lonely places at night. I'm glad the girls are with me as we make our way down the corridor.

"She's in 602," Fleeta announces, looking at a scrap of paper from her pocket.

Iva Lou is in a corner room, and as we approach, we hear her crying. We don't bother to knock, we just barge right in. Iva Lou lies in the bed, a box of Kleenex in her lap.

"Hey, girls," she says, and blows her nose.

"Are you okay?" I ask her gently. Iva Lou nods that she's all right.

"Brought you some divinity." Fleeta gives Iva Lou the tin, plopping down on the foot of the bed.

Pearl gives Iva Lou a kiss on the cheek and places her gift on the nightstand. "I know you like hand cream." I go to embrace Iva Lou, but I can't; she's wrapped in bandages and obviously in pain.

Fleeta sneezes. "Must be the lilies." She points to the wall of flowers. "So, how are ye, girl?"

"I feel odd," Iva Lou says simply. "Is this medieval or what? My coat of armor," she says, pointing to the bandages that bind her from her neck to her waist. "Now, girls, don't look at me like that. I'm not sorry 'bout my decision. Just sometimes it all hits me at once and I git sad."

"Where's Lyle?"

"My aunt Shirley Jackowski from over in Johnson City came to see me, and I made Lyle take her out for something to eat. I'll really owe him one for that—she's a handful."

"The doctor said the surgery went well," Pearl says, offering support.

"It did. I'm gonna be all right. I do a little chemo, you know, and then I'll be good as new," Iva Lou promises. "Otto and Worley came over earlier with Spec."

"Did they bring you something nice?" I ask her.

"Two dozen Krispy Kreme doughnuts. They ate about three quarters of them, and I gave the rest to the nurses." Iva Lou winks at Fleeta. "You got something to tell me?"

"Jesus Christmas. You too?" Fleeta gives the patch on her arm a slight pressing.

"Otto Olinger is quite smitten with you, young lady," Iva Lou tells her.

"Well, that's his problem." Fleeta picks a piece of lint off the blanket.

"Fleeta's a little annoyed at us because we talked about her love affair on the way over," I say.

"It ain't a love affair!"

"What do you call ridin' in a horse carriage under an autumn moon in Abingdon?" Iva Lou asks.

"A goddamn hayride to the pumpkin patch!" Fleeta says defensively. "Look. Love ain't on my radar screen. A surf and turf at Scoby's is. I like to go out once in a while, and it's nice to have company. That's the extent of it. God a-mighty, it's dry in here." Fleeta stands and reaches over to crack the window open.

"Okay, okay, we've tortured Fleeta enough. Who wants a Coke? I'll run down to the cafeteria." I take their drink orders.

The elevator is on the far side of the floor, so I loop around the hallway. As I'm following the arrows, I bump into a woman.

"Excuse me," I tell her.

"That's all right," she says.

I look into her eyes and am about to say something else when I realize that I know this woman: eerily tanned in November—it can be only one person. "Hi," I say as my mind connects a series of facts quickly.

"Hi," she says. "You're . . ."

"Ave Maria MacChesney," I tell her. How happy am I that I put on lipstick, changed into a new pair of jeans and a sweater, and lost the ten pounds that were hanging on my thighs like fat wallets. "And you're . . ."

"Karen. Yeah. I didn't know if you'd remember me," she says as she pushes a lock of hair behind her ear.

Remember you? I think to myself. You almost stole my husband, left my kid fatherless, and made a fool out of me from the pit of the Cumberland Gap to the tip-top of Cracker's Neck Holler. Remember? I'll never forget you. I wish my husband were here to see you in this green fluorescent light, so he could see what happens to "cute" as it ages. Four years have made quite a difference in my husband's paramour.

"Karen, honey?" A man emerges from a patient's room. He's around sixty. He has the biggest head I've ever seen (including Spec Broadwater's), gray hair combed a little too neatly, a pug nose (odd on a man this size and a sign of lack of wisdom in Chinese face reading, though I need to look that up, as I'm not sure what the combo of big head and small nose means), and low ears (this man would have trouble working a simple crossword puzzle).

"This is my boyfriend, Randy Collier."

"Hi!" I say so loudly that a passing nurse turns around to look at me. "Nice to meet you. I'm Ave Maria."

"Hello." Randy smiles.

"His daddy just had surgery. They took out about six feet of his intestines. He's gonna be all right, though," Karen offers, filling up the silence. "How's your family?" She and I both know what she means; she doesn't mean my family, she means my husband.

"Oh, we're great. Just great. I'm here visiting a friend. Well, I hate to keep you."

Pearl comes around the corner. "Here you are. I came to help out."

"I just ran into Karen Bell and her boyfriend, Randy," I tell her.

Pearl's mouth falls open, and then she forces a smile. "Hello."

"Nice meetin' you," Randy says.

"I hope your dad feels better soon," I tell him.

"This hospital is something," Randy says to his girlfriend, "we're always running into folks you know." He puts his arm around her and looks at us. "Yep, she's popular, my girl."

"Oh, yes. Very," Pearl pipes up at last.

We get in the elevator and Pearl leans against the railing. "What are the chances of you running into *her*?"

"Just my luck."

"She changed!" Pearl laughs.

We fill up a tray with cups of Coke quickly. I can't wait to get back to Iva Lou's room and tell her the news. She got me through the most difficult time in my marriage by giving me solid advice about how to handle Karen Bell. I don't know what I would have done without her. Iva Lou is one of the few people who deal honestly with everyone; she never holds a grudge, and if she gets angry, there's a reason. She taught me how to handle my feelings, to stay cool and think things through. Iva Lou has as clean an emotional slate as anyone I have ever met.

"Guess who we ran into?" I announce over the tray of Cokes.

"Who?" Fleeta asks.

"Karen Bell."

"No! What is that old toy doing here? How'd she look?"

"Bad," Pearl answers.

"How bad?" Iva Lou leans in for details.

"That tanning bed has given her the skin of a crocodile purse," Pearl tells them.

"How 'bout the hair?"

"The worst. I think she uses Frost and Tip from the drugstore," I tell her.

"Perox-fried." Iva Lou shakes her head.

"Like hay." Pearl looks at me and smiles.

"Good thing you dressed up tonight." Fleeta eyes me from head to toe.

"That's exactly what I thought when I was standing there face-to-face with her."

"She'll go home and beat herself up all night over how good you look," Iva Lou promises.

"You think?"

"I know. You're so lucky. Eye-talians don't age, it's like the Greeks or the Africans. Y'all just defy time. But Karen Bell? She has a soufflé face. The kind that caves in at forty and never snaps back." Iva Lou sips her Coke.

"We met her boyfriend too," Pearl adds.

"What did he look like?"

"Well, he had a hangdog face, big teeth, and a small nose."

"The kind where you can see every nose hair in his head?"

"His name is Randy Collier," I tell her.

"That old buck? Please. I dated him. He's from Pound. Cheapest man I ever went out with. Took me to Cab's over in Norton for doughnuts. Doughnuts! And it was nighttime! We sat right there in the car and ate 'em out of a sack. Then he wanted to have sex. I told him, 'I don't know what you've heard, but it takes more than a shower and shave and a sack of Cab's fresh-fried doughnuts to get me in the bed.' He took me home immediately, and I never saw him again."

Iva Lou offers us divinity from the tin and takes a piece herself. For a moment, her mind is off her troubles; she is back in the world again.

"He's no Lyle Makin, that's for sure," I tell her.

"Don't I know it? Ladies, I thank God for the man. After the surgery, Lyle climbed up here in the bed with me and wrapped himself around me real gentle-like. He was so happy I made it. I think he thought I'd die in there. I told him that things had come a long way since the days when the doc would come over to your house and do surgery on your kitchen table. You know, his people are from Lee County, and they're self-sufficient. I think his aunt took out her own appendix back in the forties."

"That's where his strength comes from," Pearl says.

"I guess." Iva Lou shrugs. "We made love right before he brought me over to the hospital. Yeah, we decided to have a formal good-bye to my breasts, and when we were done, we just laughed, because we both realized how little a part they played in our happiness, and yet like any part of a person, they're important because they're part of the whole. You don't realize *that* till you have to. And, of course, I had to. Lyle got real quiet after a while, and he said, 'Ivy, I want to get old with you.' Now, I ask you, how're you gonna argue with that?"

"I don't think you can," I tell her.

"No ma'am. You can't."

"So, why were you crying when we got here?" Fleeta lies across the bottom of Iva Lou's bed, munching on divinity.

Iva Lou takes a moment to think, looking off to the bare wall as if the answer is there, painted in bold letters.

"Because I ain't never gonna be the same. That's a tough pill to swallow when you like yourself."

"We're so sorry, Iva Lou," I say. Fleeta and Pearl nod in agreement. And it's true. I am sorry that this had to happen to one of the best people I know.

"Well, I'm sorry you had to run into that floozy," Iva Lou says.

"No, no, it was fine. In fact, I'm kind of glad it happened."

Fleeta sits up. "You gonna tell Jack Mac you seen her?"

"Not a word!"

"That's my girl!" Iva Lou pats my hand. "You're finally getting with the Wade-Makin regimen. Men want women to be adorable and no trouble. Sweet as pie, that's what they're lookin' for. And forgiving. They don't need to be reminded of past mistakes.

Fleeta looks at me. "Quickest way to lose a man is to remind him of a weakness. 'Cause when they feel bad about themselves, they go right back to the woman that made 'em feel good."

"You make men sound like idiots." Pearl takes a sip of her Coke.

We sit in silence for a moment, until Fleeta, Pearl, and I crack up. Then Iva Lou laughs with us, and it's the sweetest sound I've ever heard.

Fleeta has planned a welcome-home party for Iva Lou at the Mutual's. Spec insisted we delay the festivities until he returned from Florida, so here we are, at the height of Christmas shopping season, throwing a big bash at the Soda Fountain for our returning soldier.

Nellie Goodloe took charge of the program. She is going to read a poem; Cindy Ashley is going to present Iva Lou with a gold heart pendant (she raised the money by passing the hat at the homecoming game); Nicky and Becky Botts are going to sing one of Iva Lou's favorite songs, "Sleeping Single in a Double Bed"; and evidently, my husband has agreed to spike the punch (there was a note at home: *Bring the Rum*).

"Don't touch that icing, Spec Broadwater!" Fleeta hollers from the kitchen. I don't know how she can see Spec hovering over the sheet cakes from back there, but she can.

"You should have let me lick the spoon," Spec yells back playfully.

Fleeta comes to the doorway. "Don't you get enough sugar down in Pennington?"

The crowd has a good laugh on that one, and thank the Lord, Spec's wife, Leola, is not here yet. She doesn't need Spec's friendship with Twyla Johnson rubbed in her face, and we certainly don't need a marital knock-down drag-out at Iva Lou's party.

"I'd say you know more about gittin' sugar than I do, Fleeta Mullins," Spec says loudly. Everyone goes quiet and looks at Fleeta.

"Now, Spec." Fleeta points a spatula at Spec. Will she admit to the crowd that she and Otto are an item? The buzz of the overhead fluorescent lights is the only sound in the place. Spec takes a drag off his cigarette and looks at Fleeta. I haven't seen this kind of Mexican stare-down since the Trail Theatre showed A *Fistful of Dollars* at the Clint Eastwood Film Festival.

"You got somethin' to say to me?" Fleeta does not flinch, and the spatula stays pointed at Spec.

"No ma'am." Spec backs down. Fleeta returns to the kitchen. The chatter resumes.

"How was your vacation?" I ask Spec. "You're so tan!"

"Well, we was never out of the sun. And we was on the water a lot. Went fishin' with Leola's cousin. We had us a good time. I took a spill down there, though."

"What happened?"

"Well, I passed out. You know, Florida sun, a six-pack, and wrangling a swordfish for three hours will deplete anybody. They took me to the emergency room, so I got to see what it was like to ride in the gurney in the back instead of driving the vehicle. I can't say I enjoyed the experience."

"What was wrong?" I should be able to accept that my friends are getting older (so am I) and sometimes get sick, but it's still hard when I consider what they once were and that we'll never see our youth again.

"I had me old-fashioned heatstroke. I was dehydrated too. So I drunk me some Gatorade for the rest of the trip. Didn't have another problem." Spec shrugs. "Gonna have one helluva crowd tonight. SRO, looks like."

Fleeta returns from the kitchen with another sheet cake and sets it down on the counter.

"How many cakes did you make?" I ask her. The parking lot is filling up, and the Italian in me is always afraid there won't be enough food to go around.

"Six. Iva Lou's favorite. Chocolate Coca-Cola Cake."

"I want that recipe," Nellie Goodloe says cheerfully.

"Then go in the kitchen and git it. It's hanging on the bulletin board. Make and eat it at your own risk. This cake is rich. One of them Delph girls got addicted to it when she was pregnant and ballooned up eighty pounds beyond recognition."

## CHOCOLATE COCA-COLA CAKE

CAKE
2 cups plain flour
2 cups sugar
1 cup Coca-Cola
2 sticks butter
3 tablespoons cocoa
1½ cups miniature marshmallows
½ cup buttermilk
2 eggs, well beaten
1 teaspoon baking soda
1 teaspoon vanilla
A pinch of salt

ICING
3 tablespoons cocoa
1 stick butter
6 tablespoons Coca-Cola
1 pound powdered sugar
1 teaspoon vanilla

1. For cake: Combine flour, sugar, and salt in a saucepan, combine & heat butter, cocoa, Coca-Cola and marshmallows until it begins to boil (add marshmallows last) . . . remove from heat & stir to dissolve marshmallows. Pour over sugar & flour and blend well . . . add remaining cake ingredients and blend well. Pour into greased 9 x 13 pan and bake at 350° for 30 to 40 minutes.
2. For icing: Combine butter, cocoa & Coca-Cola in saucepan and bring to a boil . . . mix with powdered sugar till it makes a thin paste, then drizzle over the cake while it's hot from the oven.

The sound of wild cheers, wolf whistles, and applause can only mean that Iva Lou has arrived. There must be over a hundred people, including the staff of the Wise County main library, where Iva Lou re-stocks the Bookmobile. Lyle has his arm around Iva Lou, who looks slim and radiant in an electric-blue leather jacket and matching pants. Her earrings are two marcasite pyramids with enamel bluebirds swinging from the bottom.

"Thank ye all, thank ye for showing up to this shindig," Iva Lou announces from my microphone behind the counter. "I am happy to be here. So happy I don't have words. But I do have a story to tell ye." The crowd cheers. "Y'all know I am not a religious person. I was raised in several Protestant faiths, none of which I can remember, because my mama never decided where to park her soul and my daddy never much cared where his soul went on Sundays or any other day of the week. Now, I'm a believer in God and Jesus and all that, but I never liked going to church or any of the socials, because we couldn't dance or drink liquor or do any of the wonderful things that result as a combination of those two activities."

"You must've been a Baptist," someone hollers.

"Yep. For about a week." Iva Lou winks. "Anyhoo, when I was in the hospital, a kindly preacher from the Higher Ground Baptist Church came to see me, and I confessed all my sins to him. He promised me that God had forgiven me, and I felt a sense of peace. I slept through the night and felt like a new woman. Well, the next day around the same time, another preacher came to see me, this one from the AME church, and he asked to hear my sins, so I complied and he absolved me. I had another good night's rest and actually started to think, Well, maybe there is something to this confession stuff. It does cleanse the soul! Anyway, the next day, I got another visitor, this time a lovely minister from the Presbyterian church, and he took a listen to my sins too, and then, once more, graciously washed them away. But on that fourth day, when the friendly minister from the Seventh-Day Adventists came to see me and I confessed my sins, I began to wonder: Does every patient get this kind of spiritual attention when they come to this hospital? So I asked the Reverend Du Jour, who came a-callin' the following day. I don't remember what his affiliation was, but it did have Jesus in the title. He too inquired about my past. So I said, 'Rev, I've had every man of the cloth in East Tennessee come visit me. What gives?' And he said, 'Mrs. Makin, no patient in the history of Holston Valley Hospital has ever confessed a litany of sins as colorful as yours. In fact, you make Mary Magdalene look like a wallflower. I speak on behalf of all the preachers, we are truly grateful for the spice you put in our soul saving.' "

The crowd's laughter erupts into applause, wolf whistles, and general whooping. Pearl, Fleeta, and I put on our aprons and take our place behind the buffet table as the guests form a line. Iva Lou works the crowd, hugging and kissing her friends. If I ever doubted that she made the right decision regarding her surgery, I am positive now that she did. Iva Lou loves living, and whatever choice gave her peace of mind was the right one.

## CHAPTER SIX

*I*t has rained for months, so when the sun finally came out, it actually made a headline in the town paper: WINTER GONE, SPRING SPRUNG. Fleeta's so tired of hearing it that she wants to put a jar on the counter at the Mutual's requiring anyone who says "Thank God winter's over" to put a quarter in. Yet there is still cause for celebration. Pearl is a new mother!

India Leah Bakagese was born April 3, 1993, at Saint Agnes Hospital, after a long labor. Our Pearl did a magnificent job, and her husband, Taye, was so proud of her he almost insisted their daughter be named Pearl. "One Pearl in the house is enough," she told him and named their daughter after his homeland. Pearl is bringing India to the Pharmacy for the first time today. I've attached balloons to the front door to welcome her.

Fleeta enters, battling balloons as she comes through the doorway. "Turrible idea. This is a place of business, not a day-care center. I guess we're gonna put an entire nursery in the office," she grouses.

"Just a crib for now," I tell her.

"Whatever happened to the days when women stayed home with their babies?"

"What's the difference if they stay home or bring them with?" I ask her.

"It's a big difference to me. I went back to work to git away from my youngins. But I don't own the joint, so I guess I have to live with it."

"She's so cute, Fleeta. You're gonna love her."

"I ain't sayin' the baby ain't cute, I'm sayin' I don't want her around." Fleeta says this in a tone that tells me she doesn't really mean it. "Is Etta coming in for her free sundae? Ain't it her birthday?"

"This Saturday. She's having a party and everything. Can you believe Etta is thirteen?"

"Jesus, I'm getting old." With her palms, Fleeta lifts the jowls on her face up a good half inch.

"But your hair looks good."

Fleeta shoots me a look that makes us both laugh.

"Introducing India!" Pearl announces, carrying her daughter through the balloons. Taye follows with a jumbo diaper bag. He is beaming with the look of a man who has everything he wants in the world. He greets us, placing the bag on the counter. "Call me if she does anything special," Taye says with a wink.

"Yeah, I'm gonna have her make out the bank deposits, Doc," Fleeta says wryly.

"That's fine, as long as she gets her naps in." Taye kisses Pearl, then India, and goes.

"Well, well," Fleeta says as she comes from behind the counter. She studies India in the soft pink blanket. "Now, that's a brown baby."

"Well, she's half Indian," Pearl says pleasantly.

"And you're Melungeon, don't ferget that. That's some black hair on her. Now, I know them ferriners got the black hair, but this here is the shiny Melungeon variety."

"Isn't she beautiful?" I nudge Fleeta, hoping to get her off the bloodline topic. She doesn't bite.

"Every once in a while, my daughter Janine comes over and spends Fri-dee night with me. And we pop us some corn and rent us a movie. We like them Ali Baba movies set in them sand dune countries, you know, where the snakes dance out of baskets and virgins get thrown into a flaming pit on holidays. And there's always a sword fight between a homely prince and a good-lookin' poor man for the hand of the Indian princess. Somehow the good-lookin' poor man is always a real prince in disguise, but then he always gets found out and marries the princess. Well, that's what your little girl reminds me of—one of them black-eyed princesses with them Bambi eyes. She's a beauty, all right."

"Thanks, Fleeta." Pearl looks at me, and we laugh.

"Well, that's what she looks like to me." Fleeta shrugs and goes back to the Soda Fountain.

"Is she still annoyed about the crib?"

"So peeved she put it together for you," I tell her.

To Jack's amusement and my horror, we are hosting the first boy-girl birthday party ever to take place in the MacChesney homestead. Jack's family tradition for birthdays was always simple: every great-aunt and -uncle and distant cousin came for Sunday supper, and at the end of the afternoon, Mrs. Mac would bring out a red velvet cake with candles and everyone would sing. Birthdays were strictly a family affair.

My childhood birthday parties were all-girl events. Mama said I could invite boys, but I preferred my girlfriends' company. We didn't dress up, we ate lots of cake, and we played cards for hours. We were big gigglers, and that always gave Fred Mulligan an excuse not to come. Noisy girls drove him crazy, so he'd work late at the Pharmacy until the party was over.

I look over Etta's guest list. There are two Trevors, two Codys, one Jarred, one Dakota, and one Homer; two Tiffanys, one Tara, a Crystal, a Kristen, and a Chris. My daughter definitely prefers the coed birthday party.

Jack comes into the kitchen. "Everything is done. The pizza's in the oven. Fleeta dropped off the coconut cake. We have lots of pop. I borrowed the softball equipment from the church." He looks at me. "What's the matter?"

"Our girl is thirteen."

"Uh-huh. Last year she was twelve."

"You're not funny."

"You can't stop time, Ave."

"I just don't want her to grow up yet."

"We don't have a choice, honey," Jack says practically.

As I set up the picnic table on the sun porch, I look at the paper plates with Barbies on them, and suddenly they seem ridiculous, so I throw them in the drawer and pull out real china instead. I don't want to embarrass Etta, and Barbies and boys simply don't mix.

"Letter from It-lee!" Etta hollers as she comes into the house. She joins us in the kitchen. "It's from Stefano Grassi!" she announces. "It's addressed to you."

Etta stands by as I read the letter from Stefano, in which he accepts our "kind invitation" for him to come and work this summer and promises to write again soon with his travel itinerary.

Etta rolls back her shoulders—I have never seen this gesture before. She flips her hair and looks at us. "Thank you both for hosting Stefano this summer. I'm sure he'll do a good job for you, Dad," Etta says, and leaves the room.

"What was that?" Jack points in the direction of his daughter.

"She's a teenager now. She's sophisticated," I tell him.

"No, the accent. Where did that come from?"

"That was her imitation of Audrey Hepburn in *Breakfast at Tiffany's*. We watched it last night."

If the empty cake plate, punch bowl, and pizza pans are any indication, Etta's birthday party was a success. Jack is out in the yard putting away the last of the softball equipment while Etta helps me with the dishes.

"Everybody seemed to have fun," I remark.

"Yeah. Until Tara and Trevor got together."

"What do you mean 'got together'?"

"After we played softball, she chased Trevor up the path when I took everyone into the woods. Trevor Gilliam, not Trevor Bailey."

"How do you keep them straight?"

"Trevor Gilliam's cuter."

"That's as good a system as any, I guess."

"Tara got him down the path and then made out with him."

"Define 'made out.' " I try not to let my voice break.

"Ma. You know."

"I know. I want you to tell me."

"They kissed three times."

"How did they find the time?" I wonder aloud. We had the revelers scheduled with games and refreshments down to the last minute. Furthermore, how did they manage a make-out session with steely-eyed chaperone Jack MacChesney on the beat? (I'll deal with him later.)

"Tara said she's gonna marry Trevor as soon as we graduate from high school."

"She's awfully young to be thinking about marriage." This is the perfect entrée into our mother-daughter sex talk, but I am completely thrown that anyone Etta's age would even think about marriage (it's an even bigger issue than sex, isn't it?).

"Dad told me Grandma Mac got married at seventeen. That's only four years older than me."

"I know, but that was in the 1920s, for Godsakes." Etta had one grandmother who was a child bride, and the other was a single teen-age mother, and while I'd be thrilled for her to take after them in every way, this is the exception.

"Dad told me that even though they were young, they had true love."

"Etta, it was a different time. Now we have so many more options. You're going to college. Grandma Mac didn't have that kind of an opportunity."

"Tara's mom got married when she was seventeen too. She's thirty now." Etta climbs on the step stool and puts the cake plate away. "You weren't even married at thirty, were you?"

"Nope."

"I have the oldest parents in my class. But I don't care. Y'all don't act old."

"Thank you for that ringing endorsement," I tell her. "Did you have a good birthday?"

"My best yet." Etta takes the rubber band off her wrist and twists her hair into a ponytail with it.

"What did you like best about your birthday?"

"The letter from Italy."

"Can I lie and tell Aunt Fleeta it was her coconut cake?"

I'm hoping if I don't make an issue out of Etta's old crush on Stefano, it will dissipate on its own by summertime. Jack comes into the kitchen with a package. "Happy birthday, Etta. This is from Mom and me."

"But you gave me a party," she says as she rips into the package. She lifts the lid off the box, and her eyes widen with excitement. "My own telescope!"

"Dad will help you put it together."

"Not that you need my help. I think you know more about this stuff than I do."

Etta throws her arms around us. "Thank you! I love it! I'm going to go and set it up right now." Etta and Jack sort through the box, lifting out parts and directions. They go upstairs as I put away the last of the dishes.

I'm exhausted, so when I'm done, I sit on the rickety bench under the windows and rock on the leg that was sawed off short for a reason no one remembers. I hear Etta and Jack fussing over the directions upstairs, and it makes me smile. This house hasn't been quiet since the day Etta was born. If I ever missed my single life (and, I confess, I have from time to time), what I missed most was the quiet and glorious solitude of my own thoughts. As I listen to the taps the three good legs of the bench make on the wooden floor, I think about what it means to be the mother of a teenager and how fundamentally my relationship with Etta has changed. Are the best days behind me, when I could hold her and kiss her as much as I wanted? This morning I went to hug her, and she pulled away. She wasn't being rude, just her idea of grown-up. But I would be lying if I said it didn't hurt my feelings. Before I had my children, I would hear parents complain about the teenage years, and I'd think, Not my kids. I'll love them so much, they'll never push me away. Well, here it is, the day Etta pulled away, and I wasn't ready (though I doubt there is any way to prepare for this).

Mr. J's Construction Company has really grown since Jack and his partners, Mousey and Rick, began their venture as general contractors. Now, with the help of some adjunct courses from Mountain Empire Community College, they have expanded their skills to include plumbing, tile work, and even some design. The Southwest Virginia Museum has hired them to refurbish all the mantelpieces in the building (a considerable amount of work, since there's a fireplace in every room of the old mansion).

Etta works with Jack now, mostly after school and occasionally on weekends. As I pull the Jeep into the alley behind the museum, I see that the load of marble from Pete Rutledge has arrived. Glistening planks of sea-foam-green granite with black veins are stacked on the back of Jack's truck.

I find Etta and Jack in the front parlor of the museum, a grand sun-washed room with many windows. It's a construction site now, with tarps covering the hardwood floors and windowsills. Jack has removed the fireplace facade to reveal a chicken-wire web of plaster underneath. Etta is on the floor measuring small squares of shiny black marble, which will become the border of the mantel. "Well, look at Michelangelo and his daughter."

"It's more like Michelangela and her father," Jack says as he takes a brush and applies a wet coating to the plaster. "Your daughter figured out how to make a border within a border so the design pops three-dimensionally."

"Where did you learn that?" I ask Etta.

"In math class. I took the measurements and made a grid. It's not that hard." Etta continues placing the small squares in neat rows on butcher paper.

"Pete sent you a present." Jack stirs the plaster.

"He did?"

"It's on the table there." Jack points with the brush.

There's a small black velvet sack. I untie the drawstring and pour the contents into my hand. There are about ten deep blue lapis lazuli marbles the size of pearls. They are streaked with gold stripes that glisten in the sunlight.

"Cool," Etta says from behind me. "That's the same kind of marble he gave you when we were over in Italy. Remember, he gave you a square when we visited the quarry?"

"I don't," I lie. I don't want Etta to think that was a day I remember in particular, though it was the day Pete Rutledge took us to the waterfall in the Alps and told me how he felt about me. I remember the steam of the hot springs, the way the smooth stones felt on my feet, and how I felt in his arms when he carried me in the water.

"Ma, you put the marble on Joe's grave at the cemetery when we got home." Etta's voice brings me back to the present.

"Oh yeah. Right. Right."

"It's still there. God. Don't you remember anything?" Etta asks impatiently.

"I guess not," I lie. The truth is, I remember everything in vivid detail, but that isn't something I want Etta or my husband to know. Like every woman, I have secrets, moments really, that are just for me. It's a way for me to stay a whole and private person while being a part of my family. I may seem to my daughter like a practical woman, but I am every bit the dreamer that she is; someday I hope to share that side of myself with her. But for now I'm a leader in her life, and boundaries are crucial.

Stefano Grassi's much anticipated arrival date is finally here. My daughter is never on time, but today she corralled us to leave early for the airport. Etta has done a three-month countdown to this big day. I hope Stefano is as nice as I remember him to be. Otherwise, we're going to have one long summer in Cracker's Neck Holler.

"How will we know him?" Jack asks me as we stand near the gate at Tri-Cities Airport.

"He'll look foreign. And probably like the picture Papa sent." I fan myself with an old program from the Barter Theatre that I found in the bottom of my good purse. It's only June, and already we're hitting the nineties.

"I'll know him," Etta says impatiently, keeping her eyes on the gate. She looks stylish in her new jeans, white cotton blouse, and clear lip gloss. (I drew the line: no eye makeup till she's fifteen.) "There he is!" Etta points.

No one is more shocked than me when a very tall and handsome Stefano Grassi sees us and separates from the crowd of passengers to join us.

"Mrs. MacChesney?" Stefano says politely.

"It's good to see you again. Please call me Ave Maria."

"And I'm Jack Mac." My husband extends his hand, and Stefano shakes it heartily.

"My God. You grew up!" I blurt. And he did, he's a man now. He still has the same curly blond hair and mischievous brown eyes and prominent nose, but the small orphan boy I remember is now six feet tall and obviously shaves on a daily basis. You wouldn't call him classically handsome, but there is an appealing Henry David Thoreau quality to him; he looks like he belongs in another century, in a cabin with his sleeves rolled up, writing serious poetry about the woods.

"Do you remember my daughter?" I ask him.

"How could I forget Etta?"

Etta beams, and if she were on a runway, that smile would win her the Miss America crown. "Hi, Stefano."

"Did you put some Coca-Cola in the refrigerator for me?"

She nods. "And Mountain Dew."

As we drive back to Big Stone Gap, Stefano is full of questions and looks out the window often, drinking in the mountain vista. He and Jack have a long conversation about surveying and construction. Etta and I sit in the back of the Jeep. My daughter leans forward, listening intently to their conversation.

The sound of Stefano's accent brings Italy back to me, and suddenly I am homesick for Schilpario and Bergamo and my people. I understand what Etta means when she complains that she doesn't have any kin here. There are times when nothing can replace the extended family of aunts and uncles and cousins rounding out life and making it full. Today the sound of Stefano's voice will have to do. Etta and I promised to speak Italian with him all summer. I grew up speaking Italian with my mother as much as English, and I taught Etta when she was a little girl. We use it occasionally, most often when we're in public, like a secret language. It will be nice to hear it spoken with a genuine native accent every day. I'm sure that will shrink the distance between the Blue Ridge Mountains and the Italian Alps considerably.

"You didn't tell us Stefano was hot," Iva Lou says as she dips her spoon into one of Fleeta's sundaes. "That's one good-lookin' man. He's got every single girl in town in an uproar. The women around here are more excited than they were when Tommy Lee Jones came through to make *Coal Miner's Daughter.*" Iva Lou has rebounded beautifully from her surgery last fall, and evidently so have her hormones.

"It's the accent," Fleeta says, rinsing utensils behind the Soda Fountain. "Women love an accent. Especially Eye-talian accents. Makes 'em believe whatever the man is saying is true."

"Serena Mumpower is all over him. Ole Stefano came down to the li-berry to check out some books, and she followed him around through the stacks like a hungry kitten. I didn't discourage her from helping him, though. It's the first time that girl left the desk and did any work."

"That one will go for anything in pants." Fleeta sniffs.

"Serena's got appeal, I'm here to tell you," Iva Lou says, defending her assistant. "She's got movie-star looks. She resembles the young Natalie Wood, if Natalie Wood had a bigger nose."

"Has he brought any girls 'round yer house?" Fleeta wants to know of me.

"No. If he's entertaining girls, it's elsewhere."

"Where'd you put him?"

"Downstairs in our old bedroom. Jack and I moved upstairs into Joe's old room. It's nice." I don't elaborate on the reason for this switch—I don't think it's appropriate to have a thirteen-year-old girl on a separate floor with a male guest.

"I couldn't stand a boarder. When I git home of a night, I like to peel down to my underwear and walk around. I couldn't stand having a stranger mess up my schedule." Fleeta sits down next to us.

"What do you do with Otto?" Iva Lou wonders aloud.

"He ain't a stranger." Fleeta shrugs.

"Stefano isn't either," I tell them. "He's like family. He's no trouble at all. And he talks about Italy a lot, and I like that. Jack says Stefano is a great worker and very ambitious."

"You Eye-talians are good workers in general," Fleeta comments. "Not as good as them Greeks, but close."

"Thank you." Over the years, I have grown used to Fleeta's bizarre compliments (I'm not going to point out that she's probably never actually met a Greek person).

"So having Stefano around is like giving Etta an older brother," Iva Lou observes.

"Exactly," I tell her. I don't want to betray Etta's confidence. Besides, it sounds like every girl in Wise County has a crush on Stefano Grassi.

I get stuck at work with a pharmaceutical salesman out of Middlesboro who talks my ear off, so I wind up buying two extra cases of antihistamines (that's okay; it's been a terrible pollen season!). It's pitch-black as I head for home. From the lower holler road, I see that Jack has lit the mosquito torches around the house. When I pull up to park, I hear Etta's voice in the backyard, so instead of going inside the house, I follow the sound to her. She has set up her telescope and is showing Stefano the night sky. Jack is cooking hamburgers on the grill; the smell of onions and peppers simmering in a small cast-iron skillet makes my mouth water.

"That's Aldebaran," Etta tells our guest as he looks through the telescope. "It's the brightest star in the sky right now."

"Yes, it is. It sparkles," Stefano tells her as he continues to look.

"The best place to observe it this month is Schilpario, well, really any location in the Dolomites and the Italian Alps. The combination of perfect weather and position is rare."

"You're such an expert!" I say proudly.

"Hi, Ma." Etta looks up at me and smiles. "Come and look."

Stefano steps aside. I peer into the lens, and what I see is astonishing. The summer sky is a rich black punctuated by small silver stars that shimmer so, they seem to overlap like pavé diamonds.

"Do you see Aldebaran?" Etta asks.

One star glitters like the surface of water in sunlight. It is round and faceted, larger than the other stars, and a deep turquoise at its core.

Maybe the blue is an illusion, but it gives a rich center to the dazzling white around it, burning hot around the edges. "I see it, honey."

"You almost can't describe it, right?" Etta asks me.

"It's true. It would be impossible to describe something so beautiful."

Jack comes up behind me and puts his arms around me. He looks into the telescope and is as mesmerized as I am.

"Dad, the burgers!" Etta cries.

Jack bolts back to the grill and flips the hamburgers before they burn. Stefano and Etta go into the house for the plates, utensils, salad, and drinks. I sit down at our old picnic table and put my feet up on the bench. I feel the workday, too long and too hot, settle down to my bones.

"How's work?" I ask Jack.

"Stefano is a big help." Jack nods toward the house.

"I'm glad."

"He just fits in. I don't know how else to explain it. All the guys like him. Even the lunch crowd at Bessie's loves him. He's great with Etta. It's like he's part of the family."

Etta and Stefano throw a red-and-white-checked tablecloth onto the picnic table while I set the places for dinner. Jack joins us with a platter of burgers, the skillet, and roasted corn on the cob, which he wrapped in foil and grilled. "Smells delicious," I tell him.

"Mrs. Mac, could I ask a favor?" Stefano says. "Could I borrow your Jeep Friday night?"

"Sure."

"Are you going on a date?" Etta teases him.

"A gentleman never tells," Stefano says, sounding a lot like Mario da Schilpario with that accent.

"You're going out on a date," Etta says definitively. "It's Saturday night in Big Stone Gap. What else is there to do?" She acts like she doesn't care. My girl *is* becoming a woman.

"Who's the lucky girl?" Jack joins in the fun.

"Serena Mumpower."

Jack, Etta, and I laugh.

Stefano looks worried. "Is there something wrong with her?"

"Nothing at all," I tell him. "In fact, Iva Lou said that Serena likes you a lot."

"I know. She told me herself. American girls are bold."

"Yes sir, they are," Jack agrees. "Gettin' bolder all the time."

"How do you know?" I ask my husband.

"I observe from afar, honey." He winks at me.

"Why shouldn't a girl be bold? I would ask a boy out if I was allowed to date." Etta takes a bite of her hamburger.

"You would? Really?" I ask.

"Why not? It's not like when you and Dad were young and boys did all the asking. That's crazy."

Jack and I look at each other. Etta continues, "If girls can ask boys out, then it's more equal. Then boys do more stuff that girls usually do—like cooking."

"Hey, there," Jack says, feigning defensiveness.

"Or taking care of kids, or household chores like laundry," Etta says.

"Etta. Are you a feminist?" I tease.

"I didn't know there was a word for common sense," she fires back as she pours the iced tea.

"I agree with Etta. All people should take care of themselves, regardless of sex," Stefano announces. "I worked in the laundry at the orphanage. I was very good at it. The hard part was ironing the altar linens for church."

"What was the orphanage like?" I ask him, moving the conversation away from men and women.

"It was fine."

"Fine? They're usually terrible. I think of *Oliver Twist*."

Stefano laughs. "No, though I'm sure that there are many bad places. I was lucky. We lived in a converted monastery in Bergamo. It was a small group of us, boys only, and we were cared for by the nuns. They tried to be second mothers to us."

"You seemed to have a lot of access to the town."

"The nuns encouraged that. They wanted us to feel like part of a family. I was very lucky to have the Vilminores. They took care of me on holidays. Meals on the weekends. Once a year your uncle took me to buy shoes before school started. Your aunts bought me schoolbooks and haircuts."

"Do you know what happened to your parents?" Etta asks Stefano.

"I only know they both died when I was small."

"That's terrible," Etta says softly.

"But I didn't feel alone. All the boys were just like me." Stefano smiles.

As we eat our dinner, Jack steers the conversation to construction. Soon the three of them are laughing. I look at Stefano in a new way, thinking about the life he's had. I wonder if there is anyone in the world who isn't broken in some way, who isn't full of questions about the past, who hasn't wondered "what if" in the face of loss. Can a person who has lost his parents so young ever heal? Stefano seems to possess all the good qualities of a stable childhood, but can he be whole? Or is he complete in a different way, a way he earned on his own?

The best part about loaning my Jeep to Stefano on the weekends is that it comes back sparkling clean with extras like the engine tuned and the tires rotated. The perfect houseguest and the perfect contractor's apprentice has also turned out to be the perfect mechanic. Everybody's happy.

"Where are my girls?" Jack says from the bottom of the steps. It is the hottest night of the summer, and Etta and I are upstairs rearranging the furniture in her room (she's bored with the setup).

"Why do you want to know?" I yell back.

"Let's go sailing!"

Jack's idea of sailing is borrowing a pair of old canoes from Otto and Worley and heading up to Big Cherry Lake. As Etta and I pile into Jack's truck with the canoes in the back, Stefano pulls up in my Jeep.

"Don't you have a date?" Jack asks Stefano.

"She stood me up." Stefano shrugs.

"You're welcome to come with us," I tell him. He smiles and jumps in the back of the truck.

Big Cherry Lake is most beautiful in the summer, its dark blue water surrounded by trees so lush, they look like draperies of deep green. "What do you think?" Etta asks Stefano as he surveys the lake.

"It should be called Big Blue Lake," Stefano replies.

"No, it's Big Cherry because of the cherry trees. See them?" Etta points across the water to a grove of cherry trees surrounded by pine trees so tall that they could touch the windows of the penthouse in Theodore's apartment building.

"It's a small lake." Why am I apologizing for our lake?

"Ave, don't put our lake down," my husband teases me.

"Stefano's from the Italian Alps. Near Lake Como and Lake Garda. He knows big lakes. Historic lakes, world-famous lakes."

"But this is just as beautiful," Stefano says.

"Thank you," Jack and Etta say in unison, looking at me.

"Mama thinks everything in Italy is better than in America."

"Except the husbands." I put my arm around Jack.

"Too late for the suck-up. You're gonna row anyhow." He hands me an oar.

Stefano rows Etta out to the middle of the lake. Jack watches as Etta dips her hands into the water. "Are you thinking what I'm thinking?" Jack asks me without turning around.

"That our daughter is a young lady now?"

"Yeah. You don't think she's getting a crush on him, do you?"

"Getting one? She's *had* one," I tell him.

"When did that happen?"

"It happened in Italy. But she's way too young for him, so I don't think there's anything to worry about."

Etta points to the reservoir in the distance. The sound of her voice, explaining how we supply most of the water used in Wise County, carries across the lake, sounding self-assured and knowledgeable, even mature. As Stefano rows Etta across the water, I feel something very strange.

Instead of seeing Etta and Stefano in that canoe, I see Jack and me when we were young, before Etta was born. Having children makes a woman mark time in a different way. Sometimes it takes a moment to remember how old I am, but I can tell you in years, months, and days how old Etta is and how old Joe would have been.

Jack turns and looks at me. "What are you so quiet about?"

"What are we going to do when she's gone?"

"I guess we'll be lovers again."

"Just like that?"

"You got a better idea?"

"Not really," I tell him.

"Then that's the plan."

I am happy to let my husband row the canoe and answer the big questions. "Whatever you say, honey."

I'm going to miss Stefano when he goes, not just because he's good around the house but because of his personality. He's genuinely interested in everyone around him. I would say his summer in the Gap has worked out beautifully. This is his last weekend here. Tonight he's going with us to the Fold.

"Yoo-hoo, Ave?" Iva Lou calls from the front porch.

"What are you doing here?"

"Takin' y'all to the Fold. I saw Stefano down in town, and he told me to tell you he got sidetracked and to go on to the Fold without him. So shake a leg. The Reedy Creek Band is playin' promptly at eight, and I don't want to miss Dr. Smiddy."

"The father or the son?" I ask Iva Lou, grabbing my purse.

"Either one. I don't like to be late. Besides, when you're late for the Fold, the field fills up, and then you gotta park in Gate City and walk ten miles."

"Let's go, Etta!" I call up the stairs.

Iva Lou wolf-whistles. I turn to see why, and have to say, "Etta, you look beautiful." She is wearing a denim skirt, a black T-shirt, and sandals, and has on hoop earrings, just like her aunt Iva Lou.

"Those mountain boys are gonna be all over you. But don't you worry, we'll protect ye," Iva Lou says.

"Thanks," Etta says, blushing. "Where's Dad?"

"He went to the car show in Knoxville with Rick Harmon," I tell her.

"Oh. So it's just us and Stefano?"

"Stefano isn't coming either. He sent Aunt Iva Lou to take us."

"But it's his last Saturday night here," she says.

"He changed his plans, honey. Don't let that hurt your feelings."

"But he's leaving on Monday!" Etta says emotionally.

"So he's squeezing in one last rendezvous with Serena Mumpower." Iva Lou sounds impatient.

"A date?" Etta looks confused. Her posture collapses a little.

"You know he's been seeing that Serena Mumpower. 'Course, with his work schedule and her dance card forever on the full side, it's catch-as-catch-can, but Serena is a catch-can girl."

Etta's eyes fill with tears. "Excuse me," she says, and runs up the stairs.

"Did I say something wrong?" Iva Lou asks me.

"I don't think so. Give me a second." I run up the stairs after Etta. She has closed the door to her room. I throw it open and follow her up the second set of stairs. "Honey, are you all right?"

Etta doesn't answer. She is crying.

"I'll be right back," I tell her, and run back down to Iva Lou. "Iva, go without us. She's upset."

"Oh, Lordy, let me talk to her."

"No, no, it's okay. It isn't you. I just don't think we can make it tonight. I'm sorry."

"No problem. Call me later. Let me know what happened."

"Absolutely."

Lyle taps the horn, and Iva Lou hurries out the front door.

I go upstairs and sit next to Etta on the bed and place my hand gently on her back.

"Oh Mama." She's still crying.

"What is it, honey?"

"I like him so much."

"Stefano is very nice, I know. But he's eighteen, honey."

"I know."

I point out the obvious. "And he lives in Italy."

"I know," she wails.

"Is he the first young man you've ever liked?" I ask her gently.

She nods. "He's cute, and he's not stupid like the boys I know."

"Those are two good reasons to like a guy."

"And he listens to me."

"That's good too."

"But I'm just a kid to him, aren't I?" She punches her pillow, then lies down on it.

Part of me wants to say I hope so, but this is Etta's first big crush, and I have to be careful. "No, I think he thinks you're a smart girl."

"He does?"

"Sure."

"Do you think he thinks I'm pretty?"

"He'd be crazy if he didn't."

Etta kicks off her sandals, which hit the floor with a thud, and it's as though the rattan sandals have magical powers—when she wore them down the stairs, she was a young lady, but now she looks like a thirteen-year-old again, with puffy eyes, thin legs, and a broken heart.

"Why would he want to see Serena Mumpower on his last Saturday night in America?" Now Etta sounds angry, and I want to encourage that. She should let all of these feelings out. "I thought he liked *us.*"

"He does."

"Then why does he need Serena?"

I thought my husband had a preliminary sex talk with Etta, but I see that he evidently passed right over the Nature of a Man and went straight for cellular reproduction. I make a mental note to kill him when he returns from the car show. I scratch my head, hoping that the words will come. What the hell, I'm just going to wing it. "Men are funny," I say loudly. Etta looks confused. "A man doesn't necessarily go out with a girl because she's smart or beautiful or because he has similar interests. Sometimes he goes out with a girl because she's no trouble."

"I don't understand."

"Neither did I until my fortieth birthday, so bear with me."

"Okay." Etta blows her nose and looks at me with Great Expectations, as though I'm an oracle sitting on an altar with smoke coming out of my ears and soon will predict the romantic proceedings of the next century.

"Sometimes, for a man, there isn't a great romance involved. Sometimes it's just killing time. Sometimes he picks somebody to have dinner with and a conversation, so that it's light and uncomplicated, and feelings aren't so important or even involved. Sometimes he picks a girl to be, I don't know, a diversion."

"Do you think he'll marry her?"

"Oh, Etta, I don't think there's any way he'll marry her. Is that what you're worried about?"

"Yes."

"Why?"

"Because Stefano Grassi is my destiny," Etta says without a single note of irony or drama.

"How do you know that?"

"Because of the stars."

"Do you mean the horoscope in *Seventeen* magazine, or the stars in the sky?"

"The ones I see through my telescope."

"What do they tell you?"

"There are patterns to the stars and planets. And sometimes it seems like there's a big shift up there, that everything is moving, that sometimes stars get lost and disappear. But they don't disappear, they're forever fixed. They always come back to their point of origin."

"So you think that you're like a star, and Stefano is like a star, and you're somehow fated to connect?"

Etta nods, and for a moment I think she's going to throw her arms around me. Right now I *am* her friend as well as her mother, though it's a new, and probably temporary, place for both of us.

"That's beautiful. But what about stars that burn out and fall away?"

"Those weren't meant to be."

First of all, I think I just had a sex talk with my daughter by way of Copernicus, and that gives me some comfort; and second, I still can't believe that she knows so much about something I never think about—stars and constellations and universes that exist or don't—and that she believes somehow all of this plays directly into her life and affects her choices and her future. What thirteen-year-old thinks about life on such a cosmic scale? She should have a crush on Cute Trevor or Medium-Cute Trevor, not on an eighteen-year-old Italian hunk here on a work permit. But she's been hurt tonight, deflated, and I can't bring myself to tell her that this will pass and next week it won't hurt so much, that Stefano will fly home and school will start and band practice will resume and that all of a sudden boys her own age will become alternately interesting and unbearable to her, that there will be many crushes, many mini-romances, many hurts, heart-breaks, and disbeliefs on her way to True Love Town. But she won't hear that tonight even if I say it, because the object of her ardor is dancing with Serena from Appalachia to a chorus of "Hot Buttered Beans" on the floor of the Carter Family Fold. Tonight she loves Stefano Grassi, and if she's anything like her mother, it's mostly because she can't have him.

CHAPTER SEVEN

"*D*on't I look older than I am?" Etta says proudly as she looks at her new passport photo.

"You look fifteen because you *are* fifteen," I tell her.

"You're no fun." Etta smiles and goes upstairs to finish packing.

Isn't time flying fast enough for my daughter? Jack has been teaching her how to drive; the bottle of Mr. Bubble that has been a staple in our bathroom since she was a girl has been replaced by vanilla bath beads; and the cupcake tins that used to hold her pebbles, fishhooks, and spare change are filled with different colors of eye shadow and lip gloss. What other road signs do we need to direct us toward womanhood?

I promised Etta that we would go back to Italy by her fifteenth summer, and she has held me to it. Of course, I don't need much encouragement when it comes to Italy, and Jack needs even less. He hasn't been back since our honeymoon, and he wants to take his Italian cooking to the next level. To do that, he needs to be in its country of origin.

I've convinced Iva Lou to go with us this time (to fulfill her life-long dream of seeing It-lee and also to celebrate the fact that she's been cancer-free for two years). Lyle has begged off; the only foreign place he wants to go is Hawaii, so Iva Lou promised him a trip next year. She's already had a conversation with local tour organizer/high school guidance counselor Jack "Nobody Comes Home Without a Lei" Gibbs.

I invited Theodore to join us as well, but he and Max took a share in a house on New York's Long Island for the summer weekends. I'll have to send them lots of postcards to make them jealous.

Etta has dated the same boy for a year, a nice kid named Dakota Clasby. She's gone to school with him all of her life, and the part I like best is that she likes him, but it's as much a friendship as a romance. Jack thinks I'm nuts and says I don't see what's really going on. But Etta talks to me about him, and I listen, and I don't see any need to worry. Besides, she gets excellent grades and even had an internship with the Thompson & Litton architectural firm in Norton. As much as she loves astronomy, she has come to love building design and construction more (thanks to her father!).

The planning of our trip has brought out the true librarian in Iva Lou. She has been packing for six months. She kept a log for three weeks to figure out the exact amounts of shampoo, soap, and personal-hygiene items she uses over the course of twenty-one days, so she'll have all she needs. She read an article on how to roll clothes instead of folding them square (it also involves tissue paper—don't ask). She has an adapter for her blow-dryer, a mini tool kit for breakdowns, and a cosmetics case that looks like Doc Daugherty's satchel, filled with small vials and tubes. She has broken in three pairs of walking shoes and one pair of stilettos (for a night out in Venice).

I'm keeping it simple. One bag for my clothes and a backpack for everything else. Jack has a natural sense of how to pack lightly (all those years of camping), and has warned us that he isn't hauling bags all over northern Italy, so we'd better keep them light.

Gala Nuccio, my honorary sister and our family travel agent (who helped me track down my father and then conspired with Jack to bring him to Southwest Virginia for a visit), has had the time of her life planning this trip for us. She called upon many of her personal contacts in Italy so that we will have tickets waiting in Florence to go to the Uffizi Gallery; accommodations at a small private hotel in Venice; and a tour of a pottery factory in Deruta. During my previous visits to Italy, I have stayed mainly in Schilpario, but this time we're branching out and taking in more of the Tuscan countryside (bringing Iva Lou gives me a good excuse to act like a typical tourist). This way Schilpario and Bergamo will be the dessert of our grand tour.

"Ma! Spec is here!" Etta hollers from the front porch.

"Load the bags, please," I yell back from the bathroom, where I'm putting on my lipstick. I slathered moisturizer on this morning, knowing the plane ride would dehydrate me.

Jack pokes his head into the bathroom. "You look great. Let's go."

"I'm coming," I tell him, dropping my mascara wand in the sink.

"What are you nervous about?"

"I don't know."

"Fleeta's coming over to feed Shoo."

"I know."

"Are you worried about the plane?"

"No."

"What is it, then?"

"You know I get funny feelings sometimes." I wish I knew what's giving me the jitters. What am I afraid to find in Italy? (Ever since I went to Sister Claire years ago, I'm a little *too* in touch with my inner voice—sometimes it's downright noisy!)

I grab my purse and follow Jack outside. Etta and Jack have loaded the luggage into the Rescue Wagon; evidently, Spec's car is in the shop.

"I hope the mayor doesn't see us riding around in an official vehicle," I tell Spec.

Spec smiles. "I called him, he gave me permission."

"Good thinking."

"Come on, Ave. You ride shotgun, just like the old days."

Iva Lou is in the backseat with Jack, and Etta is in the way back with the bags but perfectly happy to be there.

"Honey-o, I have never been so excited in my life!" Iva Lou straightens the collar on her pale blue denim jacket. Her hair is a masterpiece, highlighted with gold streaks and styled in the upsweep made famous by Verna Lisi.

"You look like a blond Italian goddess," I tell her.

"That's what I was goin' fer! Well, that and a little Ivana Trump thrown in for effect," she says proudly.

"Let's go, Spec!" Etta calls out pleasantly.

"You got it, kid!" Spec floors it, kicking up dust as we peel down the old stone road. Spec speeds through the Wildcat Holler so fast, we're practically off the ground as we make the turn onto Kingsport Road.

"Look, Etta. Your buddies are at the Quik Stop!" Spec points.

"That's fine, Spec. Keep driving." Etta's tone is even and dry. She is not above being embarrassed to be in this bright orange station wagon with the white stripes.

"Let's send you off to It-lee with a bang!" Spec laughs and puts on the siren. Etta buries her head in her purse as Iva Lou and Jack laugh.

Iva Lou flirts with every Red Cap when we land at New York's JFK Airport, and when she tries to tip the man who hauls her bags to our gate, he won't take her money (that's never happened to *me*). Once we're on the plane, she sits back in her seat and looks out the window. "I'm so happy. How do you like my outfit?" Iva Lou is wearing a simple black jumpsuit with a cinch belt, her jacket, now thrown over her shoulders, and very cute black loafers. "I love it. It fits like a glove."

"Can't tell I'm wearing falsies, can you?"

"Not a bit."

"You wanna know my secret?"

"Sure."

"Different boob sizes."

"What?"

"Yep, I have a small case of them in various sizes. See, different outfits require different boobs. A turtleneck needs high and small; a peasant blouse requires larger and centered; a suit jacket, the classic Jane Russell torpedoes; and so on. You can bet I wasn't goin' to It-lee, the land of Claudia Cardinale and Gina Lollobrigida, flat as Fleeta's tortillas. No, I want to look every inch the American beauty rose."

"Well, you do."

"Sometimes I can't believe I made it." Iva Lou leans back in her seat.

"I always knew you'd come to Italy."

"No, I mean I can't believe I made it, period. Through the cancer. That fortune-teller was right."

"She was totally off! She told you smooth sailing, no problems. We should have gotten your money back."

"No, ole Sister Claire predicted everything."

"What?"

"Yeah. I lied to you that night. I told you that the news was good because I didn't want you to worry. The truth is, Sister told me I was in for a real tough time and to just hold on, that it would pass."

"I can't believe you didn't tell me!"

"Now, what good would *that* have done? It wouldn't have changed a thing. I still would have gotten sick. Still would have had the double mas'. And I guess in the back of my mind, I wanted to prove Sister Claire wrong. But I couldn't. She knew something I didn't. So much for knowin' myself better than anyone else does. That's the last time I don't believe a mystic."

After a smooth flight (we were all too excited to sleep), we land in Milan, then jump into the rental car and head south to Florence. Jack researched restaurants and found a jewel on a side street near the

Duomo. The decor is simple: comfortable upholstered chairs and square marble tables. Once we've ordered, Jack excuses himself and goes into the kitchen to watch the food preparation. He read an article in *Food & Wine* magazine that said Italian chefs love to be observed in the kitchen, so he's taking them up on it. He wrote letters to a couple of restaurants requesting observation time and they agreed.

"Is he going to watch the chefs make every meal we eat in Italy?" I wonder aloud.

"Ma, he wants to open a restaurant. Why do you think he tries recipes out a million times?" Etta says.

"He's a perfectionist?"

"No, he's experimenting. He says he's tired of construction." Etta shrugs.

I look at Iva Lou. "Better to open a restaurant in a midlife crisis than to buy a Harley and trade in the wife for a new model," she adds.

"Who's going to keep an Italian restaurant in business in Big Stone Gap? Stringer's is a hit because it's like a Baptist potluck supper with the steam tables and the all-you-can-eat Friday-night shrimp fries. Nobody in Big Stone is going to pay for fancy pasta," I say.

"Who says he wants to open it in Big Stone Gap?" Etta says without looking directly at me.

"Well, where does he want to open this restaurant, then?" I sound pitiful, but I am out of the loop on this one.

"Kingsport, maybe. Knoxville. I don't know. Ask him."

"I didn't think he was serious about it. I thought he was kidding around. You know, like when I say I want to go back to college and study spelunking."

Etta gives me one of those looks like I'm insane, snaps a bread stick in two, and munches on it quietly. Iva Lou looks at me and pours me a glass of wine, then pours one for herself.

"Excuse me," I tell the girls. I pretend I'm heading to the ladies' room, but instead I take a sharp left and sneak past some red-and-gold-striped curtains with enormous red tassels across the top, which separate the kitchen from the wait station. A waiter looks up at me, I smile, and he shrugs, so I enter the kitchen, hovering close to the curtains, so as not to draw attention to myself. Here is something I have never seen before: my husband is assisting the chef. The chef, a short, balding man around sixty, continues to work at a clip as he explains what he is doing. He allows Jack to take the homemade noodles off a drying rack and throw them in the boiling water; he pinches salt into the water and hands Jack a slotted spoon to stir with. When Jack stirs too hard, the chef grabs the spoon and demonstrates a gentler technique. About three minutes go by before Jack asks the chef if he can drain the noodles. The chef looks at Jack suspiciously, and Jack indicates the sink, then explains that in America, we strain the noodles in a colander and run water over them before we add the sauce. The chef feigns a heart attack and asks Jack to watch closely as he lifts some of the steaming noodles out of the water into a colander, shakes them, and puts them aside. He explains to Jack that if you rinse the noodles, you kill the flavor of the pasta and make it impossible for the noodles to absorb the sauce.

The chef then takes another pan and pours olive oil into it. In a flash he dices up some fresh garlic and throws it in. As it sizzles, he takes strands of pancetta, a salty ham sliced so thin it's see-through, and lays them in the pan (it reminds me of the hunk of pork fatback Fleeta uses when she makes collard greens). Then the chef dumps in about a cup of fresh cream, followed by some pasta. Quickly he cracks two eggs on top of the mixture and, just as fast, tosses the eggs through the pasta and the sauce below until all the noodles are coated evenly. The pasta is whispery golden, like yellow rose petals when they've faded.

You'd think I would know this from my mother's cooking, but the truth is, we rarely ate pasta. Mostly we had risotto, a creamy rice dish, in many variations. When we did make pasta, it was often baked in small pots, or layered like lasagna in a pan, or gnocci (which means "knees"), a pasta made from potatoes and flour (rolled by hand into

small round puffs light as clouds and coated in a light cream sauce).
Spaghetti with tomato sauce was not a typical meal in my mother's
hometown of Bergamo.

Jack is still unaware that I'm watching (a testament to his passion
for cooking) and asks a question. The chef motions for Jack to remain
quiet, and what he does next is pure art. He takes the pan and turns to
a butcher block behind him. He has only to pivot, like a ballerina;
every spoon and pot, strainer and lid, hangs within overhead reach,
and his pristine cutting board and knives are lined up along the
counter. The chef flips a wooden cap off a wheel that is a foot and
a half across and about ten inches deep; at first I don't know what
it is, but then I realize it's Parmesan cheese. He takes the steaming pasta, now coated with the buttery mixture, and throws it into
the wheel—which is dug out deeply in the center, from many such
dishes, I imagine—and then, putting the hot pan aside, he picks up
two wooden instruments (they actually look like hands) and tosses the
pasta while a thin layer of cheese peels off the sides and bottom of the
wheel and onto the pasta.

"Hi, honey," Jack says, looking up at me. I am startled and smile
back. "*Mia sposa*," my husband says, introducing me.

"Italiana?" the chef says, smiling in approval at me.

"I'm a better one having seen you cook," I tell him in Italian.

"*Andiamo!*" he tells the waiter, who takes the plates from the work-
table and hurries them to our table. "Go. Go. Eat!" The chef pats
Jack on the back. I practically run to the table. I can't wait to taste the
masterpiece.

When it arrives at our table, Iva Lou rolls the tender pasta around
the fork and takes a dainty bite. "Jesus Christmas. This is better
than—"

"You can say it," Etta says as she dives into her spaghetti puttanesca.

"It's better than sex," Iva Lou declares. "And you know for me to
say that, well, it's a mouthful."

I take a bite and agree. Jack chews carefully and closes his eyes, then he reaches for his wine and takes a taste.

"I think this is the best meal I have ever had," he says, opening his eyes.

"Me too, honey," I tell him, squeezing his leg under the table.

"Now, y'all, none of that. This is Mood Food and therefore dangerous," Iva Lou says as she savors another bite and nudges Etta. "We single gals have to be very careful tonight. This sauce has magical powers. We may fall under the spell of some Eye-talian man."

"But you're married," Etta reminds her.

"You sure know how to bring the groove down."

"Uncle Lyle would want your groove down." Etta laughs loudly, and Iva Lou joins her.

For a moment I wish I had the camera out; I would capture this moment forever. But I decide not to. I want to retain this night in the warmth of memory, this meal consumed in an Italian bistro where the walls are washed in an iridescent gloss the color of pumpkins, where the candlelight makes us all look like movie stars, and where, behind the striped curtains, the chef stands proudly, watching with delight as we eat.

I am so glad we rented a car instead of taking trains, I'm thinking as we drive through the hills of Umbria, the gentle green gateway to Tuscany. The four of us feel safe and at home in the familiar landscape of small towns connected by single roads.

Jack has been very cagey about plans for Tuscany. He knows that I wanted to spend more time in Florence because I love the Duomo, the art galleries, and the Ponte Vecchio, loaded with more gold treasures than Cleopatra's jewelry box. "Ladies, next stop is Loro Ciuffenna," he announces.

"She sounds pretty," Iva Lou teases.

"She is a place, Iva Lou," Jack corrects her.

"Why do you want to go there?" Etta asks as she studies her map.

"I want to meet the King of Olive Oil," Jack says.

We girls have a good laugh. "Is there such a person?" I ask him.

"According to Renzo, the chef in Florence."

"What's the king's name?"

"Giuseppe Giaquinto."

"He sounds sexy," Iva Lou decides.

"I don't know about that. I do know that some chefs will use only Tuscan olive oil when they cook or bake, but Renzo uses only Giaquinto olive oil."

"That's a pretty strong commitment."

"I thought so. Renzo gave me the address and called ahead."

I can't believe that this is *my* husband making plans with total strangers in a foreign country. He's from Big Stone Gap, a place so small no one's ever heard of it, and yet when he ventures outside its borders he becomes daring, curious, and bold. This is not the man I married, but I have to say, I like him.

Loro Ciuffenna is south of Florence and west of Siena at the foot of the mountains. We drive up a mountain pass that is worse than any in Wise County: extremely narrow, hollowed out, and pitted from wear, with no guardrails on the driver's side. On the opposite side is a menacing wall of jagged rock, which, if you drive too close, could peel the car doors off like the lid on a can of tuna fish.

"This is a tight space," Iva Lou says, shutting her eyes and sounding like she feels slightly ill.

"Wait till we go to Schilpario. The Alps are really, really high. And the roads are more narrow than shoelaces," Etta warns her.

I hadn't mentioned any of this to Iva Lou. Why scare her so far in advance? Luckily, we begin our descent to the town through a picturesque passage. The road widens, and the terrain becomes smooth. On one side is a deep green valley, and on the other, a hillside dotted with olive trees almost precisely the same distance apart.

"That ground under them trees looks mighty dry," Iva Lou observes.

"It's supposed to. That's how you grow good olives," Jack tells her.

Etta makes Jack stop so she can get a picture of a white Tuscan farmhouse with a brown tile roof, set back off the road behind a spectacular iron gate. Even the most ordinary things are artful in Italy.

"That's the two-story traditional farmhouse I've been looking for. I want examples of architecture from the eighteenth century on," Etta says as she gets back into the car. "See the front? That opening on the ground floor is where the animals stay, and the second floor is where the family lives."

"I don't know if I'd want a cow that close to me," Iva Lou says. "'Course my mamaw had a goat that lived in her kitchen. Fresh milk on tap. So I guess it ain't so bad to keep an animal indoors."

"Everything stays warmer that way in the winter," Etta tells us.

"You could be a tour guide," Jack tells her proudly.

I turn to look at Etta, who reloads her camera and smiles.

"This looks mighty modern," Iva Lou comments as we pull up to the metal gates outside the Giaquinto olive-oil plant in Loro Ciuffenna.

"Look up," Jack says, pointing to the hill above the factory. "There's your old Italian town with the castle." He presses the speaker panel. When he mentions Renzo's name, the gates open instantly, revealing a simple stone building, a long rectangle whose only marking is an olive tree in relief over the glass doors. Iva Lou quickly powders her nose and snaps her compact shut. "I ain't meeting the King of Olive Oil with a shiny nose."

A young woman around thirty greets us on the steps of the factory. "Welcome!" she says in an accent that can only be described as American Deep South.

"Lordy mercy, honey, where you from?" Iva Lou wants to know.

"Mississippi."

"Bless your heart!" Iva Lou looks at us and nods in approval.

"My name is Elaine." She is tall and slim, with long brown hair tied back in a simple bow. Her heavy-lidded green eyes are rimmed in soft brown, but that is her only makeup; she is a natural beauty. We follow her into the hallway; several doors lead off it to small offices. She takes us to the back, to the largest office. The sign on the door reads G. GIAQUINTO.

Mr. Giaquinto motions for us to enter, though he is on the phone shouting every Italian curse word I know. We do enter the office but hover by the door, afraid to interrupt. Giuseppe motions for us to sit, in a broad sweeping gesture that tells us to follow his instructions immediately. He continues to rant to the person on the other end of the line. Iva Lou's nose is now shiny, as is the rest of her face. She's nervous, poor thing; she's never heard anyone go full-out Eye-talian before. Suddenly, without warning, Giuseppe slams the phone down. Etta jumps in her seat a bit, then quickly shifts.

"Welcome," he says, looking up at us. The King of Olive Oil stands. He's around five feet eleven, trimly built, and simply dressed in black trousers and a white button-down shirt. He is in his mid-forties and has a handsome face, not rugged but refined. His nose ends in an elfin tip that swoops up (he's optimistic), and he has a high forehead with a widow's peak.

"You study me intently," he says to me with a smile.

"Tell him," Iva Lou says under her breath.

"Tell me what?" Giuseppe looks at me.

"I'm Iva Lou Wade Makin." Iva Lou extends her hand. Giuseppe takes it and shakes it with both hands. "I'm a librarian, and my friend here studied the ancient art of Chinese face reading. And she's right good at it."

"What does my face say?" Giuseppe asks, turning to me.

"That you're a brilliant perfectionist," I tell him. Elaine laughs from the doorway.

"You think that's funny?" Giuseppe says to her with a wink. "You met my girlfriend?"

"I find it hard to believe that a robust Eye-talian such as yourself had to go all the way to Mississippi, U.S.A., to find himself a woman," Iva Lou comments.

"She found me. At a food show in San Francisco."

"And my life has never been the same," Elaine says dryly.

Jack Mac introduces himself, and then all of us, with beautiful southern manners. Giuseppe seems soothed by my husband's tone and latches on to him as we tour the factory. I don't mind being left out of their conversation as I look at the rows of dark green glass bottles. The labels are beautiful, and some have gold leaf on the edges, an elegant touch. The explanations of the contents are pure poetry.

"You really believe in your product," I tell Giuseppe.

"Olive oil is a religion to me. I worship its natural perfection."

Iva Lou learns that olive oil is the best moisturizer. Etta takes pictures as Iva Lou rubs olive oil into her hands.

"Can you use olive oil for everything?" I wonder aloud.

"Absolutely. If it's good," Giuseppe tells us. "Good olive oil, meaning it is made from the olives grown here in Tuscany. When you eat olive oil, it nourishes your body. When you apply it topically, it soothes your skin. You need never use anything on your skin but olive oil, and if you ingest anything but this natural oil in cooking, I think you are insane."

I rattle off brands sold in the States. Giuseppe grandly dismisses them with a wave of his hand. "I would not put those oils in my car."

I name an expensive brand.

"I would not wash my feet with that!"

"Why?"

"Because the olives come from all over the place and are picked whenever it's convenient, not when nature dictates. Those brands take olives from Tunisia, for example, Greece, where the standards of pressing are not good, so the product is not pure. They mash everything and anything together. Stems! Leaves! Crap! They add colors to olive oils. Either green dye to make it look extra virgin, or gold to make it look standard. This is a black mark on our industry, but it happens all the time."

"How can you tell good olive oil from bad?" Iva Lou asks.

"Once you taste my oil, you cannot ingest another. The other oils taste like gasoline. You'll see. My family has made olive oil since nineteen thirty. I've been running the company for the past twenty years. To not be educated in this, I would have to be the village idiot. Let me show you."

We pile into Giuseppe's van to tour the farm where his olives are picked. As we drive along a long, dusty road, he points to the trees, small and spindly with a sprinkling of green leaves, many anchored to the ground by string. "I use the best pickers. Some have been doing this for fifty years. It takes a trained eye to know a good olive. They can feel if the olive is good as they pick it. I never have to check their work. They are more selective than me!" He laughs.

"I find *that* hard to believe, Big G," Iva Lou tells him, giving him a nickname now that she feels at home.

As Giuseppe explains the evolution of olive oil from tree to bottle, we are mesmerized. It really is a simple process, with three steps: growing, harvesting, and mashing. Etta is amazed that the pits, as well as the meat of the olive, are crushed to make the oil.

"I work in the only pure manufacturing business in the world. Nature does the work, I collect the gold." Giuseppe raises his hands in victory. "But I must be a soldier, watching every step without taking my eyes off it for a second! If I look away, maybe an imperfect olive makes its way into the tubs, or the storage drums are the wrong temperature, or God knows what could happen. I have to watch everything!"

"Now you taste." Giuseppe gives Jack three small pieces of unsalted bread, then pours three types of oil into small cups and sniffs the first before handing it to Jack. Giuseppe taps the side of his nose. "This, this is my la-bore-a-tory."

Jack sniffs the oil, then dips the bread into the cup and tastes it. "This one is spicy."

"Aha! Good taste buds. This oil is made from olives that have just begun to ripen. Full-bodied, yes?"

Jack nods and tastes the next oil sample. "This is . . . flowery."

"You are a genius! This oil is made from olives about to peak. We snatch them at the last possible moment." Giuseppe claps his hands together. "I may have to hire your husband."

Jack tastes the third sample. "This is very mild."

"Because the olives it comes from are very ripe! Now try this one." Giuseppe gives Jack a sample from an unmarked bottle. He tastes it and makes a face.

"What is wrong?" Giuseppe asks.

"I'm sorry. This is bad."

"Of course it is! Tell your wife! It is the brand she cooks with in the States! Terrible! I would not use this to —"

"Wash my feet!" Etta, Iva Lou, and I say in unison.

"There is a huge difference. Really, you cannot compare," Jack says to us.

As we pile back into our car, Giuseppe and Elaine wave from the steps of the factory. Iva Lou snaps a few pictures of them from the car. Elaine promises to ship a case of olive oil to Big Stone Gap. "We can be in Bergamo by sunset," Jack promises.

Etta puts her hand on my shoulder, and I reach back to take her hand. She is as happy as I am to return to Bergamo and Schilpario, to our Italian Alps. I grasp her hand tightly and look back at her. Etta loosens her grip first, but I continue to hold her hand, pulling it close to my face. We're both a little embarrassed; it reminds us of when Etta was little and we were close. Then she does something she hasn't done in years — she leans forward and rests her head on my seat. I think about what I have learned from my daughter over the years. She taught me that the stars, even when they seem to disappear, always return to their origins. And here we are, back to the place we came from, only one generation after my mother left to find her destiny in America. Who knew we would return so soon?

"There. Dad. Turn there." Etta leans between us into the front seat, pointing to the turn to Via Davide.

"You know where it is?" Jack can't believe she remembers.

"Third house on the left," Etta says confidently. "Black shutters. Lemon trees. There!"

"It's adorable." Iva Lou climbs out of the car. "How long's it been since you were here?"

"Seven years," I say.

"And it hasn't changed a bit!" Etta says excitedly, running up the familiar walkway with tiny purple flowers.

My cousin Federica peeks out the window (her brilliant red hair gives her away instantly) and shouts for Zia Meoli when she sees us coming up the walk. Federica greets us at the door. She is very pregnant, and luminous. Her red curls are cropped close to her head, and a three-year-old girl hovers around her knees. "Welcome home!" Federica throws her arms around me, remembers Jack, cannot believe how much Etta has grown, and is delighted when Iva Lou presents her with a gift of Outdoor Drama baseball caps from Big Stone Gap.

"This is Giuliana." Federica picks up her daughter to introduce us at eye level.

"She looks just like you!" I tell her.

"The hair, no?" Federica laughs and runs her fingers through Giuliana's thick curls.

"Ave Maria!" Zia Meoli stands in the entryway with her hands on her hips. She is older, her hair nearly white now, but her posture is still perfect and her energy as vital as ever. I give her a good long hug.

"Etta! Etta, you are all grown up! I can't believe it! *Bellisima!*"

Etta is thrilled to see her aunt, so happy she cries. Iva Lou fishes in her purse for a tissue. "Jesus, now you're gonna make *me* cry."

"How is Zio Pietro?" Jack wants to know.

"Come see him."

Zia Meoli leads us back through the house to the sun porch, through the familiar hallways that smell like lavender, past the old photographs in simple gold frames, through the sparkling kitchen with the white metal cabinets and the black and white harlequin floor. "Everything looks beautiful, the same," I tell my aunt, and then "Zio Pietro!"

My uncle sits in a wicker rocking chair with his hands folded in his lap. He opens his eyes when I call to him. At first he is overwhelmed by the sum of us, but he sees who we are and smiles broadly. "How are you?" I kneel down and embrace him.

Jack introduces Iva Lou, and Etta makes a big fuss over Zio Pietro, reminding him of how she learned to make boxes in his woodworking shop.

"I haven't made anything in a long time," he says.

"I could help you," Etta offers.

"Too much for me now. I am old," Zio Pietro says, and smiles.

"Hello, everyone." We hear a familiar voice in the doorway.

"Stefano Grassi!" Iva Lou throws her arms around our old friend.

"How are you, Miss Iva Lou?"

"How do I look?"

"Magnificent."

"Then that's how I am!"

"It is so good to see you all again," Stefano says graciously as he shakes Jack's hand and kisses me on the cheek.

"You remember Etta?" Iva Lou pushes Etta toward Stefano. Etta doesn't lurch; in fact, she is refined in her movements and extends her hand.

"Etta has grown up!" Stefano's eyes narrow and he looks at me, then to Jack and then back to Etta.

"Little Rose here has blossomed," Iva Lou says smugly.

The term "sparks fly" takes on new meaning as we stand with Stefano and Etta. He looks at Etta as though this is the first time he has ever seen her.

Etta is tall and lean, her light brown hair falls below her shoulders in waves, and her eyes are soft, tilting upward, the color of mossy green velvet. The only Italian element I can see in her face is the set of her mouth: her lips are full and her front teeth have a slight overbite, which gives her an endearing pout. Here in Italy, her Scottish-American coloring stands out.

"How have you been, Stefano?" Etta asks him, sounding grown up.

"Very well. Thank you."

Iva Lou nudges me as she notices how Etta smiles at Stefano. I look over at my husband. He too has not missed a beat of this. He puts his arm around Etta's shoulder.

"We're all so happy to see you again. We've planned a wonderful dinner in Città Alta," Stefano says.

"That will be wonderful," I say, speaking for the American contingent. Federica asks for a rain check. She will stay home with Zio Pietro, who is too tired to join us. We do our best to convince him to come, but he is stubborn, so we promise to bring him something from the restaurant. Zia Meoli joins us, and I'm very happy about that; we have so much to catch up on.

Stefano takes our group to Bergamo Alta (also known as Città Alta), the ancient town above the modern city (known as Bergamo Bassa), to a hillside restaurant with a view of the valley. Stefano is a delightful host, ordering such local delicacies as risotto with fresh truffles (it's the hunting season for them now) and costolette, veal cutlets coated in bread crumbs and pan-fried in butter. Etta fills Stefano in on all the news in Big Stone Gap, and Iva Lou, her loyal sidekick, adds the spicy details, while Jack laughs.

"Zia, how have you been?" I ask her.

"It's hard to get old."

"You're not old!"

"Eighty-three. And Zio Pietro is eighty-eight. We are old."

"You look terrific."

"I am doing well. I have shrunk a bit, though that's what happens to old bones. But Zio has had some problems with his heart, and his memory is not so good anymore."

"Does he go to the wood shop?"

"Not in several years. He likes Stefano to come by and talk to him about architecture and building. That was always his passion." Then Zia says with admiration, "Etta is a woman now, isn't she?"

"Almost. She looks so much older than she is."

"What are her interests?"

"Zia, she is a complex girl. She's sensible but headstrong. Sometimes that serves her well, and sometimes it causes problems."

"She is very different from you, isn't she?"

"Very."

"It's difficult to know what to do. We think our daughters will be just like us, or at least appreciate who we are. It wasn't really until Federica had her daughter that she realized that I wasn't crazy or old-fashioned. It took a long time." I sit back and exhale a long, deep sigh. Zia takes my hand. "It's difficult now, but eventually, you will be happy you have a daughter."

"Oh, I am happy I have her."

"No. What I mean is, a daughter will stay by the mother all of her life. A son is different. A son will leave you. Sons are easy until they are grown. But when they're grown, they're gone." She sighs.

"There's an old expression in America. 'A son is a son till he marries a wife; a daughter's a daughter the rest of her life.'"

"Exactly," Zia says, nodding.

We're staying the night on Via Davide. Papa is due to pick us up in the morning. Federica has prepared our rooms beautifully with all the details we remember—the embroidered sheets, the down comforters,

the silver cups on the dresser filled with wild roses. Iva Lou is setting
her hair in the bathroom down the hall, so I know Etta is alone, and I
go into the room they're sharing. She is writing in her journal, which
she closes gently when I enter.

"I'm not interrupting, am I?"

"No, come on in."

"That was fun tonight, wasn't it?"

"Yeah."

"What did you think?"

"Of what?"

"Stefano Grassi."

"He's the same, Ma."

"How so?"

"Well, he's very self-absorbed."

"Really." I'm taken aback. Where's my daughter who had a mad
crush on the older Italian boy?

"Yeah. He talked about his work a lot, and where he's been. He
spends a lot of time in Rimini, on the coast. He went on and on about
the Adriatic Sea. Iva Lou asked him if he had a girlfriend, and he said,
'Several,' which I thought was cheesy."

"That *is* cheesy."

"He's got a big ego."

"He's young. He's Italian. No surprise there," I tell her.

Etta leans back on the pillows. "I think about things too much. I
analyze stuff to death. I'm too critical."

"Sounds familiar," I tell her.

Etta smiles knowingly. If I've had fifteen years to observe her, she's
had the same fifteen to mirror me.

"I've always been that way. It's the one thing I wished I could
change about myself. I admire people who can be light, and move
through life like small birds, you know, landing, pecking a bit, and
then flying off. Not getting too involved. Not caring too much."

Etta looks at me as though she understands exactly what I am saying. "You know when Stefano was leaving Big Stone Gap? And I got so upset?"

"I remember."

"I promised myself that I would never let any boy upset me like that ever again."

"How's that worked out?"

"Pretty well. I don't let myself get too wrapped up, Ma. I keep a distance. Boys are just too fickle, whether they're American or Italian."

Part of me is thrilled that my daughter is so poised and confident, that she has A Plan when it comes to boys. But another part of me worries that she will isolate herself, much as I did for so long. I don't want Etta to be repressed, as I was; that's part of my personal legacy that I hope she rejects. But there is something within the women of my line that spends too much time worrying about being worthy, and being strong in the face of love, and rejecting it to avoid the pain if it doesn't work out. Etta is only fifteen, too young for some of these concepts. And now that she is opening up to me, I want to encourage her to continue. I don't want to say the wrong thing.

I sit down on the foot of the bed. "You know what my mother always told me?" I ask.

"What?"

"That all the answers to all your questions are already inside of you. You just have to listen."

"Is that true?" Etta asks, putting her book aside.

"I think so."

"How do you learn to listen?"

"Well, that's something that comes with experience. And trusting yourself. At night, before I go to sleep, I think about what is troubling me. And then I ask myself to work it out while I sleep."

"And you wake up knowing the answer?"

"Sometimes. But I always wake up feeling as though I'm on the right track."

"That's interesting," Etta says as she braids the tip of a lock of hair.

"What do you see yourself doing, honey? After you leave Dad and me and go off in the world. How do you see yourself?"

"Well, I see myself working. I like cities, but I hope I'll live in a small one."

"You don't see yourself in Cracker's Neck Holler?"

"Maybe when I'm older."

"Do you see yourself married?"

"Ma." Etta's tone tells me not to go down this road.

"I was just wondering."

"Did you?" She turns the question on me.

I guess I'll be honest. "No."

"But you married Dad."

"And no one was more surprised than me. I guess that's what I'm trying to get at, Etta. Stay open to the big surprises, because I swear, they'll come."

"What are you two yammering about?" Iva Lou wants to know as she comes in. Her hair is rolled on curlers the size of orange-juice cans. "Oh, it's serious." She turns to go back out the door.

"No, no. We're done." As I stand to go, I ask Iva Lou, "Are you having a good time?"

"Do you have to ask? Look at me. I'm spillin' over with joy unabandoned. My pap used to say that, and I have no idea what it means exactly, but it sort of fits how I feel about It-lee."

"We're happy you're here."

"I feel like family. I can't thank y'all enough."

As I go down the hall to my room, I hear Iva Lou squeal with delight, just as I did, when she lies down on the poufy cloud bed for the first time and sinks a good foot or two into the soft goose feathers. I stand in the hallway and listen to her and Etta laughing and realize that maybe my daughter did miss out on a big family life as an only child, but what she got instead was just as valuable. How many girls have an honorary aunt like Iva Lou? Sometimes what we don't get in life makes way for something even better.

CHAPTER EIGHT

"**W**here are my girls?" my father yells up the stairs at Via Davide in his rich Barbari baritone. Etta and I fly down the stairs into his arms.

"Does that include me, Mario da Schilpario?" Iva Lou says from the top of the stairs.

"Of course."

Papa is in good health, robust and youthful. He is wearing faded jeans (with pressed creases, of course) rolled about a half inch at the hem, with a beige cashmere V-neck sweater. His face hasn't aged much since his last visit to Big Stone Gap. The sharp angles of his jaw and cheekbones and thick arched black eyebrows are as pronounced as ever. I'm glad I was born when he was young, because now I have him in my middle years. The thought of this makes me wince. I hope I will be around when Etta needs me later in *her* life. "Where's Giacomina?"

"She's in Schilpario, preparing for your arrival."

"Couldn't take that mountain road I've been hearing about, eh?" Iva Lou teases.

"No, she doesn't mind the road."

"Mario da Schilpario, is that road as bad as these folks say? Should I be nervous?"

"Not with me as your coachman."

Iva Lou, Etta, and I ride with Papa, who has a thousand questions for Etta about school, her internship, and even Shoo the Cat. (We put Iva Lou in the front seat in case the winding roads get to be too much for her.) Jack Mac follows us in the van with the luggage. I offered to ride with him, but I think he'd like some time alone; he has been surrounded by women since the start of the trip. It's times like these that I think of my son—he should be here for his father, who was so proud of him; no matter where we go or what we do, Joe is always missing. When I look back and see Jack following close behind, I feel sad for him.

"Should I have ridden with Dad?" Etta asks me. I think she's reading my mind.

"He looks like he's okay."

"Are you thinking about Joe?"

"Always."

"Me too."

I wonder what life would be like if my son were here. Or what life would have been like with more children. We tried, but it didn't happen. I took it as a sign not to push things, to enjoy Etta, to focus on her. I wonder what she wishes; surely she hoped to have sisters or brothers. I was an only child and used to imagine a house full of siblings and what joy that must be. Jack was an only child too, but he looked at it differently. He liked being alone and loved having the attention of both of his parents. Jack still can't speak of his father without getting emotional. They were very close, and Jack has told me he would never change that.

"Whenever I'm really happy, I think of Joe and feel bad he's not here," Etta says to me softly.

"Me too," I tell her, knowing that I shouldn't encourage that kind of guilt. "He would want you to be happy, Etta."

"I know."

"Remember the day of the big snowstorm?"

"The one where we made ice cream?" Etta asks.

"The very one," I tell her.

"It was so cool. You and Joe and me got all bundled up and went out into the woods with a bucket and lifted clean snow off the branches. Joe and I were so little, you had to do it all. And then we went back inside, and you took sugar and cream and stirred it into the clean snow. It tasted so good."

"That was a great day, wasn't it?"

Etta doesn't answer me. She looks out the window, still remembering. Sometimes I forget she was there through the whole ordeal, and think I'm the only person who lost Joe. Maybe that's because I'm the mother and he was born of me. But it's really not true; Etta lost her brother and Jack lost his son, and there isn't one of us who will ever be the same. No matter where we go, we are always looking for him, whether it's on a curvy alpine road or in the field behind our house in Cracker's Neck Holler.

Iva Lou makes sounds I have never before heard from her as Papa takes the sharp curves, then speeds up on the straightaways, then decelerates around dark corners, only to emerge speeding higher and higher up the alpine road. "Does anyone ever go over?" Iva Lou asks Papa, gripping the handle on the dashboard like the hand of God.

"Not often."

"How often is not often?"

"Every few years or so." Papa smiles, keeping his eyes on the road. "You make your living as a driver of the Bookmobile, no?"

"Uh-huh," Iva Lou squeaks.

"You know that nothing can go wrong when you know your road."

"Whatever you say, Mario," she replies weakly.

"Papa, pull over so Iva Lou can look down," I say.

"I don't want to look down," Iva Lou insists, her eyes shut.

"It's really cool, Aunt Iva Lou," Etta tells her.

Papa pulls over at a roadside viewing spot, and Jack follows suit. Iva Lou takes deep breaths while Etta coaxes her out of the car.

"Come. Over here," Papa orders. "Is this spectacular? Lago d'Iseo!"

"Lordy, now, that's deep." After taking a peek, Iva Lou turns back for the car.

"Iva Lou, you shouldn't miss this. Look," I tell her gently.

Lago d'Iseo has all the elements of a perfectly imagined place: a thin, milky mist and pink morning light and the movement of the wind that is almost musical as it brushes over us. The air is full of the scent of sweet grapes, growing over simple arches of wood down a never-ending footpath connected by small bridges. The bridge swings out over a mighty waterfall, which pours off the mountaintop so loudly that we must shout to hear one another. The waterfall begins somewhere high in the hills in giant white waves and cascades down the mountainside like silver streamers, falling into a pristine sapphire-blue lake below. The far side of the mountain has a steep crag that is filled with rock formations protruding from the ground in a series of shivering stone fingers that reaches to the sky.

"What are those, Papa?" I ask, pointing to the rock formations.

"We call it the Forest of the Fairies. They're a mystery. A natural wonder. No one knows how they got here."

"Must've been magic. How would anything get here? This high. Or that low," Iva Lou wonders aloud.

"Worth the ride?" Papa asks her.

"Definitely."

We make the turn to enter Schilpario, and Papa takes us through the old town, down the twisting main street, through a series of connected white stucco houses with dark brown alpine beams and shuttered windows. Papa gently taps the horn, driving slowly as the pedestrians move single file to one side of the narrow cobblestone street. When we emerge out into the sun, the familiar town square comes to life, the waterwheel spins grandly, a woman waters her garden patch of snow-white edelweiss, and several girls around Etta's age come from the bakery with long loaves of twisted bread, making their way up the mountain toward home.

At Via Scalina Number 5, Giacomina meets us on the front porch. "Welcome!" she says, with her arms open wide. Giacomina wears a straight navy blue skirt and a pale blue sweater set, and her reading glasses dangle on a pearl string around her neck. She has lovely classic features.

Nonna joins Giacomina from behind, pushing her aside a bit. "Ave Maria!" my grandmother announces at a volume normally reserved for football coaches. Nonna doesn't age. Perhaps with Papa's marriage to Giacomina, she has something to fight against, and that has given her a new lease on life.

"Etta!"

We turn around to the road to see who could possibly be shouting so enthusiastically at our daughter. It's her cousin Chiara, who is jumping up and down at the sight of her pen pal.

"Chiara!" Etta shouts back.

The two girls run toward each other and embrace, but the word "girls" no longer applies to these two. Chiara is an eighteen-year-old woman. Her black hair is full and wavy, and her once gangly legs are now long and womanly. She has found her style in a long linen skirt and an embroidered white peasant blouse tucked in and accented by a wide belt. Her espadrille sandals are tied up her ankles Roman-style, and her gold hoop earrings give the whole look a touch of Spain. To say that Chiara has turned into a beauty is to underestimate the whole process—she is a knockout. After Chiara greets Jack and me, Etta introduces her to Iva Lou, who takes an instant liking to the brunette bombshell, perhaps recognizing an alpine Iva Lou in the making. Chiara's English is excellent. She attends the university in Bergamo, where she is studying journalism, with the goal of becoming an international correspondent.

Jack and I take the room that Etta and I shared. Just being in this room again fills me with a sense of belonging and security. I feel it is *my* room in my father's house, and somehow Giacomina understands how important that is to me. She has placed Etta next door in a lovely single room with a daybed and a small desk. Giacomina has papered the room in a print of small daisies; I feel as though I'm inside a candy box.

Iva Lou is given the suite, which has a fireplace and a window seat that faces the road leading off Via Scalina and up into the Alps. Giacomina even left a pair of binoculars on Iva Lou's dresser, so she can look at the stars or up to the top of the mountain peaks.

After a hearty lunch of pansoti—delicate folds of pasta filled with ricotta cheese in a sauce of olive oil and pine nuts—crusty bread, and a plummy, rich Dolcetto wine, we all part ways for various side trips. I convince Iva Lou and Jack to go on a hike with me. Iva Lou takes to the mountain paths like a goat; after all, she was raised in the Blue Ridge Mountains. She stops occasionally to drink in the wonder of what she is seeing. "Picture books just don't do this justice." She sits down on a rock and swigs water from her shoulder carrier (which matches her overalls and pale blue kerchief).

"Isn't it amazing how close together everything in Italy is?" I wonder aloud.

"Perfect place to vacation because you can take in so many different places," Jack adds. "I'm going to wander ahead. You girls take your rest."

"Don't get lost!" I shout after him.

"I'm just gonna follow the sound of the water, honey," he shouts back, disappearing up the path.

"I know you told me about this place, and you showed me the pictures you took, but I really can't believe it." Iva Lou rolls up her pants to get some sun on her legs. "How can a place have a hot sun and cool breezes at the same time?"

"I don't know."

"Where's that field of bluebells?" Iva Lou whispers.

The famous field of bluebells where I took Pete Rutledge and almost broke my wedding vows. That day could have changed my life forever if I had let it. That field is my place of secrets, and I'm not too anxious to share it with anyone, even Iva Lou.

"It's in the other direction," I tell her. I think Iva Lou gets the point and doesn't press me.

"How does it feel to be at the ole Eye-talian homestead?"

"When I come here, I never want to leave."

"I can understand that. And how about that waiting on you hand and foot? Now I know what it feels like to be a princess. This Eye-talian hospitality is no joke. It puts the southern brand to shame."

"They care about details, you know?"

"No kidding. Giacomina even left me a fresh nightgown in the bureau. I mean, come on. That's thinking ahead! Your nonna is a pistol, though."

"Poor Giacomina. I don't know how she puts up with it."

"Well, ole Grandma was part of a package deal."

"I couldn't do it."

"Me neither. Why do you think I married a man ten years older than me? I was looking for an orphan. I did not need to be forty-plus and dealing with a mother-in-law."

"I'm sure Lyle feels the same."

"Nah, he would've loved my mama. But my daddy, now, that would have been a different story. Lyle doesn't like anyone who shirks responsibility. And my daddy was the all-time shirker. I've been thinking about ole Pap a lot lately. About how he left us. Why he left us. How that formed me. Maybe spending time with your daddy got me to thinking about it. I don't know."

"What was your dad's name?"

"Jessie Creed Wade. I said if I ever had a son, I'd name him Jessie. I guess I wanted to replace my dad all my life."

"I like that name. It's strong."

"He was Scotch-Irish and French-Indian."

"I guess that's where you got your cheekbones."

"That's what Mama used to say. That and my temper."

"What was he like?"

"I remember him being nervous. Skittish almost, around us, like family life was too much for him. You know, a lot of folks have bad nerves when it comes to raising children, and he certainly was one of them. And he'd get sad when he had to leave us. You know, when there was no work, he'd head north to Michigan to work in the factories. And then one time he left, and by God it was a good eight years 'fore we saw him again. Mama was devastated, kept trying to find him, and eventually, you know, she tracked him down. Somehow he always made his way up north. Mama would complain that he didn't love us. But I always looked at it differently. I thought he loved us so much it was painful for him. He didn't come from a happy home, and he didn't know how to make one. Skeered him to death, I think."

"You don't sound very angry."

"I never was. Mama didn't like that neither. She thought I should hold him accountable, I guess. But I understood the man, even as a youngin I just understood him. I knew what he was made of, and I didn't expect anything more from him. And then, of course, you know, I've known me some men, and it's held me in good stead never to expect too much."

"So when Lyle comes through and is there for you . . ."

"I'm surprised. And happy to be surprised, by the way. No, Lyle Makin is a shocker. I can't believe how well he handled my cancer, or how he stuck by me when I'd get that fidgety wandering feeling in my bones, my wantin' to be alone a lot. I guess I'm just like my daddy. I want to move, find the action."

"You're a mountain girl who longs for the ocean."

"I guess I am. I can't believe I'm here. Me. The Wade girl from Appalachia. I'm in the Eye-talian Alps. And how, I ask myself? How did this happen to me? Number one in her steno class, president of the Lucky Leafs Library Club. And now a goddamn world traveler. What a life."

As Iva Lou and I follow the trail after Jack, we don't say much. I'm thinking about my father, Mario, and the man who raised me, Fred Mulligan, and my mother, who loved Mario until the day she died but served Fred until the day *he* died. I thought as I grew older that my parents would become less of a focal point for me, that my child would take precedence. And I do put Etta first in all my decisions, but it is also true that I have never really resolved how I was parented or let go of my sadness that my mother revealed the secret of my real father only after her death. I often wonder if my life would have been different without the shame of that secret. Would I have been more daring? Would I have stayed in Big Stone Gap? Once a woman falls in love, her vista changes. She becomes a helpmate, an organizer, and leaves behind her solitary existence. Men seem to control their destinies. Didn't Iva Lou's father walk away when, for whatever reason, family life was too much for him? Fred Mulligan, who raised me but never really embraced me — didn't he find a way to carve out his solitude even with a family to support? And Mario da Schilpario, his whole life a testament to his choices and not his obligations? I never like to say it's a man's world, but it often seems like it is, and it will be for my daughter. And I know, as surely as I pick up these loose rocks on this path and toss them into the woods, that my own daughter will feel an obligation to take care of me in my old age. I don't know that my son, had he survived, would have done the same. He would be off pursuing his life. The daily care of his old parents would be woman's work. And I know that no matter how I would have raised him, sensitivities and all, his selfhood would have won out over any responsibility he would feel toward me.

"Girls, this way!" Jack Mac shouts from a distance. Iva Lou points toward the sound of his voice, and I follow her up the path.

"What's all the noise about?" I ask as we reach my husband's side.

"I'll be damned. Peacocks. A slew of them," Iva Lou whispers.

"Watch." Jack whistles, and the sound makes the peacocks scatter, leaving the safety of their group to create individual spaces in the field where they strut solo. Suddenly, making a big flapping sound, we see the first of the peacocks' fans unveiled. The peacock stops, poises his neck, and spreads his glorious feathers, a mix of bright turquoise and pure white plumes that open wide, revealing tips of burnished orange and horizontal stripes of polished black. Each feather has a circle in the center of its design that shimmers like the horn of a seashell.

"You know, the peacock is the symbol of eternal life," I whisper to Iva Lou.

She doesn't say anything, just watches the spectacle like a little girl, not missing one detail of the show and in awe of every movement, as though it were choreographed just for her.

"You know, this is Italy," I tell her. "There's always something around the corner that you weren't expecting."

Etta and Chiara go into the old town for *La Passeggiatta*, the traditional after-dinner stroll, while Jack, Iva Lou, Giacomina, Papa, and I sit in the front yard and eat fresh berries from the bushes behind the house.

"I must show you the pictures of Pete and Gina from when they came to visit last year." Giacomina gets up and goes inside.

"Have you met Pete's wife?" Papa asks us.

"No, we haven't. They were supposed to hike through Big Stone but postponed it," Jack tells him.

"We had a good time with them."

Giacomina returns with a pack of pictures and shows them to us.

"That's Gina." Mario points to the petite woman with a chic blond haircut. She wears sunglasses and smiles in the picture. Good teeth.

Lots of them. Long. Narrow. White. Pete looks, well, Pete looks gorgeous.

"Well, that is a fine-looking man," Iva Lou says, studying a photo. "And woman too," she adds quickly, looking at me.

I'd like to stand up and say, "This is all too weird," but I don't. I just smile and look at the pictures with everyone else. I'm crazy about my husband, but the truth is, when I look at Gina in these pictures, I envy her a little. She got the guy who talks poetry and is as sensual as he is intelligent.

"We have a gift for you," my father tells Jack and me.

"Papa, you've done enough," I say.

"No, this is one that's just for the two of you." Papa hands me an envelope. "My cousin Battista helped with this one."

I open the envelope. There is a single card trimmed in gold, written in Italian, inviting Jack and me to two nights at the Villa d'Este on Lake Como.

"Battista Barbari is one of the managers of the hotel. He is your second cousin, and when he visited us last month, he wanted to meet you. So, this came in the mail. You really should not miss it." My father rarely endorses something this strongly.

"When should we go?"

"Tomorrow. You can drive. It will take you about an hour and a half. You have to go down the mountain and then north a bit until you get to Cernobbio."

"What about Iva Lou and Etta?" I turn to her.

"Honey, I have a list as long as my arm of stuff I want to do around here. You and ole Jack Mac could use a set-down in a romantic setting."

Giacomina pats Iva Lou on the back and looks at me. "Don't worry. I will take good care of Iva Lou. Your father and I will take her to Bormio to the spa for a facial and a steam, and then we'll shop in Clusone. She won't even miss you! And don't worry about Etta. Chiara will keep her busy for the entire visit."

Laughter coming from the kitchen rouses me in my royal bed on the second floor of Via Scalina. I wake up happy, as this is the day Jack and I depart for the Villa d'Este.

The aroma of rich coffee and sweet steamed milk greets me at the door of the dining room. Everyone is around the table, talking, enjoying crusty bread with soft butter and raspberry jam.

"Stefano!" I'm surprised to see him.

"He missed us, Ma." Etta laughs.

"I thought you could use a tour guide." Stefano smiles at me.

"Jack and I are off to the Villa d'Este today."

"He knows already, Ma. Dad told him all about it."

"We're making big plans while y'all are gone. Stefano here is gonna take us all up through these hills," Iva Lou assures me.

Jack rushes me to pack a small bag to take on our trip. Iva Lou follows me upstairs to help.

"Iva Lou . . ."

"Honey-o, you don't even have to say it. I will watch Etta like a hawk watches raw hamburger. Don't you worry."

"Thank you. I really appreciate it."

"Ole Stefano has that look in his eye. Well, the look might be in his eye, but his entire body is electrified with possibilities, if you know what I mean." Iva Lou takes one look at my face and knows I'm concerned. "Now, don't worry. If there ever was a chaperone who knows the wily and secretive ways of men, it is yours truly. I'll keep 'em apart, and just friends, I promise!"

The Iva Lou plan is in place, but I don't hedge my bets. I pull Papa and Giacomina aside and tell them to please watch Etta while I'm gone. I know Etta has a good head on her shoulders, but even I was tempted by romance in these Alps. This is a place made for love, and my daughter is young. Even though she *says* she's not interested in Stefano, she might become enchanted under the right circumstances. Giacomina understands more than Papa, who you'd think would have instant insight into this but does not. He knows Stefano is a good guy and doesn't believe that he would try anything. "It's not just Stefano I'm worried about," I tell Papa. This, finally, he understands.

The gates to the Villa d'Este are so impressive, I feel I should be in a glass carriage and wearing a tiara to enter. The guard, with his long, serious face, checks a clipboard for our names. When he finds them, he grins broadly and waves us in. I order Jack to drive slowly, as I don't want to miss a detail of this entrance that looks like the start of a winding road in a fairy tale, with its perfectly manicured bushes, beds of red satin begonias, trees plumed with open cups of white magnolia, and a family crest carved into the hillside in flowers. The gardens are the least of the beauty, though. There is a low walkway with a rococo handrail along Lake Como, which might very well be made of midnight-blue lapis and not water, as it glitters so brilliantly in the sun.

As in all fairy tales, the road leads to a castle, known on this lake as the Cardinal's Palace. The Queen's Pavilion, a burnt-umber-faced villa with a boat launch at its base, faces the main building, where Battista has booked us. Jack says nothing, as he has never seen anything like this either. Only the most glamorous and elegantly dressed, coiffed, and perfumed belong here. No wonder Ava Gardner and Frank Sinatra honeymooned here; Caroline of Brunswick, Princess of Wales, was kept in exile here; Clark Gable roamed these grounds; and Ginger Rogers swam in the pool that floats on the lake. This is heavenly, and stars belong here. Jack and me? We'll do our best not to gape our two days away in awe of all we see.

"I am so happy that you decided to come," Battista, my cousin who looks like an elegant duke, says as he leads us to our room. We banter in Italian, and Jack turns and looks at the architecture. The high ceilings are shades of yellow, and the marble staircases with their flecks of silver reflect light in every direction. Battista takes a large key from an envelope (even the key has a tassel on it) and opens Room 218, a suite with a view of the lake. He opens the windows and lets the lake breeze play through the draperies, which are boldly striped in shades of dusky blue. The living room has a gray velvet couch and blue-and-gray-striped chairs; there is a bowl of fresh yellow roses on the glass-topped table. The bedroom is set off by more draperies and boasts a walk-in closet, and French doors lead out to our own private balcony overlooking the lake. Battista can see that I am overwhelmed. "But you haven't eaten a meal here yet. The cuisine is what we are famous for!"

He leaves us to our unpacking. Jack and I keep looking at each other as though we have landed on another planet.

"We only have two days!" I wail. "Let's stay right here on the lake and see everything we can."

As soon as we have unpacked and made plans for the morning, like visiting the statuary and going to the floating pool, we want to start for the lake. But before we get out the door, Jack turns to me and sweeps me into his arms and kisses me like the first time he ever kissed me in Iva Lou's trailer park so long ago. He takes the camera out of my hands and the sunglasses off my face and we tumble onto the bed. As we make love, I can hear the gentle waves of the lake and smell the jasmine that coils around the balcony. I feel young again, utterly connected to Jack, not just by our vows but in this moment. My husband, I know, feels the same. He looks at me and understands what I am thinking (one of the pluses, or minuses, of being married for so long). We laugh at our urgency and our passion—where is *this* coming from? I learn something very important today: environment matters! When a country girl is in a castle, she behaves like a princess and expects as much from her man.

There is a formal dinner dance each evening on the veranda. Thank God I brought my mother's vintage dress, a simple pale blue silk off-the-shoulder sheath with a ballerina-length skirt. Jack looks handsome in his navy suit and red tie. Battista promises something special tonight, and we can't wait to see what awaits us. (Fine dining and cuisine has become a theme in our family; in New York it was Max, in Florence, Renzo, and now the Villa d'Este!)

The waiter seats us at the water's edge and tells us that Battista has ordered for us. As soon as our drinks arrive, Jack points out over the lake. "Look, Ave!" By the Queen's Pavilion, two hot-air balloons, one with the face of the moon and the other with the sun, float over us, with two trapeze artists twirling from their baskets. The dinner guests erupt into applause, and I hear a woman at the next table tell her husband that this night is called "A Midsummer Night's Party." No wonder Papa wanted us to come right away. We won't have to dream tonight—what could be more fantastic than this?

Later, as Jack and I prepare for bed, we keep looking up at each other and laughing. This tops our honeymoon, or maybe we're just old enough to appreciate a night like this, to savor it.

"You know what I love about you?" Jack wraps his arms around me as we lie in bed. I am studying the trompe l'oeil doors on the closet, depicting a scene of a picnic on Lake Como.

"What?"

"You have a sense of wonder."

"Who wouldn't have a sense of wonder in a place like this?"

"I know lots of people who wouldn't." He pulls me closer still. "You know I never loved anyone like I love you."

I don't know what to say. My husband never talks like this. Well, not until recently, anyway; maybe it was the champagne. Or the Courvoisier after dinner. I don't care. I like it. And frankly, I'm going to pump him for more. "Why's that?" I ask demurely.

"I just never have, and I don't think I ever will." Jack kisses me good night and turns over. The soft warm breeze off the lake and the smell of gardenias take me back seven years to the summer in Schilpario when I left Jack to bring Etta to Italy. I think of him alone, back home, and his friendship with Karen Bell. It seems long ago, almost as though it happened to someone else. Instead of yanking at the picks in the fabric of our past, I leave it alone. We survived our problems, I remind myself. Love or something else saved us. Maybe it was just the timing, but we made it through. I know I was meant to take care of my husband, and I've seen him grow contented with our life together. I must remember to always be tender with him, because he always has been with me. I cover my husband with the duvet, centering the embroidered crest on his backside like a label. This makes me giggle.

"What's funny?"

"Honey, you have a royal ass. You are actually stamped and certified."

Jack and I want never to leave the Villa d'Este, but we also can't wait to go back to Schilpario to tell everyone what we saw. We decide to tour the quaint village of Cernobbio on the way back and to have lunch in Bellagio, which we saw from our boat tour of Lake Como. Our captain, Sergio, would speed down the center of the lake until he saw the home of a celebrity, and then he would turn off the motor and tell us about the owner as we bobbed on the water. The homes often matched their owners. The house of Fiorucci (the madcap shoe designer) was lime green with forest-green shutters; Catherine Deneuve (the regal French film star), a tasteful three-story beige villa with brown shutters; the Versace family (fashion designers), an old Hollywood-style white castle trimmed in gold and black. At the Ratti silk outlet, I buy six yards of silk wool in a multicolor bouclé to have a coat made for Etta. I hope she likes it. My mother would swoon at the quality of this fabric. Jack picks up some wine and cheese in Saronno on our drive back. I call ahead and tell Papa that we won't make it for dinner, we'll probably roll in around midnight.

There is a single lamp on in the front window at Papa's house when we pull into the driveway. We load ourselves down with the parcels so we only have to make one trip and enter the house through the garage. I take the perishables to the kitchen.

"What's that racket?" Jack asks as he drops a bag on the table.

"What racket?"

"That." Jack points to the street. We go to the window. Four figures come down the narrow street singing. And it's a song we know. It's the theme of the Outdoor Drama, "The Trail of the Lonesome Pine."

"Jesus, it's Iva Lou. She's drunk," I tell Jack as he follows me to the door.

The volume of the singing escalates. "Etta?" Jack asks, obviously hoping it's not her.

"Daaaa-dee," she says, one arm slung over pie-eyed Iva Lou and the other over Chiara, whose mascara has smeared into two black triangles under her eyes. A man, holding Iva Lou upright, emerges from the shadows.

"Stefano? Is that you?"

"Yes ma'am."

"What is going on here?" I sound like everyone's mother now, including Iva Lou's.

"We went to the disco up there!" Iva Lou points to the hill above us and attempts to do a couple of dance moves that look slightly dangerous. Jack stops her before she topples over.

"And had bell-eeeeee-knees." Etta throws her head back and laughs. My daughter is dead drunk.

"Get in the house," I say sternly; even in her inebriated state, Etta can tell I mean business. "Now."

Jack helps Etta and Iva Lou into the house. Chiara, also tipsy, follows. "You stay here tonight, Chiara," I tell her.

"*Va bene*," she says. Evidently, she loses her ability to speak English when she's wasted.

"Bye-bye, Stefano!" The trio of lushes waves good night to him as Jack pushes them through the door.

"Are you drunk too?" I turn and face Stefano.

"No."

"How could you let this happen?"

"I didn't think—"

"No, you didn't think. Etta is only fifteen years old."

"I know how old she is, Mrs. Mac," he says evenly.

"Then you know that she's too young to be at a club drinking."

"I understand." He turns to get into his car. "I'm sorry."

Iva Lou is snoring by the time I check on her. Chiara is facedown and sound asleep on the trundle in Etta's room. Etta is throwing up in the bathroom, and I decide it's better for her long-term health to let her father hold her head while she hurls, as I might kill her.

"She washed her face and got into bed," Jack reports when he comes to our room.

"Do you believe this?"

"She's a teenager."

"Jack, she was drinking!"

"We let her drink wine on this trip."

"This is different. This is going-out-partying drinking!"

"We're on vacation."

"That is no excuse."

"Iva Lou was a wreck too."

"Iva Lou can get drunk. She's over twenty . . . *fifty*-one!" I bellow.

"What happened to Stefano?"

"He went home. I yelled at him."

"Iva Lou gave me the whole story before she passed out."

"Didn't you see how he looked at Etta down in Bergamo? She's a pretty young thing, and he's Italian and he was giving her That Look. I don't like it."

"Honey, I think we'll all be better off if we don't make a big deal out of it. Okay?"

"She should be punished!"

"And ruin the vacation?" Jack says sensibly.

"Here we go again. Mr. Loose, Mr. Let Her Do What She Wants, thinks all of this is just fine, a natural part of growing up. 'Go on back to the still and git you some hooch!' Well, I don't go for it. I never came home drunk, and I don't want a daughter who is underage and drinks. Call me a fanatic, call me too strict, I don't like it!"

"Ave, I can't do this tonight. I'm beat. Can we table this till the morning?" Jack sounds genuinely weary. Besides, I don't want my yelling to wake Nonna, Papa, and Giacomina, so I let it go for now.

This is a recurring pattern, I think, as I lie down in bed with my husband: he goes right off to sleep, and I spend my time stewing. There is a pattern with Etta too. We have a coast period when we get along great and she follows the rules, and then suddenly, she does something completely out of character and ruins whatever good behavior points she has built up. I am speaking of her as a prisoner, and I know it. I'm not proud of that. But I don't know how else to mother her. When I'm lenient, she takes advantage, and when I press the discipline, she sulks. She knows she is not to drink, and she knows that wine with dinner is not the same thing as champagne cocktails while partying. No, she figured we wouldn't be back tonight, and she was going to test the rules. And what a chaperone Iva Lou turned out to be. What was she thinking?

Jack, Giacomina, Papa, and I are the only ones at breakfast. Not much is said as Papa reads the paper, and the cuckoo clock behind him ticks loudly. Jack and I drink our caffe lattes and Giacomina fills the sugar bowl. We look at one another when we hear the Less Than Holy Trinity come down the stairs.

"Keep your cool," Jack says to me quietly.

Iva Lou, in sunglasses, Chiara, looking far younger than eighteen with her disco war paint washed off, and Etta, still a bit green, sit down quietly at the table.

"Well, y'all look like a pack of river rats," Jack says as he surveys the damage of the night before.

"Don't rub it in," Iva Lou says.

I can contain myself no longer. "What happened last night?" Giacomina offers the girls bread, and in unison they slowly shake their heads. Instead of the usual large mugs of steaming milk, Giacomina serves them espresso, black, in tiny cups (good hangover cure).

"We was dancin' at the club. And we all started with OJ and ice. Right, girls?" They nod in agreement. "And then we thought we'd try the bitters, 'cause I ain't never had bitters. So we chugged them back. And then there were these broad-shouldered alpine hunks at the next table, and they bought us a round of drinks. Now, Stefano put out a warning that maybe we shouldn't take the offer, but I figgered why not. So you see, all of this is my fault." Iva Lou adjusts her sunglasses and continues, "Well, I tasted the bellini first, and it was delicious. I told Etta she could have a sip. And the rest is, well, the rest is a hangover."

"Etta?" I look at my daughter, who looks contrite, but that could be due to the fact that she's on the verge of vomiting.

"I'm sorry," she says softly.

Jack nudges me under the table.

"Apology accepted," I say in a tone that implies it's not. "Let's not ruin the rest of our trip."

The remainder of our vacation goes smoothly (Iva Lou became a teetotaler after Bellini Night). We make our way through the Milan airport, hauling more bags than we brought (boy, did we shop). When we reach the gate, Etta asks if she can go and buy magazines. There's a bit of a line to check in, so I let her.

"Mrs. Mac?" I hear from behind me.

"Stefano! What are you doing here?" Jack and Iva Lou greet him.

"I wanted to apologize again for the disco," he begins.

"It's all been settled," Jack tells him politely.

Stefano looks around; he must be wondering where Etta is. "Etta went for magazines," I tell him.

"Could you give her this for me?" He gives me a small parcel.

"What is it?"

"A lens for her telescope. This one is high-definition."

"I'm sure she'll love it. Thank you."

Etta rejoins us in the line and lights up to see Stefano.

"Stefano brought you a present," Iva Lou announces.

Etta rips into the package and pulls out a small lens. "Thank you." She looks up at Stefano, and there's that heat again. "I can't wait to try it out!" I thank God when they announce that it is time to board. Jack looks relieved too. Maybe now he sees what I see.

"Good-bye, Stefano." I give him a hug, and Iva Lou and Jack Mac say their farewells. The three of us turn away, though I nudge Iva Lou to keep watching. She leans down to pick up one of her carry-ons and whispers, "Kiss on the cheek. That's all."

Iva Lou eats everything the flight attendants offer on the trip home, including the mixed nuts (hers and mine). "I was too excited on the way over," she says, apologizing.

"No, no, eat."

"It-lee triggered my appetite. For food. For shoes. For jewelry. And Lyle Makin better watch it. My sex drive increased in the land of love."

"I'm sure he'll be thrilled about that. And, of course, the crocodile loafers you bought him."

Jack Mac stands and stretches in the aisle. He is sitting with Etta, who is reading a novel in Italian. Jack motions for me to meet him in the back of the plane, and when I do, he says, "Okay, she's suffered enough."

"Jack, I am not torturing her."

"You've hardly talked to her since the incident."

"I have a problem with teenage drinking, okay?"

"Ave, it wasn't a typical thing. She's on vacation in a foreign country, with *your* girlfriend, her cousin, and a young man I respect. It got out of hand, she told you how. She drank bellinis and—"

"I'm not interested in the 'how' of all of this. I only know that she got drunk. If we act like it's okay, you're going to find her on High Knob with the Alsup brothers drinking Night Train."

Jack laughs.

"I don't think it's funny."

"You know what? I am sick and tired of being the referee in my own family. You put me in the middle, and I don't want to be there. You work it out with your daughter however you want to. I'm out of it." Jack turns to walk up the aisle.

"I'll talk to her," I say.

"Good. I told Iva Lou I'd help her with her customs form, anyway."

We go back up the aisle and Jack sits with Iva Lou, while I take his seat next to Etta.

"Etta?"

"Yeah?" She answers without taking her eyes off the book.

"I'd like to talk to you."

"I really don't want to talk right now."

I look over at Jack, who is chatting with Iva Lou. He completely set me up. Etta is furious at *me*, probably more angry than I am at *her*.

"I don't want to end our vacation not speaking to each other."

"Too late for that."

"Wait a second. You're the fifteen-year-old who came home drunk."

"How many times a day are you going to remind me how old I am or that I drank too much at that stupid disco?"

"Till it sinks in that you're not twenty-one."

"I'm well aware that I'm your prisoner till I go to college."

"I resent that."

"I resent that you treat me like I'm a kid."

"You *are* a kid. You're my kid. And I don't want a daughter who drinks when she's underage."

"You're forever judging people." Etta turns and looks out the window.

"If you mean you, yes, I am judging you. That's my job. I don't like to be your warden. But you scared me. You did something that makes me think you don't understand the consequences of your behavior."

"You're old-fashioned. You don't get it."

She's got me there. I am old-fashioned (emphasis on the "old"). Most of the kids her age have mothers in their early thirties. I have two decades on them, so I am coming at things from a different perspective. And I know I'm alienating my daughter. She's not really *bad*. She's no Pavis Mullins, who spent more time in the county jail than he did in his mother's house. Why do I treat her this way? Why do I treat her like Fred Mulligan treated me? The thought of this makes me cry.

"Ma, please."

"Oh, Etta."

"What?"

"You have to try and understand: part of my nature is that I try too hard. I'm afraid for you. And I express myself in ways that hurt you, and I don't mean to do that. You're plenty mature. Usually you do just great with everything. But it seems like whenever we have a good run for a while, something like this happens and ruins it."

"Was your mother like this?"

"My father."

"Grandpa?"

"Fred."

I haven't told her much about Fred Mulligan. I felt I resolved almost all of that, but I can see by my actions that I haven't, really. On some level, the man I first knew as my father was a consistent parent. He controlled me, and I behaved. I hadn't realized that I have subconsciously taken that path with my own daughter because I know it works.

"You have a great future ahead of you. I don't want you to compromise that with some dumb choice, like drinking, that you'd look back on and regret. That's all."

"I've told you I'm sorry. I meant it, Mom."

"I believe you."

"You're mad at me all the time."

"I don't like being mad at you."

Etta goes back to her book. I should feel that our situation is better. She has promised not to drink again, but I can't promise I will ever be the mother she might wish I were. Jack looks over at me. Iva Lou had plenty to declare, but they've run out of things to do. I motion that he can come back to his seat. He looks at me as if to ask, *How did it go?* I give him a peppy thumbs-up. But I feel far from a thumbs-up. I wonder how I'm going to get through the next three years. And then there's four years of college, worrying about Etta from afar. This motherhood thing just doesn't get any easier.

## CHAPTER NINE

The timing of the United Methodist Church's "First Call for Fall" Covered Dish Supper is coming on a good night. Our vacation photos are back from Kingsport and everybody in town wants to see them, so I figure I'll just haul a bagful over to the church basement and form an assembly line.

Fleeta has whipped up five pounds of Swedish meatballs in a jumbo baking pan, which will be our contribution (that and a case of Coca-Cola, which is standard to-bring fare at a potluck when you come in a party of three or more).

"Hi, Mom." Etta and Tara come into the Pharmacy. Etta shows me a pack of gum from the display case and tears into it, handing Tara a piece. "Hi, Mrs. MacChesney."

"You girls look great. What's going on?"

"I got a perm." Tara twirls to show me her curly hair. "Ethel Bartee said you're only supposed to git one perm every six to eight months, but mine fell out, so she bent her rule and give me another one."

"Thank God. We can't have our lead flag girl with a flat head of hair."

"That's what I told her," Tara says soberly.

"Is Dad going to the church supper?" Etta asks.

"He's meeting us there."

"Can Trevor come with us?" Tara asks softly.

"Cute Trevor or Medium-Cute Trevor?"

"Ma," Etta says in a tone that means I've said something wrong. As a mother, I make it a general rule to remember only the things that embarrass my daughter and then, of course, to say that exact embarrassing thing in front of her friends.

"Oh, he's the cute one," Tara informs me.

"Then he can come. Aunt Fleeta made plenty of food, so we haven't hit our head-count limit yet."

The Methodist Sewing Circle has decorated the church basement with fall leaves made of construction paper and glitter. The main table has been set with a white tablecloth trimmed in twisted orange crepe paper.

"From Fleeta," I tell Betty Cline as I hand her the enormous tray.

"Good. We're short on meat," Betty says as she takes it. Then she lowers her voice. "If you're a deviled-egg fan, you better make haste to the Apper-tiff Table. I already caught Lottie Witt stuffing a few in her purse. They's almost gone."

"I'll get on it," I tell her.

It's so much fun to see everyone after the long summer. Nellie Goodloe has her first tan, compliments of a trip with her grandkids to Myrtle Beach. Kate Benton, the band director, has a beau in tow, a transplant out of Norton named Glenn who sells mining equipment. Iva Lou is entertaining the Dogwood Garden Club with stories of the natural wonders she observed in Italy (not many plants, mostly men).

"Father Rodriguez! Did the Methodists invite you?" I ask.

"Catholics have to eat too. How was your trip?"

"Great. I brought lots of rosaries back for you to bless, if you don't mind."

"I'm happy to do it," Father Rodriguez tells me.

I smell a cigarette, so I turn to look. In the corner, Spec is having a smoke by one of the basement windows, ashing out into the drainage area. "Spec!"

"I wondered how long it would take you to say hello."

"The place is packed."

"I know." Spec smiles. "Sorry I had to send Otto and Worley to pick you up at the airport, but we had our all-county Rescue Squad picnic at the Natural Bridge, and I couldn't get out of it."

"No problem."

"What did you bring me from It-lee?"

"Gina Lollobrigida wouldn't fit in the suitcase."

"Damn." Spec laughs so hard, it turns into a cough. I pat him on the back.

"So I brought you a tie and handkerchief set. Silk."

Spec whistles long and low. "You didn't have to do that."

I feel a tugging at my pant leg; it's little India Bakagese. She looks up at me with her huge brown eyes. I lean over and scoop her up.

"God, she's gorgeous, she's gotten so big," I tell Pearl.

"I know. She's already two and a half. Welcome home."

Fleeta, still wearing her Mutual Pharmacy smock, interrupts us. "Y'all took off without the serving utensils," she says, waving three large slotted serving spoons.

"Sorry."

"Use your heads, people. Vacation time is over. We all need to git back in the groove. Looky there. They let the Tuckett sisters out of Heritage Hall Nursing Home for the night. I'll be damned."

The Tuckett twins, wearing matching housedresses in a loud iris print, occupy side-by-side wheelchairs at the head of one of the picnic tables. Nellie Goodloe sits on the bench conversing with them.

"See how they tell 'em apart? The slippers. Edna's in the white scuffs, and Ledna's in the blue." Fleeta waves us off with the spoons and goes to the serving table.

"Ave, can I stop by later?" Pearl asks.

"Sure. You guys did a great job while I was gone. You really kept up with the prescriptions."

"Had to. We have to compete with twenty-four-hour chains. Can't let any grass grow under our feet." Pearl looks off into the distance.

"Are you okay?" I ask her.

"Why?"

"You seem upset about something. What is it?"

"Well, I do have news."

"I hope it's good news."

"It is. But it's also big. It would mean big changes."

"How so?"

"I was gonna wait till later to talk about this. But you know me, I can't keep anything from you."

I smile. It's true, Pearl has confided in me ever since she was a girl. In many ways, our relationship reminds me of the one I had with my mother.

"Taye got offered a job at the Boston Medical Center."

"Boston, Massachusetts?"

She nods. "He wants to take it. But it means that we would move with him. India and me, that is."

"Of course. You have to be with your husband." My mind races. This town without Pearl? This pharmacy? How would we do it? She is the passion behind the growth, she is the visionary. How would I manage without her? "But I'm worried about the business," Pearl says plainly. "I told you about selling the Lee County branch, well, it's a lot harder to do than I thought. There aren't any buyers for our kind of operation, and if I have to move soon, I can't really do a statewide search for partners."

"So you want to sell the business? All three pharmacies?"

"The problem is, I can't sell them even if I wanted to. I've been to the banks, and they said that Big Stone Gap is essentially a bedroom community now. Most of the young people commute to Kingsport to work. We haven't had any new industry move in, except for the wild-cat coal operations, and you know how folks feel about them."

"I do."

"I wouldn't do anything without asking you."

"Pearl, you're the president. You're in charge. I'm just your partner on the Big Stone Mutual."

"I know. But there isn't anyone else I trust to oversee the three operations. I can sign this pharmacy over to you, but that's a full-time headache. The three branches are really interdependent. I've set it up so that costs are spread over all three. They work together, in a way."

"How can I help?"

"Lew Eisenberg seems to think I should put the company in trust and have you as the guardian. That way, the places could function until we find a buyer. I can't be in two places at once. When we move, I have to devote myself to something new in Boston."

"I understand."

"I've been agonizing about this." Pearl's eyes fill with tears. "I've been struggling to figure out what to do."

"Honey, when I gave you this place sixteen years ago, I did it without strings. There still are no strings. We'll find a way to keep the places open until we find a buyer, and if we don't find one, we'll figure out how to proceed."

"Hello, gorgeous." My husband interrupts us, giving me a kiss. "You two look serious. What's wrong?"

"Nothing," we say in unison.

I give Jack a look that tells him I will explain later. Reverend Manning calls us to stand as he blesses the food. I take Pearl's hand and hold it firmly. I don't want her to worry. We've been in this position before, and we made it through, and we'll make it work again.

Jack helps me fold down the quilt on our bed. I open the windows a bit to let the fresh air in, all the while filling Jack in on Pearl's plans.

"Pearl in Boston?" he wonders aloud.

"It's a great opportunity for them."

"Big change."

"She can handle it."

"Do you ever want to move?" Jack looks out the window.

"Are you serious?" I go to him and put my arms around him.

"Don't you ever want to try someplace new?"

"And do what, open a restaurant?" Why do I always say the first thing off the top of my head? Jack winces and sits in the easy chair.

"I'm sorry," I tell him sincerely.

"I'm getting tired of construction."

"I know." Before our vacation, I noticed that Jack had grown weary of the late-night phone calls, the haggling over bids, and the long hours. Rick, Mousey, and Jack have kept their operation small (the only way to make money), but it has taken a toll on them, since they do the primary labor. I tell him gently, "Honey, I want you to be happy. But we have Etta going to college, and with the Pharmacy in flux financially, I think we should stay the course for a while, if you can stand it. We need your income."

He nods and knows this is true. "But don't you ever just want to shake things up?"

I look at Jack and want to say sure, I love to shake things up. But truthfully, I don't. I like to have a plan that goes off without a hitch. I like knowing that Etta's schedule is consistent, that we do the little things that add up to a strong family life, things like eating dinner together every night. I know I'm set in my ways, but I don't know how else to do it. "Do *you* want to shake things up?"

"I do."

"How would you do that?"

"Move."

"Where?" Why am I asking? Why would I care? I used to dream of picking up and moving. Why does the idea of it scare me now?

"I don't know. Charlottesville. Kingsport."

I make a face.

"Tuscany." Jack smiles.

"Tuscany!"

"Giuseppe said he could use a man like me in his operation."

"Giuseppe? The Olive Oil King? Really?"

"Yeah."

"What did you say?"

"I said I'd think about it." Jack looks at me. "Life is going by so fast. I want to take some chances. I hope you do too."

We lie down in bed. I'm so surprised, I can't think of anything to say. Maybe I discourage Jack from dreaming big because I'm always worried about practical things, but I've never pegged him to be an adventurer. He always seemed happy here, living in the house where he was born, in the mountains he grew up around, with me, a girl he loved all his life and finally married. What more is there? Evidently, a lot.

The phone rings.

"It's probably for Etta," I say as I reach for it.

"It's always for Etta," Jack replies.

"Hello?"

The caller speaks so softly, I can barely hear her. She asks for me.

"This is Ave Maria."

"This is Leola Broadwater." Leola is Spec's wife. I wondered why she didn't come to the Covered Dish Supper.

"Leola, are you all right?"

"No. It's Spec. He's had another heart attack. Worse than the one he had in Florida."

"Florida?" I can't believe Spec lied to me. I sit down as my heart begins to pound. "Where is he?"

"He's in the ICU up at Saint Agnes. He's asked for you. I think you ought might hurry," she says, and then she starts to sob.

"He was fine at the supper tonight!" I tell her, trying to be upbeat. "He looked great."

"Oh, Ave," Leola cries.

"I'm on my way."

Jack wants to drive me, but I tell him I don't want him to wake Etta or to leave her alone. The truth is, I need to be alone. It's strange, but I have to sort out things like this for myself. Jack understands this about me and doesn't give me an argument. I promise him that I will call once I'm at the hospital.

As I walk to my Jeep, I look down and realize I have two different loafers on. I wipe the dew off the windshield with my sleeve, feeling an odd sense of familiarity that keeps me from crying. This night reminds me of the times I joined Spec on emergency calls at all hours with the Rescue Squad. I never thought I'd be making an emergency run on his behalf.

The night receptionist at the hospital knows me. By day, she works as a clerk at the Norton Mutual's. She waves me in, and I take the short hallway to the ICU. Leola stands beside Spec's bed, and surrounding him are his five children. His son Clay cannot stop crying. I grab Dr. Stemple as she exits the ICU and introduce myself.

"He was asking for you," she says, looking back at Spec through the small viewing window.

"How is he?"

"You know he has a bad heart. He had a bypass a few years ago, but it's not the arteries that are failing him now, it's the actual heart muscle."

"Is he going to make it?" She does not answer me, and I already know the answer. "Was he at home?"

"No, he was at work. He had some mechanic working on the fire truck or something and was staying to oversee the job, and then he collapsed. The mechanic drove him here."

"Is he conscious?"

"Yes ma'am."

A nurse summons Dr. Stemple, and she hurries off. For a moment, I stand and look at Spec and his family. I refuse to let this man go. It's too soon.

I push back through the doors and go to Leola. I put my hands gently on her shoulders. She does not turn to look at me. She just places her hand on mine and continues to watch Spec, who is on oxygen and, as the doctor said, wide awake.

"Was it the Swedish meatballs, Spec?"

He smiles as I take his hand.

"Doc said you were gonna be fine."

Spec rolls his eyes. I should know better than to bluff a trained emergency technician.

"Let's give Pap some privacy," Clay tells the rest of the family.

Spec lifts the oxygen mask off of his face. "Git Ma some coffee," he tells the kids. Leola kisses him on the cheek, then moves to the doors, sheltered by her children.

"I'll be right back, you old mud turtle," Leola promises from the door.

"Mud turtle. Now, there's a sexy picture for you," I say.

Spec tries not to laugh. Then he pushes the oxygen mask from his nose and mouth onto his forehead. "This is just for show. They want it to look like they can save me."

"They *can*."

"No, this is the end of the road fer me."

"You may not go. That's an order." It's not much of an order as my eyes fill with tears.

"Don't cry on me."

"Sorry." I wipe the tears away with my sleeve.

"We had us some fun, didn't we?" Spec lays his head back on the pillow and smiles.

"God, yes. Liz Taylor choking on a chicken bone. Naomi and her buck. That Sturgill boy when he shoved a dime and three nickels up his nose."

"Made change for a quarter." Spec sighs.

I reach for water on the nightstand and try to help Spec with the straw, but he takes it from me and sips at it himself.

"It's a funny thing. I'm lying here on my way to God knows where, and all I can think about is John Wayne. All my life I modeled myself after the Duke."

Spec was forever quoting John Wayne's lines from the movies, and encouraged Jim Roy Honeycutt, the owner of the Trail Theatre, to have at least one Duke Film Festival a year.

"Yep," he goes on, "when I was a youngin, it was *Stagecoach.* And then when I got to be a man, it was *The Searchers.*"

"And now?"

"*True Grit,* I guess."

"You know I love you, Spec."

"I know." He exhales slowly. "I was thinkin' of your Joe and how I was his godfather."

I remember the day we baptized Joe. He looked like a tiny doll in big Spec's arms. Spec held him so gently, Joe didn't even wake up when the priest splashed water on him.

"My mamaw would've shot me if she knew I was in the Cath-lick church."

"You did it for me."

Spec nods. "'Bout broke my heart when that boy died."

"I know."

"It wasn't right. Now, me? I'm old. I seen a lot. I lived. But I never did understand why the Lord took him."

"I never will either. I keep looking for the answer."

"You ought to stop," Spec says plainly.

"I know."

"I want to ask you to do something for me."

"Sure."

"Don't be so hard on Etta. She's country. You know, like us. She's got her own mind. You'll see in time that that's a good thing. Now, my youngins, they ain't gonna do too well with me gone. I set it up all wrong."

"How?"

"I didn't cut 'em loose. I hung on to 'em. Now, they's followers, all except for Clay, so it's partly their nature. But it's mostly how I raised 'em."

"You were a wonderful father." I want to say more to my friend, to tell him what he has meant to me, but I don't want to cry (Spec hates weeping and wailing).

Spec looks off in the middle distance and cocks one eyebrow. "I done tried my best. God knows I ain't perfect." I'm sure Spec is referring to his long friendship with Twyla Johnson, and I wait for him to say something about her, but he does not. Instead, he reaches back and tries to adjust the pillow. I help him. "Now I'm gonna sleep." Spec closes his eyes. I slip the oxygen mask back on his face and check the levels on the machine. His mighty chest heaves in deep breaths. The nurse comes over to check on him.

"You should get the family," she says to me quietly.

I go into the waiting area, where Spec's children are gathered around their mother. They look up at me. I cannot speak, but they see why I came for them and rush into the ICU to gather about their father. The boys help their mother onto the bed, where she lies next to her husband with her arms around him. It is only minutes until Spec takes his last breath. The heart monitor hums a low whistle that tells us he has died. Spec Broadwater, the Mighty Oak, is gone.

Spec's funeral is not to be a simple Baptist affair with a service and a burial at Glencoe Cemetery. It is going to be a full-out, all-county memorial festival. Rescue Squads from Wise, Lee, Dickenson, and Scott have gathered (in uniform) to parade down Wood Avenue to the church, led by the town fire truck and brought up in the rear by the National Guard. Iva Lou insisted that the Bookmobile be in the parade as well, even though Spec said he never finished a hardback book in his life. Some folks are calling it a volunteer-military funeral, but for me, it is an appropriate send-off for a man who devoted much of his life, including his spare time, to serving others. Leola told me that Spec would be buried in his Rescue Squad windbreaker, a dress shirt and pants, and the tie we brought him from Italy. That made me very happy.

Nellie Goodloe organized the luncheon following the funeral. Fleeta has stayed up for two nights baking three coconut cakes, three chocolate sheet cakes, and pies from pecan to shoofly (Spec's favorite). Pearl opened the Mutual's kitchen for the prep. Jack made five trays of his lasagna, I bought out every head of lettuce at the Piggly Wiggly, and Hope Meade made so many rolls, she had to borrow our pickup to transport them.

"Do you think there's enough food, Nellie?"

"I sure hope so. Ole Spec had a bigger turnout than Eisenhower."

Etta is fanning the napkins on the buffet when she calls to me to look out the window.

"What is it?" I ask her.

"Bless their hearts," Nellie says aloud.

Emerging from their cars (there must be a dozen of them) are women opening their trunks and pulling out cooked hams in baking pans, roasted turkey, large pans of casseroles, even a case of champagne (they must be Episcopalians, not Baptists).

"Tennessee license plates, Ma," Etta comments.

We open the doors to let the ladies in. A tall spindly woman, around sixty, leads the group.

"We're from Johnson City. And we heard about Mr. Broadwater, and we wanted to do something, so we hope you have some use for this food."

"Thank you kindly." Nellie accepts a large platter.

"I better go get a couple more folding tables," Jack says, motioning to Otto and Worley, who are setting up the seating area.

"You're from Tennessee?" I ask the tall woman.

"Yes ma'am."

"How do you know Spec?"

"We had a fire at our rec center about eight years ago. And he came and helped put it out. Then, later, when we were rebuilding, he showed up to help with the construction. We don't know a finer person, and when we heard he passed, we just had to do *something*." The other ladies nod in agreement.

"He'd be very grateful to you."

"Well, we're very grateful to him."

I don't hear much of what is said at Spec's funeral. My mind is off in the past, when I was single and young and rode shotgun with Spec all over Wise County, working with him on the Rescue Squad. I learned so much from him. I learned to not panic, to keep my emotions in check, to not jump to the worst-case scenario in a crisis. He was always level and clear in times of tragedy. And he never went to a funeral, not even my son's, didn't believe in them. He had some kin way back who were Cherokee, and they had a philosophy about death. You don't dwell on it, you bury your dead, and you walk away from that grave never to return. Now, that's a hard concept for someone raised Catholic, like me, who every Sunday visits her mother's grave with fresh flowers. And it's hard for the Protestants, who hold somber picnics at the cemetery on Memorial Day. But to Spec, the Indian way made sense. "Life is about the living," he'd say.

Jack, Etta, and I are exhausted as we make the turn up to our house. By the time the last of the Rescue Squad workers left and we put the Baptist Church Fellowship Hall back the way we found it, it was late afternoon.

I'm proud of my daughter. She helped her dad set up, and served and stayed for cleanup. Her friend Tara tagged along and served punch. Etta loved Spec; he's one of the first people she remembers from her childhood. He spent many early mornings here having coffee and telling us the local gossip while she was having cereal in her pajamas.

"Ma, whose car is that?" Etta points to a chartreuse four-door with a black cloth roof parked in front of our house.

"I have no idea."

As we pull in, I get out of the truck and go to the mysterious car.

"May I help you?" I look into the car. There is a woman alone, probably in her early sixties, as the slight lines on her forehead indicate. Her car has the scent of polished leather and Youth Dew perfume. She wears a pale, shiny lipstick but is not smiling.

"You don't know me."

"I can't say that I do, ma'am."

"I'm Twyla Johnson."

I hope I didn't gasp when I heard the name, but the truth is, I've always wanted to meet her. Really, I know very little about Twyla Johnson. She works at the Farmers and Miners Bank in Pennington Gap and she had a relationship with Spec. After his bypass, I thought Spec would leave his wife to be with her, but he never did. And since then, the only mention of her has been Fleeta's joking references.

"Please, come in," I tell her.

I introduce her to Jack and Etta. Jack has heard tell of her but gives no indication when he repeats her name aloud and shakes her hand. Etta has no idea who she is.

"Would you like a cup of coffee?" I ask Twyla as I turn on the lights.

"I would love it," she says graciously. Shoo the Cat makes a beeline for Twyla and sniffs her patent-leather high heels. She wears a trim navy blue suit with a crisp white blouse. She has twisted a floral scarf around her neck and anchored it with a gold brooch in the shape of a bird. Her handbag matches her shoes, and there is not a smudge on its shiny surface.

"Mama, I'm gonna go to bed. I'm beat," Etta says.

"Go ahead, hon. You were a big help today."

I show Twyla to the kitchen as Jack goes outside to unload his truck. "What a beautiful old house," she says.

"My husband's family homestead."

"All hand-done stone- and woodwork."

"You could never match this craftsmanship today." Do I think Twyla Johnson is here to talk about construction?

As I make the coffee, Twyla makes herself at home at our kitchen table, neatly placing her purse in the chair and unwrapping the scarf from her neck.

"You know about me, don't you?"

"Yes ma'am, I do."

"Spec often spoke of you. I know it must seem odd that I know lots about you but you never met me."

"It is a little strange," I tell her, placing a dish of cookies before her.

"I loved Spec very much."

"You must be so sad."

"I am," she says, her eyes filling with tears. I give her the Kleenex box from the phone table. "There was no place for me today. I wanted to be there. I even got there early and went into the church, but when I saw people driving up and getting out of their cars to come inside, I went back to my car. I didn't want to cause any trouble."

"Did you see the parade?"

"I did. I had no idea that he was so well known."

"Everybody knew Spec Broadwater. Do you mind if I ask you something?"

She takes a tissue and wipes her eyes. "Go right ahead."

"Why so many years with Spec when you couldn't marry him? You seem like the marrying kind."

"Well, there was only Spec for me. And he was already taken."

Under normal circumstances, I would never ask personal questions of someone I just met. But Twyla needs to talk about Spec, I can see that. She loved him too, and she has no one to turn to in her grief. "How did you meet him? Did the bank catch fire?"

Twyla laughs. "No, no, nothing that grand. He had an account at our bank, an old account that was left to him by his parents. And every once in a while, he'd make a deposit and we'd chitchat. He'd comment about my hair or my clothes, but all of it seemed to have a double meaning."

"Spec was a flirt."

"But he meant his flirting, it wasn't silly. He was a real man. A man's man. He made me feel safe, maybe because he was so tall and sturdy. I remember the second time I met him, this was twenty-three years ago. I was operating the drive-through window at the bank, and we were very busy. I said good morning into the microphone and didn't look up, and pressed the button for the automatic drawer. Well, was I stunned when the drawer flipped open and inside, instead of a deposit envelope, the thing was stuffed with field daisies. I mean stuffed!" She laughs. "So I looked up, and there in the car was Spec. I asked him what I was supposed to do with the flowers, and he said, 'Put 'em in water.' I went to lunch with him that day, and it was the start of our friendship."

"Were you married?"

"I never was."

"It must have been hard for you on holidays." Could I possibly say anything more lame?

"It was. And really, except for our lunches, we couldn't see too much of each other because of his work. He called me a lot, though."

I think of Iva Lou, who told me one of the sure signs that a married man is having an affair is that he frequents phone booths.

"Did you get to see him at the hospital?"

She shakes her head sadly. "I didn't get there. I got a phone call telling me that he was in bad shape."

"Who called you?"

"Fleeta Mullins."

"Fleeta? Do you know her?"

"I never met her. Do you know her?"

"She works with me. She has for years."

"She was very curt. But she said that Spec would want me to know."

I don't know what to say. Fleeta called Twyla? How could that be? Fleeta is so principled about fooling around.

"I'm not proud of being the other woman."

"I can tell that you're a very good person. Spec was a deep person, even though he never said much. I'm sure he wasn't happy about the situation either."

"He had his family. I knew they came first."

I want to ask Twyla why she settled for third place, after Spec's family and his work. How could lunch once a week with the man you love be enough? But this woman is in pain, and I put aside my own judgments (and, for Godsakes, my own experience in these matters) and ask her a simple question instead. "Would you do it all over again?"

Twyla thinks for a moment as she stirs her coffee. "No, I don't think I would."

"Really?"

"You give up everything when you give up the privilege of saying good-bye."

I make an excuse that my coffee needs a warm-up, but my eyes are stinging with tears. "When Spec survived his bypass, he came down to see me afterwards," Twyla continues. "We felt so lucky that he had dodged death. And I had it in my mind that I was going to break it off that day, but when I saw him, I couldn't do it. So here we are." Twyla reaches for her purse and pulls out a small square of tissue paper. "He said when he died, he wanted you to have this. When he came back from Florida, he went to the doctor, who told him that he had more scar tissue than heart left. Spec took this as a sign that he may not have a lot of time, so he began to settle things."

"He never said anything to me."

"Spec was too proud to admit any weakness. That's the one thing he saved for me. He could talk to me when he was afraid." She gives me the tiny package, and I hold it for a few moments, not wanting to open it; knowing that if I do, Spec really is gone.

"It belonged to his mother," Twyla tells me.

I carefully unfold the paper and pull out a fine gold chain with a fairy stone dangling from it. A fairy stone is a small brown wooden cross, delicate, squat, and square. Every girl in our mountains gets one at some point in her life as a gift, from either her parents, a friend, or a beau. There is a story behind how these fairy stones came to be. We are told that there is a valley in the neighboring Cumberland Gap where there is a grove of dogwood trees, and on Good Friday hundreds of years ago, the birds in the trees wept, and when their tears hit the ground, they changed into fairy stones. And until the end of time, the birds will cry every Good Friday until their sorrow is released on Judgment Day. This is an old Scottish myth brought here by the immigrants, but it has never died.

"I never had a fairy stone."

"Now you do," Twyla says softly and smiles.

I shake Twyla's hands as she goes. She promises to be careful driving home, and we make murky plans for lunch sometime down the road. I know as I watch her back down the road that I will never see her again. We met when we had to, and our business is done. She took a big risk in coming here. I'm sure Spec shared my troubles with her and that she knows how I feel about fooling around. But I guess that now I understand, specifically because of Twyla, how these things happen. It's not like she planned this; how could she know that it was where the road would lead? As I turn out the lights and lock the doors, I feel unsure and full of questions. I am at a point where I need answers, and there is only one man who can provide them.

Jack is lying on the bed watching TV when I come up. He quickly turns it off. "What was that all about?"

"That's the famous Twyla Johnson."

"I figured that when she introduced herself."

"She gave me this fairy stone that belonged to Spec's mother." I lean in and show Jack Mac the necklace around my neck.

"She is an attractive lady."

"Spec liked beautiful women. It's so sad, though. There was no place for her today." As I undress, I think of her perfect suit and shoes and bag, and how there was a time when a woman never left her house without shoes that matched her bag, an appropriate hat, and gloves. Twyla Johnson is one of those women who live in a bygone era and refuse to give up the artifice. Maybe that stubborn nature kept her in a relationship with Spec. "She loved him very much, she told me."

"Complicated, isn't it," Jack says.

"Well, we went through it." I sit on the bed and look at Jack, who turns the color of the red throw pillow propped behind his head.

"We did," he admits.

"Yes, we did."

"Uh-oh," he says flatly. This makes me laugh.

"I always told you that I didn't want to know the nature of your relationship with Karen Bell."

"It's so far in the past."

"It seems like a lifetime ago."

"It does. And it is. We're happy now, and that's what matters."

"I learned something tonight that left me peaceful about all this stuff."

"What's that?"

"Spec and Twyla were friends. Outside of the romance part, which I'm sure was there, there was a friendship. A kinship. Spec wasn't a big communicator, and I'm glad that there was someone he could unload on who would listen. She was a sounding board, someone he could talk to. Isn't that the most important thing?"

Jack doesn't answer me. "Let's go to bed, honey," he finally says, softly.

"Jack."

"What?"

"There's something I didn't tell you about when it happened. I thought it was best not to say anything at the time. I saw Karen Bell at Holston Valley when Iva Lou had her surgery."

"She wasn't important to me, Ave," Jack says quietly.

"Yeah, but she listened to you when you needed somebody to talk to. I wasn't there for you. She was. That's the truth."

Jack considers this for a moment and then nods in agreement.

"That was really how you became friends, right?" I ask him.

"I don't even remember."

"Did you make love to her?"

I'm expecting Jack to bite my head off or roll over and dismiss my question, but he doesn't. He looks off for a moment and then looks directly into my eyes. "I've never lied to you, Ave Maria."

"But we have skirted issues sometimes. I need to *know* now, honey."

I'm not nervous in the pit of my stomach asking this, maybe because I feel secure in my husband's love for me now. Maybe I want closure. Or maybe I want to understand Spec. I do know I won't rest until Jack tells me what really happened.

"I didn't make love to her," Jack says simply.

I know that he is telling me the truth. I would like to tell him that it doesn't matter anymore, because I know now what we have in this marriage. Sex is sex, but deep emotional commitment makes a soul mate.

Jack continues, "She helped me through a rough patch. That was the extent of it. Now, I'm not going to lie to you. She fell in love with me, and I was very tempted, and I wasn't sure you wanted me. So I thought about that, and I decided that if you left me, I would have to go on. And I went into a sort of survival mode where I figured out scenarios that could happen. I think like that, analytically. But you came home when she began to really press me to leave you."

"Oh my God." The nerve of that woman, I'm thinking. I should've slapped her at the hospital instead of giving her a big ole hidee-hello.

"That summer you were gone, Spec came to see me."

"Why?"

"To scare the hell out of me. One night I came home, and he was sitting on the porch steps. He must have been waiting there for a couple of hours. Well, he got up and put out his cigarette and motioned for me to come closer. When I got about a foot in front of him, he reached for me with those giant hands of his and he took me by the collar, yanked me to about an inch from his nose, and he said, 'You hurt Ave Maria and I will kill you.' "

"No!"

"He meant it too. He told me that he didn't want me to mess up your life."

I lean back on the pillows and think about this for a moment. Spec Broadwater was more than my friend. He looked out for me like a good father, offering protection and asking nothing in return.

I get up off the bed and go to the bathroom.

"Wait a second."

"Yeah?" I turn to him.

"What about you and Pete Rutledge?"

"Why do you ask?"

"Something went on there, didn't it?"

"What do you mean?"

"Etta told me that you and he were close that same summer."

"Etta said that?"

Jack nods. "Were you?"

I don't know which is worse, that my husband is asking the question or that my daughter noticed something and felt it was important enough to tell her father.

"He's a friend." I try to sound casual.

"He is now."

"And that's all he was back then."

"Etta wouldn't make up a story. What happened between you two?"

"You know, I don't really know."

"Now who's skirting the issue?"

"I didn't make love to him, if that's what you're asking."

"I figured that."

"How?"

"I'm married to you." Jack smiles, and in his smile I see relief.

"What does that mean?"

"You never create a new mess without cleaning up an old one first."

"Oh." I go into the bathroom and brush my teeth.

Jack joins me in the doorway. "When we were young, the thing I wanted the most was to get to here."

"Here in Cracker's Neck?"

"No. Here. To this stage of our lives." He continues, "I want to get old with you. Real old. And then, when the time comes, I want to die in your arms."

I put down my toothbrush and pull my husband close. I realize that I have exactly what I have been looking for all of my life. When you honor someone, he owns you. Jack MacChesney owns me, and maybe that's the only part of love that lasts.

The lunch crowd at the Mutual Pharmacy is proof that life goes on after someone dies. Spec's seat at the counter is left empty (at least for now). Otto is on the stool next to Spec's. Fleeta pats his hand as she refills his mug with coffee. This is the first sign of public affection I've seen Fleeta give Otto; I guess it's true that grief binds folks together. Fleeta takes a break to join Iva Lou and me in a booth for a cup of coffee.

"I heard you had a visitor." Fleeta cocks her head toward me.

"Who?" Iva Lou wants to know.

"Twyla Johnson." Fleeta drags out "Johnson" like she's singing it.

"You're kidding." Iva Lou's eyes widen.

"Where'd you hear that, Fleeta?" I ask her.

"I ain't tellin'." Fleeta chomps on a straw. "I guess we can expect her to start sneakin' up to the cemetery of the nighttime and puttin' a lone rose on his grave. That's how they do it, you know. The other woman. She wants the wife to know that she ain't the only one."

"That's an awful lot of effort to make a point." Iva Lou cuts her brownie with her fork.

"Well, don't you think an extramarital affair is a lot of work?" Fleeta sniffs.

"Too much for me. Why do you think I gave it up and got married?"

Fleeta turns to me. "So. What did she say?"

"She said that she and Spec were just friends."

"Oh, come on." Fleeta laughs. Then she studies me for a moment and asks, "Really?"

"Swear to God. She said Leola was the great love of Spec's life and that she could never hurt another woman or take their daddy away from his children."

As Fleeta considers this, her stress-lined forehead smoothes out like polished marble for the first time in years. "Twyla Johnson is a goddamn saint," Fleeta says reverently.

"I think so."

"You know, Spec could piss me off worse than a blood relative. But I liked the man. I knew he was a good egg. I didn't want to think he was like all the other men, you know, that hit fifty and run around the county with their tongues hangin' out, looking for action." Fleeta gets up and goes behind the counter.

Iva Lou looks at me. "That was a crock of bullshit and you know it," she says quietly.

"And it's the story you repeat every time you stamp a book and someone inquires about the nature of Spec and Twyla's relationship. Okay?"

"You got a deal."

———

April is a month of great celebration in the MacChesney home. Jack is in the kitchen making homemade spaghetti. He's putting together a special supper for our seventeenth wedding anniversary.

"Happy anniversary!" Theodore sings.

"Thank you very much. Where are you?"

"At the office. I got your message about Spec. Jesus, that was fast."

"I know. How's Max?"

"Still cookin'."

"When am I going to see you again?" I ask Theodore sadly.

"Anytime. What's the matter with you?"

"It's just so depressing around here. Etta just got her driver's license. Pearl is moving to Boston with her husband. And I really miss Spec." I could go on, but I stop.

"Lots of changes in Cracker's Neck Holler."

"Too many," I tell him.

"You need to look at what you have, not what's missing. You have a good man who loves you, and if that's all you get, you've already won the lottery," Theodore promises me. He fills me in on his life, and I do feel better. When Theodore talks about Max, I hear such happiness in his voice. Max brings out things in Theodore that I have never seen before, all of them positive. Love hasn't changed Theodore but has made him more open and willing to take chances.

Jack has already written in our anniversary book. I still haven't had a chance. Usually I'm the one pushing *him* to write in it. This tradition of writing to each other every year has served us well; we look in it and see each other's thoughts as our marriage has grown, and there is always something that we have written in the past that helps us in the here and now. This year his passage is simple but slightly arty. At the top of the page he glued a picture that Sergio took of us kissing on the banks of Lake Como. Next to that he affixed a small wild rose he plucked from the bushes outside our room at the Villa d'Este. Then he wrote:

Dear Wife:

When I was young I thought seventeen years was a long time. And now I know it is just the beginning.

With all my love, J.

He has left the book next to my place at the table to remind me to write in it.

I'm using the good china tonight, and feeling in a generous mood. I invited Etta to bring her new boyfriend to dinner. He's a senior at Appalachia High School, an honor student who plays basketball. He has an old-fashioned name: Robbie Ramsey (his parents were not inspired by the Old West, as were so many other parents of his generation, judging by all the Austins, Dakotas, and Cassidys in Etta's class).

I hear the motor of Tara's cranky 1988 Dodge Dart coming up the road. Etta jumps out, and Tara toots lightly on the horn as she backs down the mountain.

"I'm home!" Etta calls out.

"Come on back," I holler.

"Where's Robbie?" I ask when I see Etta is alone.

"I decided not to invite him."

"Why not?"

"I just like it when it's the three of us sometimes." Etta shrugs and goes to wash up. When she returns to the table, Jack serves his excellent meal. At the end of it, our daughter presents us with a gift, a first edition of *The Trail of the Lonesome Pine*, the novel by John Fox, Jr., that our Outdoor Drama is based on. "I thought you guys would like it. Since you used to direct and Dad used to play in the band."

"We love it." I look at Jack, and he beams.

"I'm going to clean up. You guys go and relax," Etta says, standing to clear the dishes.

Jack looks at me, raises both eyebrows, and says nothing. I thank Etta and follow him out of the kitchen. We grab our jackets and go for a walk in the woods. We always promise each other we are going to take long walks, but we usually get too tired after supper and scrap the plan. When we were in Italy, we often did *La Passeggiatta* after dinner, and we were amazed at how it relaxed us for a good night's sleep.

"We have a good kid," Jack says after a while.

"We sure do."

"She knows you've had a rough winter with Spec gone."

"She misses him too."

"I know. But she understands what you're feeling."

"Is that the same kid who got plowed on bellinis last summer?"

"The very same."

Jack takes my hand and leads me down the old path behind our house, the one that carries a creek in the summer and becomes a dry gulch in the winter. The old trees planted years ago by my mother-in-law hover around the property, their top branches leafless and reaching like old fingers up into the sky.

When you live in the mountains, there are signs every day that life is changing. The terrain shifts when the mountains settle, and sometimes streams disappear never to return. One year you might find sweet raspberries growing by a field, and the very next summer they're gone. Take nothing for granted, because if you do, it will surely go. If an old tree gets leveled by lightning, it reminds you that you're vulnerable too. And even though these woods are loaded with trees, when one falls, you miss it.

"Next year I'm going to take Etta up to Saint Mary's to check it out. What do you think?" I ask.

"She keeps talking about UVA."

"I just want her to see my college. She doesn't have to go there, just consider it."

"You won't get bent out of shape if she decides not to go where you went?"

"I won't."

Jack pulls me close and kisses me. It's one of those good, long anniversary kisses (it goes on for a full forty seconds, not that I'm counting). As he holds me, I'm thinking that it doesn't feel like seventeen years at all, it feels like seventeen days. Jack reaches into his pocket and gives me a small package.

"What's this?"

"A present, you dummy."

I tear away the pink wrapping and ribbon (this is from Gilley's Jewelers; the gold monogram gives it away) to find a small black velvet box. It's dark out, so Jack pulls out a lighter and flicks it so I can see the contents of the box.

"They're gorgeous!" And they are. They are gold hoop earrings with a dangling diamond charm. "So Italian!" I throw my arms around my husband and kiss him again. "Thank you."

"Ready to go back?" he says, putting his arm around my waist.

"Your present is in the truck."

"What is it?"

"A table saw. I'm sorry. You asked for it." And it's true. I asked him what he wanted, and that was his choice.

"You always give me what I want, honey."

As if there weren't enough changes around here, the most seismic of all is happening now. Pearl must decide the fate of the Mutual Pharmacy. Lew Eisenberg is on his way over to meet Pearl and me in the Soda Fountain. Pearl and Taye are moving to Boston, and we have to settle our business. Pearl doesn't say much as she takes the last bite of her BLT. Fleeta wants in on the meeting, as she feels that she has the most seniority (and she does; she has spent more years in this Pharmacy than I have).

"Hello, girls." Lew ambles in and squeezes into the booth, taking one of Fleeta's cigarettes. Fleeta does not actually smoke them anymore. Her quitting technique is quite original and has worked for her where the patch, hypnosis, and the classic "cold turkey" have failed. She simply dangles the cigarette from her lips without lighting it.

Lew begins, "So, here's the deal. We're creating a trust for the business, in which Ave Maria is the trustee. And this will ensure the operation of all three pharmacies until an appropriate buyer makes an offer or you decide to close the places down. Right now business is profitable in Big Stone Gap and Norton; the Pennington Gap branch is barely breaking even. You have six employees there, and the manager is recommending that the place stay open twenty-four hours a day to compete with the chain. That's something for you to consider."

"Ave Maria, I know this is more work for you. But the managers of the other stores have agreed to come here every Friday with their weekly reports. This shouldn't be too much of a drag," Pearl promises.

"Whoa. Doesn't anybody want to know what I think?" Fleeta takes the unlit cigarette, now rimmed in "Mad for Melon" orange lipstick, and taps it on the table.

"Sure," Lew says, looking at Pearl, sorry that Fleeta was included in the meeting.

"My Janine just graduated from Mountain Empire in business management. She ain't a kid. She's thirty-six. Top of her class. And she's lookin' for a job. She's lookin' into managing something or another. Why can't she be the overseer of all these stores and report to you"—Fleeta points to Lew—"and to you"—she points to me—"and file some damn thing in the computer every now and agin so you"—she points to Pearl—"can keep up with what the hell is goin' on around here."

Pearl looks at me. I look at Lew.

"I like that idea," I say aloud. "Janine is a great girl."

"I think it could work," Pearl adds.

"Y'all are forever jacking your jaws about giving people jobs 'round here; now, here's your opportunity." Fleeta leans back in her seat.

"When can I meet her?" Lew wants to know.

"She's out in the car right now. I'll fetch her." Fleeta puts the unlit cigarette back between her lips and starts to slip out of the booth, then stops. "One more thing."

"What do you need?" Lew asks her.

"I put my sweat and blood in this here Soda Fountain. All the cookin' is mine and all the bakin'. I think it ought to be called 'Fleeta's.' "

The three of us look at one another.

"I think that's a good idea," Pearl tells her.

"Well, it's about damn time." Fleeta goes to fetch Janine.

Pearl laughs, and then Lew and I join her. Who'd have thought Fleeta Mullins would have a viable business plan and the ego of a mogul?

Pearl lives with her husband and daughter on Poplar Hill, in an old house they renovated, down the road from her mother, Leah, and her stepdad, Worley Olinger, who still live in the house I gave to Pearl when I married Jack. Otto lives with them now, and Pearl likes that India has her grandma, grandpa, and honorary great-grandfather under the same roof. All that will change now, and that's very hard for her. I don't think Pearl ever imagined leaving Big Stone Gap. She made the big change in her life when she moved from the housing project in Insko into my old house in town. She commuted to college at the University of Virginia at Wise, and then took on the huge job of running the Mutual Pharmacy and expanding to other towns.

"I know this is best for my family," Pearl says as she packs dinner plates in bubble wrap.

"You'll have an adjustment period. But think of the fun you'll have in Boston. So much history there! You can take India up to Concord to see Walden Pond, and the house where Ralph Waldo Emerson lived, and the Alcott homestead. It'll be great."

"I wasn't thinking about side trips."

"What were you thinking about?"

"Not having you to talk to."

"I'm a phone call away."

"I know. But it won't be the same."

"Honey, you're goal-oriented. You like to set a plan and follow it through. Think how fulfilled you'll be when you invent new challenges. A long time ago I went to a fortune-teller, and she told me that when you have a dream come true, you must then redream. You must not stay in the past. Because all of life changes anyway, and if you try to hang on to happiness or success or even the people in your life, you will be unhappy. You have to set new goals. Look where you started. And look where you are. Aren't you amazed?"

Pearl thinks about this. "Not really. When you start out with nothing, anything you achieve is a surprise."

"Look at the move to Boston in the same way. You're starting over again, except this time you have nothing to prove, you're already a success."

Pearl smiles gratefully. When I give her advice, I'm never heavy-handed or preachy, I speak from my heart and she understands. Maybe it's easier to mother a girl who is not your own, to give advice freely when you don't feel personally responsible for her every choice. If only I could be this way with Etta.

Pearl tells me that she and India will fly to Boston in the morning and join Taye, who has begun his residency at the hospital. Their furniture and other belongings will follow in the moving van by the weekend. As Pearl lists what is left to do, there is a knock at the door. "They're early," Pearl says as she goes to answer it. I stop stacking dishes, and when I look up, I'm instantly glad I'm not holding anything breakable when I see who stopped to visit.

"Dad?" Pearl says in a whisper.

"Yep, it's me."

I haven't seen Albert Grimes since the Trail Theatre burned. After he was taken to the hospital and discharged, he seemed to want contact with Pearl, so she invited him to her wedding. I'd hoped that Pearl's wedding was a new start for them, but evidently it was not. Pearl hasn't spoken of him in years, and I sensed it was a painful topic for her, so I never asked. Albert looks much better than he did back then (I think he has new teeth). He has a close-cropped haircut, and he's wearing a neatly pressed khaki uniform. The tag on the shirt says GUARD.

"How are you, Pearl?" he asks.

"We're moving."

"I heard."

"You're working?" she says kindly.

"Yeah. Up to the Wise County prison. And I murried me a nice girl out of Pound. She was an Isover. I don't know if you know you any Isovers, but they're good people."

"I think I've heard the name. Congratulations." Pearl looks away and says softly, "You have a granddaughter. Her name is India. If you'd like to see her, she's over at Mama's."

"I'll do that directly."

"We're leaving in the morning."

"I know all about."

"How'd you hear about it?"

"Funny thing. One of the guards is moving, and you're sharing the truck with him. So I asked about when the truck was comin' down here and figgered I'd catch you."

"I'm glad you came."

I realize that Pearl and Albert have been standing in the doorway the whole time, and say, "Should I throw on some tea or coffee or something?" They look at me. "Albert, I'm Ave Maria."

"I remember you," he says nicely.

"You look great," I tell him sincerely.

"Well, a good woman will do that to ye." Albert and Pearl stand in silence for another moment until Albert fumbles into his pocket. "Pearl, I want to thank ye fer looking out fer me fer so long when I had a hard time. This here is a check. I kept track of what you give me, and I want to pay you back."

"That's not necessary, Dad." Pearl's voice falters.

"No, no, you take it. My wife and I agreed you ought to have it. It's yorn. You got a girl to raise, and you may need this. Please." Albert gives Pearl the envelope, and she takes it. "I know it was hard fer ye, to take care of me. I know that I must've been a disappointment to ye in some ways, but I hope this lets you know that I believe in paying back and puttin' back. I'm just happy that I got me a job and can pay off my debt to ye."

Pearl wipes her eyes with the dishcloth she's holding, then reaches up and embraces her father for a very long time.

"I always knew you were a good man, Daddy."

"I was hopin' you did."

I'm mostly in the kitchen, but I can see that Albert Grimes has tears in his eyes too. I hear Spec's voice inside my head: "People do the best they can." And here's proof that they really do.

## CHAPTER TEN

"Ma you know I want UVA. It's where I want to go." It is the fall of Etta's senior year, and she already has a plan in place. We spent the past year visiting every college in Virginia from William & Mary to Hollins, collecting applications, postcards, and sweatshirts, so that Etta would keep an open mind. But she's been set on UVA since she completed her internship at Thompson & Litton. I think she even has her dorm picked out.

When Etta was born, like every mother, I made a lot of plans for her. I made lists of my favorite books to share with her, most of which she has read (she's in the middle of *Pride and Prejudice*, next up *The House of Mirth*). I wanted her to see the world and have a fine education. I still hope she'll consider my alma mater, Saint Mary's College up in South Bend, Indiana.

"I know you're set on Charlottesville. But can't we just take a ride up to South Bend so you can see the place?"

"Okay. But don't get your hopes up," she tells me.

Jack begs off from the trip I've planned for Etta's fall break (smart man). I think the flat farm fields and never-ending countryside of Indiana, and its midnight-blue night sky with stars so low they dangle like crystals on a chandelier, might woo her to change her mind. It's a football weekend at Notre Dame, which adds to the excitement. Maybe when she sees the girls in their wool pea coats and Fighting Irish baseball caps, she will reconsider.

As we drive onto the campus, Etta is impressed by the lane, anchored on either side by hundred-year-old oak trees, so high they meet over the center of the road, forming an orange canopy over our heads. The buildings, so beautifully set beside a lake with an island at its center (the ducks are out, how picturesque), create a scene that far exceeds the beauty of the photographs in the brochure. Etta laughs when she sees an old Packard, painted white with silver fins and stuffed with nuns in black and white habits, whiz by. "They look like a tin of Aunt Fleeta's iced brownies," she observes.

Etta's never seen a nun in a habit. Catholics are rare in Southwest Virginia. The only nuns she knows are at Saint Agnes Hospital in Norton, and their habits are more like the traditional nurses uniform, not the long flowing robes of the order of Saint Joseph. Our priests down home are worker priests, missionaries really, so they rarely wear their collars. Etta is amazed by the first Catholic place she's ever been. The statues of saints tucked in alcoves, the angel statuaries in the gardens, and the heavy cross in Le Mans hallway are all new to her. I'm not sure she relates to it all.

Etta has a meeting with the admissions committee, who, I can see by the looks on their faces, would love to have her. Etta tells them that she is grateful for their time, but she remains noncommittal, saying that she wants to check out the art department in Moreau Hall. A B.F.A. would be the closest match to the architecture studies Etta has in mind, and she wants to see what the facilities are like. As we tour, I remember taking photography classes, and when we enter the Little Theatre, I remember the plays I saw when I went here.

"Isn't this gorgeous?" I ask Etta as we walk across the empty stage of the Little Theatre.

"It's really nice." Etta looks at me with that *Don't press it* expression, so I don't. Why am I selling this so hard? Don't I know that if she picks where she goes, she will make it work? Doesn't the University of Virginia have the best architecture school in the state? What's the matter with me—haven't I learned to pick my battles?

The ride back home goes quickly, and soon we find ourselves in the blue hills of Kentucky near the border of Virginia. Etta has been quiet most of the way back (she slept a lot), and I notice that by the time we stop for food, her mood has visibly lifted.

"You're in a better mood," I say, handing her the ketchup for her hamburger.

"We're almost home."

"And that makes you happy." I don't pose this as a question.

"Yeah." Etta has a swirl of sarcasm in her voice.

"You didn't like Saint Mary's, did you?"

"It was nice."

"It's traditional and old and grand and well respected. I wouldn't call it nice."

"Ma. I don't want to go to Saint Mary's."

"Why?"

"Because it's not for me. I knew you were gonna do this. I knew you wouldn't make it a fun trip, you'd make it about getting what you want."

"I've already gone to college. I don't want anything except the best education for you."

"No, you want me to do what you did."

"You'd love those girls once you got there."

"No, *you'd* love those girls once I got there. I didn't see one person like me."

"What are you talking about? You're smart and you have a great personality. You'd fit right in."

"I don't want to fit in there."

"You really want UVA."

"You make it sound like a mail-correspondence college. It's the state university of Virginia, founded by Thomas Jefferson. It's not some dump."

"No, I know it's a great school."

"Then why don't you want me to go there?"

"I don't *not* want you to go there."

"You've never once said, 'Great choice, Etta.' Most of the kids in my class don't even go to college. Why can't I decide what's right for me? If you don't get your way, you act like the world's gonna end. You're so spoiled."

"Spoiled? Me?" The last thing I consider myself to be is spoiled.

"You're an only child, and you've gotten your way forever."

"You're an only child," I retort.

"No. I had a brother." Etta takes a sip of her Coke. I can see that if we weren't in a truck stop in Kentucky, she'd get up and leave. But she is trapped, and so am I. "You forget that I lost someone too."

"I'm sorry." I try not to cry, wiping my eyes with the napkin.

"And don't do that either. Apologize all the time. You can't say whatever you want to me and push your agenda with heaps of guilt and then apologize for it like you didn't mean it. You do mean it. It's your way or nothing."

"That's not true."

"It is true. You think you know best for everybody! You think you're above people. You even think your family is better than Dad's."

"I do not. I loved Mrs. Mac very much."

"As a friend. She died before she was family to you."

"What does that mean?"

"You could deliver her medicine and hang out with her, but that's not being family. You never get attached to people, Ma. Don't you notice that?"

"I have dear friends in Big Stone Gap. Aunt Iva Lou! Aunt Fleeta! What about Spec?"

"Ma, I'm a mountain girl. I'm a MacChesney. Look at me. I have brown hair and green eyes and freckles. I'm built like Dad. I like mechanical things and astronomy. I couldn't sew a button on my coat or work in a pharmacy. I'd be claustrophobic. I like soup beans and corn bread and divinity candy. I like mountain boys who talk like me. I like my girlfriends who live in the hollers and have babies when they're young enough to chase them around. I love the country, the back roads, the Powell River when it floods, and the fact that you don't need much money to survive in Big Stone Gap. I'm one of them, and I will be until the day I die. And whether I live there after college or not, I'm gonna carry all that inside me all my life. That's who I am."

I can't say a word. I hear her, and I know she believes what she says. I guess I was hoping that it wasn't true. I wanted more for her. I wanted her to love the world outside these mountains as much as the world within them.

"I guess when you were born, I thought I'd have a daughter just like me. And that was wrong. You are who you are, and you have a right to be that person."

"Thank you." Etta sounds relieved.

"I didn't want you to be like me because I thought I was better than everybody else. I wanted you to be like me because I was very much like my mother, and I found great comfort in my relationship with her. I'm letting go of hoping that you and I could be like my mother and me. It just wasn't our fate, I guess."

"Is this really what you're sad about, Ma?" Etta looks at me. "Is it really about me? Or is it about Joe?"

"I don't understand."

"All my life I just wanted you to be happy like you were before Joe died. You used to laugh more, and it seemed like you weren't scared of anything. I know I was little, but I remember that everything changed. I don't know what it's like to be a mother, I can't even guess, but it doesn't do you any good, or me, to be scared for me all the time. You can't protect me by putting me in a school in Indiana any more than you can lock me in an attic. If something were to happen to me, it would be because it was supposed to happen, and there is nothing you could do to stop it."

"Don't say that."

"It's true. It wasn't your fault, Mom. You didn't do anything wrong, and Joe died anyway."

She's right. I look at my daughter, and I don't see a little girl anymore, and I don't see a teenager. I see a whole person who thinks deeply about things and searches for answers. I set out on this journey of motherhood with a plan in place. I knew exactly how I was going to handle every challenge and what my rules were. What I did not consider was what kind of a child I would get. And I have to say that, even though I was hoping for something different, I was very lucky to have Etta for my daughter. She is far more intuitive than I ever was, and certainly more honest about her feelings.

"I'm happy you want to go to UVA, really I am."

"Are you sure?"

"Totally sure."

Etta smiles. "Thank you, Ma."

And those are the most important words my daughter can say to me. Mothers who try hard (I lead the pack) need to know that once in a great while, they do something right.

Jack and I sailed through the milestones of Etta's senior year of high school, including the spring musical (Etta was set designer for *Carousel*), the prom (she went solo with a group of girlfriends), and graduation (Jack cried, I didn't). Papa has sent Etta a round-trip ticket to Italy for her graduation present. We took her to the airport yesterday; it's her last fling before she starts college.

Theodore has been awarded an honorary degree by the University of Tennessee. I convince him and Max to drive down a couple of days early to stop in Big Stone Gap on their way to Knoxville. Theodore wants to show Max "Where the Big Orange Reigns Supreme" and, of course, Big Stone Gap.

There are many people who want to see Theodore, so I've parked him at Mutual's during lunch to have one central location for folks to stop by and say hello.

"I don't know what you were talking about. The food here is interesting," Max chides Theodore.

"I lived here eleven years, and I couldn't get past the first bite of soup beans and corn bread."

"That's your problem. I think they're delicious." Max goes back into the kitchen for seconds.

"So much for my cosmopolitan boyfriend," Theodore tells me. "Do you think the folks wonder who Max is?"

"Are you asking me if they think you're a couple?"

"Yeah."

"I think that everyone here is so old now that if they might have cared at some point, they don't anymore. Gay, straight, or tuckered out entirely, I think they just want everybody to be happy."

Theodore throws his head back and laughs. "I think you're right!"

One of the things I missed the most after Theodore left was spelunking into the caves of these old hills. I couldn't find anyone else who had the passion for it. I took Jack once, and he said he'd rather be in a coal mine. Another time, I took Etta, and she was busy measuring the walls for potential collapse instead of examining the lichen and stone formations. So I'm thrilled when Theodore agrees to go to Cudjo's Caverns with me while Jack gets a lesson from Max on how to make profiteroles.

Everything is as we remembered it: the low ceiling entrance, the unwieldy footbridge, and the underground stream. "Isn't it weird nothing has changed?" I ask Theodore.

"This isn't like Disney World. They don't upgrade. It's whatever nature does. It took hundreds of years to get this way, and it will take hundreds more to change it."

"If I tell you something, will you laugh?"

"Never."

"I'm getting early empty-nest trauma. Every time I think of Etta leaving for good, I can't breathe. What's wrong with me?"

"You're like everybody else. You want to hang on to what you know. It's going to be strange not to have your schedule arranged around Etta. Work won't matter in the same way because you won't be doing it for your family, you'll be working for you. So you have to rejigger the whole picture. And it's scary to start all over again at our age. Who really does? No one. And you know why? Because it's too hard."

"Thanks. Now I feel worse."

Theodore laughs. "It's true. Sorry."

"That does not explain my physical ailments, like palpitations."

"Are you going through the Change?" Theodore asks bluntly.

"What?"

"You know, the Change. When your eggs take a vote and decide to close down the factory."

"I know *what* it is, I can't believe you asked me about it."

"Why? It's completely natural. And it also makes very sane women lose it over nothing in particular, and you've certainly been doing that lately."

"For your information, I *am* going through the Change. Well, really, it's the Changeover. I'm at the end of the ordeal. And the process made me realize why these mountain girls are brilliant. There's a reason to have your children at twenty. When you have them in your late thirties, they leave you just as your cycles do. It isn't pretty, and it sure ain't easy."

"Contrary to your standard self-recrimination, you are doing just fine with everything."

"Thank you for the support."

"Max and I are planning a trip to Lake Tahoe at the end of the summer. You want to come?"

"Jack and I always wanted to go there."

"You could drop Etta and join us after. I promise I won't let you ruin my vacation with your pity party. You'll have to leave your Etta wailing back in Virginia. Think you could do it?"

"Yes, I do." And I mean it. I don't want to spend a moment of sadness around Etta's great achievement. She's going to the University of Virginia to be an architect—what mother wouldn't be thrilled about that?

Throughout July, we get regular postcards from Etta, detailing her travels up the Mediterranean with Chiara, Giacomina, and Papa. Meanwhile, I'm here making lists for whatever she might need for her freshman year at UVA. Iva Lou and I drive over to Fort Henry Mall and pick up all sorts of dormitory necessities: new towels, bedsheets, and a leather book bag (I hope she likes it). Iva Lou helps me unload the packages when she takes me back to Cracker's Neck, and Jack meets us on the front steps. His face is ashen. I drop the bags on the porch. "Did something happen to Etta?"

"No, no. She's fine."

"Why do you look like that?"

"She called while you were gone and said she'd call us back in fifteen minutes. She wants to tell us something."

"But she's flying home tomorrow. Is something wrong with the ticket?"

"She didn't say."

"Why didn't you press her?"

"She wouldn't be pressed, Ave."

"It's probably nothing. She probably bought y'all matching ID bracelets on the Ponte Vecchio and wants to know how you want 'em engraved. For Godsakes, don't jump to conclusions." Iva Lou looks as though she might shake me.

The longest fifteen minutes of my life commence. Oddly enough, they give me ample time to play out several horrible scenarios in my mind. I don't have a best guess, but the feeling in the pit of my stomach is one of dread.

At last the phone rings. Jack motions for me to pick it up in the living room, while he sprints up the stairs to talk on our bedroom phone. Iva Lou pours herself a Coke in the kitchen.

"What's wrong?" I say without a hello.

"Ma."

I breathe deeply.

"I'm getting married."

I can't say anything, I drop the phone. Iva Lou runs into the living room, takes one look at me, and motions for me to sit down. She picks up the phone and hands it to me. Then she sits down next to me, sharing the receiver, and we listen together.

"Etta, what do you mean you're getting married?" Jack asks this question like he heard it wrong.

"I'm getting married."

"After college?" I ask weakly.

"No, next month."

"Next month!" In the back of my throat, I feel the cheeseburger that Iva Lou and I had at Pal's.

"Aren't you going to ask me who?"

"Who?" Jack, Iva Lou, and I say in unison.

"Aunt Iva Lou?"

"Sorry. I picked up the phone to see if Lyle wanted me to stop at Stringer's for a takeout."

"Stefano Grassi has asked me to marry him, and I said yes."

"What about school?"

"I'm going to go to the University of Bergamo. They have a great architecture school."

Jack raises his voice and sputters into the phone, "What about UVA? Are you abandoning all your plans just like that? Where is this coming from?" Every bit of his protest is lost on Etta, who sighs into the phone.

I blurt out exactly what I'm thinking. "Have you lost your mind? You're eighteen years old. Marriage? What in God's name are you thinking?"

"Mom. I'm an adult, and I can do what I want."

"The fact that you're eighteen, dumping out of college, and getting married tells me that you are far from an adult!"

"Please. Talk to Grandpop." Etta hands the phone to my father.

"Ciao," he says quietly.

"What is going on over there, Papa?"

"They're in love," he says simply.

"Jesus. Where was Chiara?"

"She's not a very good chaperone."

"No kidding. Neither are you!"

"I'm sorry, but you can't stop this sort of thing. I know she is young, but she knows her own heart. Stefano is a good man. You know him. This is what they want. It's like a boulder coming off the mountain. You have to let it be and get out of the way."

"Papa, I'm going to be sick."

"Ave Maria, listen to me. You cannot stand in the way of her happiness. You will lose her."

"Too late for that."

I hang up the phone. Let Jack deal with them, with her. I can't. I can't believe this is happening.

"What a shocker." Iva Lou gets up off of the couch. I begin to cry. Iva Lou doesn't know what to do, so she paces, then says, "Look, it could be worse. She could be miserable or hurt or something horrible. She's in love, and she sounds happy. Why is this so terrible?"

"She's a kid."

"Not according to the government."

"What do they know?" I wail. Jack joins us in the living room. He comes and puts his arms around me. "That kid is trying to kill me," I tell him.

"No, she's not."

"She deliberately pulls this stuff. She's ruined my life."

"Come on, Ave."

"We sat up here and did homework with her every night, sent her to Mountain Empire for college prep classes, supported her when she did her internship. . . . For what? It's all gone."

"She says she's going to go to college over there."

"Dream on! When? How? Who's going to support her? You know what happens to teenage girls who marry? They have babies and they get trapped and it's over. Over!"

"That's a little prejudiced," Iva Lou says politely.

"It's the truth!"

"This is a shock. And when the shock of it wears off, we will figure out how to proceed."

"Jack, wake up. The horse has left the barn. She's getting married. Did you hear her? She didn't ask for our blessing. She doesn't care. She does what she wants when she wants, and doesn't listen. She's never listened!"

"She's got a mind of her own."

"And look where her mind got her!"

"We know Stefano —"

"Him? I'd like to kill him."

"You don't mean that."

"Yes, I do. With my bare hands, I would like to kill him. How dare he subvert her college plans? What kind of a man discourages a woman from getting an education? I'll tell you what kind. The kind who wants a slave to cook and clean and wait on him."

"You know better than that. He's an educated man himself."

"Oh, please."

"He is. He's a good man. This could be worse. She could have called home saying she was going to marry a stranger."

"What am I going to do?" I walk to the window and consider running all the way to Lee County, until my heart gives out and I fall over dead.

"You're gonna have a drink." Iva Lou looks to Jack. "Where's the hooch?"

The problem with drinking when you're upset is that it doesn't take quickly. I have several shots before I feel the first one. I'm not proud that I turned to Jack Daniel's in my crisis, but I realize there is a first time for everything. Iva Lou went home after a couple of hours of hearing me rant. She took all she could and then slipped out. Jack is in the kitchen making us something to eat. I muster all my strength and go into the kitchen. Iva Lou has stacked all of Etta's college supplies on the bench under the windows. The sight of them makes me cry.

"Come on, you need to eat." Jack puts the food out on the table.

"I'm not going over there."

"We have to go."

"I'm not going. I am not going to support this."

"Ave, it's too soon to say that."

"Plenty of people disown their children and go on to lead happy lives."

"Name one."

"I don't actually know anybody personally, but I am sure they're out there."

Jack sits down and takes my hand. "Ave?"

"Jack, how could she do this to us?"

"I don't like this any more than you do. But I don't think she's doing this to hurt us. She's following her feelings. She's in love."

"Ugh."

"I want you to remember when we fell in love."

"We were thirty-five years old!"

"Okay. Bad example. How about my mother? She was sixteen when she fell in love, and seventeen when she got married."

"That was in colonial times."

"Folks have always married young in these mountains. Now, I'm not saying this in defense of what she's doing, I'm just making the point that this is not a new concept to her."

"We didn't raise her to do something like this."

"You have to get past this feeling that she did it to spite you."

"Okay, let's say they are in love. A girl at eighteen can't know what love is. She's dated two boys, both of whom she dumped because they were too dull. She's throwing her life away without exploring any of the possibilities. He's probably the first man she's had sex with, and she got hooked." I can't believe I said that, but I believe it's true. She got caught up in the moment, and in that moment, she gave away the rest of her life.

"I don't think that's what's happening here."

I look at Jack and see that he is as wounded as I am; but he's better than I am, he is giving her the benefit of the doubt, trusting that he did a good job as a parent and that this will all work out. I wish I had his perspective.

"You're a cockeyed optimist," I tell Jack.

"Aren't you happy that she's marrying an Italian?"

"I don't want her to marry anybody right now!"

"Your father is there. Giacomina. Nonna. She has a loving family around her. It's not like she ran off to Albania with a convict."

"Jack, any way you look at this, it's wrong. She's out of her mind! She flip-flops! When I took her to Indiana, she went on and on about being a mountain girl, and being a MacChesney, and how she loved these mountains, and now she turns around and decides to live in Italy with her childhood crush. I don't get it."

"If all that is true, it must mean she really loves him. She was excited about UVA, thrilled about it. She wouldn't throw that away on a whim."

"I don't know her at all, Jack. I can't figure this out." I can barely get the words out. I'm drunk. I sound like an old booze hound somebody found on the floor of Ray's Café on a Sunday morning after an all-night binge.

"We have to accept this."

"Why is it so easy for you?"

"Because I know it's her life and she has to live it."

I shove all the college supplies off the bench and lie down on it, curling up in a ball so small you could play field hockey with me. I'm so sad and disappointed. It's like I built a beautiful castle and turned away for a moment, and a fire has broken out and burned it to the ground. Now I understand why people drink: there are days when the news is just too hard to take.

The flight to Italy is so turbulent that Jack and I have a moment where we truly believe that we won't make it to Etta's wedding. Our initial plan, to stop this thing, entirely backfired on us. When we threatened to come over to bring her home, Etta pushed the date up. Jack and I went to Father Rodriguez to talk things through, and he helped me understand that I have to find a way to accept this because my daughter needs me and surely will more in the days to come. I haven't accepted this marriage yet, but I have decided to act like I do, and then hopefully one day I will have a change of heart and embrace my daughter's decision. Of course, this is my rational mind talking, not my heart.

Theodore will be meeting us at Malpensa Airport in Milan. When I called him to tell him about Etta, he quickly dropped the Lake Tahoe trip and rearranged his plans. Jack and I invited Max too, but he felt he'd be in the way, so he's going to see his family instead. We've rented a car and will drive directly to Schilpario, where the wedding is to take place a week after our arrival. Five weeks have passed since the fateful night of Etta's phone call, and we have spoken since, but the conversations are strained and overly polite. I received a five-page letter from Stefano Grassi, who outlined in nearly mathematical terms why this union would stick. I read it through once and haven't had the strength to read it again.

Jack thinks I'm doing better with the whole thing, but I find it hard to talk to him about it, because he is overly optimistic. I can't find a single soul who understands why I'm devastated. Even Fleeta said, "It's not like she's fifteen. She's eighteen. She's legal." The only person who is on my side is Theodore. Thank God he will be there for this wedding. I really need him now.

Jack falls asleep after the meal, which gives me a chance to think. Once again I feel cheated out of happiness. By getting married so young, Etta has deprived us of that natural order of maturity: graduation from high school, then college, then a life on her own in some new and exciting place, after which she finds a good man to settle down with, and then, at a mature age, children, if she so desires. I had so many plans for Etta's wedding day. I cut out pictures from magazines of bridal cakes and Italian *regali* — gifts left on the wedding table for the guests. I thought about what kind of gown and veil she would look good in, deciding that bright white was bad; an eggshell beige would go better with her skin tone. I would make her day a happy one, filled with sweet surprises and beauty. I would welcome her husband's family with open arms, and be a hostess with largesse and good manners. Instead, I've had nothing to do with the planning of my daughter's wedding. She has not asked for my input, telling us only where and when the service will be, and the address of the reception.

Malpensa Airport is packed with people. I doubt Theodore will be able to find us, and the way things have been going, I wouldn't be surprised. Jack corrals the luggage through automatic doors. I hear Theodore calling my name and see him in the crowd.

"I have the car. Let's go." Theodore kisses me, shakes Jack's hand,

and takes a couple of bags. We pack everything into the trunk of the black Volvo and pile in.

"We're going to make this a happy trip, aren't we?" Theodore says, eyeing me in the rearview mirror.

"I'm doing my best."

"She really is," Jack tells Theodore.

"This could be worse," Theodore says.

"Yeah?"

"She could be marrying that Boggs boy who broke into the Mutual's and stole the Valium that time."

"True, Theodore," I say halfheartedly.

All the magic that makes the Italian Alps my dreamscape is lost on me as we ascend the regal cliffs. I might as well be on my way to the guillotine. I feel as though everything is ending, even though I know that my daughter is at the beginning of a new life. Despite everyone's protests, I still have an aching feeling that this marriage is doomed.

Papa and Giacomina meet us in the driveway. His embrace reassures me, and Giacomina's warmth makes us feel as welcome as always.

"Where's Etta?" I ask.

"She's at the church. She'll be home any minute."

"You should be pleased that she's getting married in church," Theodore says to me under his breath.

"Don't push it," I whisper back.

Giacomina shows us to our rooms and, when she gets the chance, pulls me into her and Papa's bedroom. "How are you?" she asks me tenderly.

"I'm here."

"I know this is hard for you."

"I wish I was an actress, so I could invent a character to be throughout all of this. I'm going to try really hard to be nice. To be happy. How's Etta?"

"She's in love," Giacomina says simply. Papa calls her from down-stairs, and she excuses herself and goes.

*Love.* What a tiny word that is used to describe everything and can mean nothing. These Italians. They're all for it. Love is the point of life itself, love is the great healer, love is the energy behind all things that are beautiful, whether it's a silver cup of berries or lovers on a bi-cycle built for two. Dreamers. They're all dreamers.

"Mom?" Etta stands in the doorway and looks at me.

"I'm sorry, honey. I'm so angry at you," I tell her quietly. I look at her and, of course, my heart melts. This is my daughter, and I want her to be happy more than I want it for myself. But I cannot hide my disappointment or my fear.

"I know." She sits on a chair and motions for me to join her. "How was your trip?"

"Not great," I tell her.

"You think I'm too young."

"Oh, Etta, it's more than that. You don't trust my judgment. You don't listen and benefit from my experience. Yes, you're young, but you're also impulsive. If you're really in love, and it will last, why are you rushing into this? Can't you come home and get your degree and then marry Stefano? Why are you doing this?" The questions I have longed to ask her come tumbling out, and not eloquently.

"Because it's right for me."

"How? You were accepted to college and you were excited about going. Aren't you sad about giving up your future?"

"I'm not giving anything up, Ma. I'm adding to my life. I'll have my studies and my husband at the same time."

"When did this happen?"

"Ma, I've known I would marry Stefano since I was eight years old."

My memory takes me back to the house on Via Davide, where Etta slept in the trundle next to my bed and told me that someday she would marry Stefano Grassi. At the time I thought it was cute, that she believed she was wise and could project into the future. I sure as hell didn't think she was serious. As I play through all the key events of her life, like I have done so often over the last few weeks, I realize that there was never a time when Etta lied to herself. She looks at me, waiting for me to say something. I can't. I hold my arms out for my daughter, and she rushes to me. I begin to cry.

"I'm sorry this is so hard for me," I tell her.

"It's okay."

"No, you deserve to be happy."

"So do you, Mom."

"Don't worry about me. I'm okay." Who am I kidding? I will never be the same. I'm letting her go and she may come back to me, but she won't ever be mine again. But that's my problem, not hers.

"I have so much to show you." She takes my hand.

"Is there anything I can do?"

"Tons!"

Etta takes me to her room on the first floor, which looks like a bridal showcase. She has made favors for the tables, small gold silk purses filled with pastel almonds, tied with a peacock feather.

"They're beautiful. How many people are coming?" I ask.

"Just family and a few friends. Maybe thirty of us in all."

"Do you have your dress?"

Etta nods excitedly and unzips a garment bag. "In Italy, the gown is white, but it's accented with color." Etta pulls a pristine, high-waisted, scoop-necked beige silk gown from the bag. It is embroidered with tiny pink and blue rosebuds on the hem, and down the back are satin streamers that match the roses.

"It's exquisite," I tell her.

"Do you think so?"

"I love it. It's exactly what I would have picked for you."

Etta hugs me so hard, I feel I might snap in two. "Oh, Ma, I'm so happy."

"Tell me about it. How, when, the whole thing." I sit down on her bed, and she sits down next to me.

"When I got here, Chiara and I went to Sestri Levante to hang out at the beach. When we got there, we heard that Stefano Grassi was working on a project there, and did I want to see him? He had come by Zia Meoli's house and asked me out to dinner. So we went."

"Did it happen just like that?"

"No, it took a while. But Mom, I think Stefano said when he wrote to you, he's loved me since our last visit. I know I was young, but he was seeing a girl seriously and gave her up because he felt like a phony with her and was hoping someday that he and I would be together."

"I remember that part in his letter."

"Mom, when I was little and you told me the story of your mom and Grandpa, it was so romantic, how they fell in love and would sneak around to see each other, right here in Schilpario like Romeo and Juliet."

I could kick myself for planting these romantic notions in her head, even though they are true. This is all my fault! But I say nothing and motion for her to continue her story.

"Anyway, we began a proper courtship with Grandpa sort of chaperoning, and then Giacomina, and we just spent a lot of time together, and it was almost time for me to leave, and Mom, I couldn't get on the plane. Stefano wanted me to go home and go to college and come back when I had my degree. But I couldn't imagine leaving him. I tried. I knew that I had obligations back home, but nothing else mattered, only Stefano. I want to be with him for the rest of my life. And I don't want to wait. There's no point in waiting."

"But you told me you were a mountain girl."

"Ma, look out the window. There are mountains here too. They just have a different name. These folks are just like the people of Big Stone Gap. They have their own music and their own cooking and their own ways. They don't like outsiders to come in and change their way of life. They like that they're remote and that visitors get lost trying to find them. The lady who runs the patisserie is just like Aunt Fleeta, crabby but she'd do anything for you. There's another woman who works in the dress shop, she's just like Aunt Iva Lou, a free spirit. They even have a Spec Broadwater here, he's the forest ranger who checks for floods. It's not really different. I feel at home here."

"And I'm glad you do. Because it will be your home for the rest of your life. Stefano is Italian and not likely to leave his country."

"I'm fine with that."

"I accept that you're in love and swept away, and all the good stuff. But take it from an old bag: I'm not worried about your happiness this year or next, I know you'll be flitting around on the wings of bliss for a long spell. It's your future that concerns me. I'm worried about when you're thirty, or forty-one, when you wake up and realize that you've given up your youth to a grand romance. This is a time in your life that you can never retrieve. And I'm not trying to change your mind. Look, there's the dress and the shoes and the *regali*. You're all set. But I wanted to explain why I couldn't jump up and down when you called. I was worried sick for you."

"Mama, you're always going to worry about me."

"I know. I've done my best, and I tried to instill in you the values that my mother instilled in me. There wasn't anything complicated or fancy about what my mother taught me. It was to honor myself and be true to what I believed. And when I reacted the way I did, I realized that I was imposing my beliefs upon you. This is your life, not mine."

Etta embraces me, and for the first time since the day she was born, I feel that she needs me. "I want to promise you something," I tell my daughter. "By next Saturday, your wedding day, I will be where I need to be for you."

"I know you will, Ma."

Theodore and I take a long hike up the mountain, and we try in vain to find the peacocks. Either they moved or I took a wrong turn at the pine tree near the stream. Even so, the views are spectacular, and we reminisce about our days spelunking in Lee County.

"You're almost yourself again, Ave."

"You think?"

"I knew when you saw her, you'd come around."

"Yeah, you're right."

"The phone isn't your thing. Long letters bore you. Besides, you had to stew before you let Etta go. It's your way."

I put my arms around Theodore, so grateful for his friendship. Who drops their own vacation plans to suffer through a teenage wedding? Who else stays upbeat and sunny for me when I give in to my dire predictions? There is one constant in my meltdowns, and one person who consistently pulls me from the abyss: the one and only Theodore Tipton.

"So, what do you think of Schilpario?" I ask.

"I want to know where they're hiding Heidi."

"It *is* just like *Heidi,* isn't it?"

"Any minute I think your father is going to send me to the attic with a bowl of hot milk and melted cheese. Remember that?"

"That's all that poor kid ate, goat's milk, cheese, and every once in a while a slab of crusty bread." I can't believe I remember the story so well.

"The town is amazing. I love the architecture, and the people are so interesting."

"Thank you for coming all this way."

"First of all, I had no choice. You were suicidal. Second, who gives a flying fig about Lake Tahoe? I can rent *Guys and Dolls* if I get a yen for gambling Reno-style. No, this is big. This is your kid's wedding, and I belong here. I'm her godfather, for Godsakes. Who else could give a kick-ass toast this high above sea level?"

"No one."

"Damn right."

"Giacomina said she's making risotto tonight."

"I want those Italian babes slaving over the stove every moment I'm here. I want local dishes out the yin-yang. Before we head down, can you show me the field of cockerbells?"

"Bluebells. No. It's in the other direction. Way way way over there."

"I get it now." Theodore laughs.

"What?"

"How you got entangled with Pete Rutledge up here. It's like the rest of the world doesn't exist."

Theodore and I get back just in time to wash up for dinner. It's amazing to me, how I can bounce back when I'm on my home turf. Everything about these Alps soothes me: the air, the fragrant nettle, and the water, so clear and icy that it cleanses the deepest part of me. Jack meets us in the hallway on our way to the dining room.

"Stefano's here."

"I thought he was coming tomorrow."

"He wanted to see us tonight."

"Have you talked to him?"

"For two hours."

"Good. He's warmed up," I tell my husband.

"Back off, Kitten with a Whip. This is your future son-in-law. Leave some flesh on him for the ceremony," Theodore reminds me.

"Oh, I will."

This house has never been so quiet. I think even the stones in the wall are frightened that I may tear this place down board by board when confronted with the man who stole my daughter from the University of Virginia, Cracker's Neck Holler, and the American Academy of Future Architects.

The dining room is set for dinner. Stefano stands near the windows

alone. He looks out as though he is watching something, but it is suppertime, and Via Scalina is empty.

"Stefano."

"Hello, Mrs. MacChesney." He extends his hand.

I embrace him instead. "Thank you for your letter. You covered
every detail. So I'm going to make it short and sweet. I wish you all the
happiness in the world."

"Etta told me you reconciled."

"We did. Thank God."

"I'm sorry if we caused you any pain."

"Oh, you did. But I'm getting over it."

"I will take good care of Etta."

"I know you will. And I know she'll take good care of you. But I
want you to promise me something."

"Of course."

"I want her to finish college. It's very important that she have her
education."

"I agree, and so does she."

"Don't let that fall by the wayside, or I will have to get on a plane,
come over here, and make your life a living hell."

"Yes ma'am."

Theodore has thrown himself into the local culture and has arranged
to go down to Bergamo with Stefano, Etta, and Jack. Papa insists that
I rest before the wedding, and I agree I need it. I would like to look
good in the photographs, and when you're over fifty, that requires an
additional four hours of sleep per night. I remind myself that all the
great Italian beauties are luminous in their fifties. There is a reason I
keep a picture of Sophia Loren in my wallet. She is over ten years
older than me but still the most gorgeous dish on the continental
menu. My Etta trauma has put me in the smallest size I've worn since
I was a teenager, and what Mother Nature streaked through my hair
has turned a natural chestnut brown at the behest of Lady Clairol. I'm

going to look good on Saturday, maybe the best I've ever looked. I'm wearing a pewter-gray party dress with a full skirt (my mother's, of course), and if I'm feeling daring, I'll wear a gardenia in my upsweep.

I love the mirrors in my father's house, because they are old and mottled and give off a golden aura that blurs lines and wrinkles. At my age I thank God and the Italian gene pool for my strong nose and jaw, because, as my mother promised, they hold everything up and take off ten years when you really need it.

"Ave, you have company!" Nonna shouts from the kitchen. No one has seen her for days. She's baking the wedding cake, and evidently, it takes more concentration than cracking World War II spy codes. I skip down the stairs, finally feeling myself again. I bounce into the kitchen and stop short.

"Pete?"

"Ave."

"Oh my God. What are you doing here?"

"Etta invited me to her wedding." Pete Rutledge smiles.

"She did?"

"She didn't tell you?"

"No."

"Well, it's all right with you, isn't it?"

"Yes, absolutely. It's wonderful that you came," I tell him. "It all happened so fast. She was going to go to college this fall and came over here for a final vacation, and fell in love, and here we all are, and here you are, and oh my God. Where's Gina?"

"We're getting divorced."

"No!"

"It didn't work out."

Now, Nonna is listening to all of this, even though she doesn't speak English. She looks at me, expecting a translation. Instead, I tell her that I am going to go for a walk with Pete. She shrugs and goes back to forming cherubs out of marzipan.

Pete and I walk almost instinctively up to the road beside the chapel of the angels. I try to swerve us up toward the rec center so I can show him the new ice rink, but he takes my arm and leads me to the old stone path that goes up the mountain.

"Where are we going?" I ask him.

"I don't know. Let's not plan it."

"Jack is in Bergamo. He'll be back tonight." I say this peppily, though what I'm really saying is, You may be divorced, but I am still very married, so please obey the rules.

"Great. I'd like to see him."

"So, what happened with Gina?"

"You can't get married to get married. You have to want it badly. I really think that's what makes it work."

"Who wasn't it working for?"

"Both of us. I travel a lot, and it seemed that whenever I left and returned, we started all over again, instead of picking up on what we had built. It was strange. I thought I loved her, I hoped she loved me, but we both found out that marriage is another matter entirely. It has to work separately from love, almost. Don't you agree?"

"I do, I guess."

"You don't sound so sure."

"The older I get, the more I believe in luck."

Pete and I catch up on his work as we climb the path. He keeps one foot in the marble business and one in academia at NYU. He finally took an apartment in New York City near Washington Square Park (and, therefore, Theodore). He comes to Italy a lot, mostly because he loves it, but often on business.

"Where are we going?" I ask, but I can tell where we're going from the direction we're taking. He's climbing up toward the field of bluebells.

"You know."

"This is a bad idea." I stop on the path.

"What?" he says innocently.

"The altitude is bad up there. Makes me do things I shouldn't do." Then I breathe deeply. "Things I don't want to do," I correct myself.

"Are you sure?"

"Yes. I love my husband. He's really the man for me. Of course, it's taken me almost twenty years to figure it out. No matter what happens, no matter what I do, he stays true. He was there when I went through menopause and had hot flashes so bad I almost drove my Jeep into Powell Valley Lake to cool off. When my friend Spec died, it was like losing my father, and Jack was there to comfort me. When the call came that our eighteen-year-old daughter was getting married, he held me together when I was falling apart. Maybe I have limited experience in these matters, but I don't think it gets any better than Jack MacChesney."

"I understand," Pete says quietly.

"So, the truth is, I'll never go back up there. Not with you, not alone. Not with anybody. I want to remember what it was, how it was, with you. We can have that, but that's all we can have. Okay?"

"Okay."

As we walk down the path back to town, I am thinking one thing, and one thing only: wait until my daughter gets home.

I help Giacomina clear the dinner dishes. The crew returned from Bergamo, happily surprised to find Pete Rutledge at the dinner table, but then thrilled as the wine flowed and stories of Etta's first trip to Italy when she was little and Pete's trip to Big Stone Gap were told in Technicolor detail amid much laughter.

Theodore comes up behind me at the sink. "We need to talk," he whispers.

"I'm almost done."

"Now." Theodore takes my arm and pulls me out the kitchen door. "Are you trying to sandbag me? Why didn't you tell me you invited Pete? You shouldn't scare me in this high an altitude."

"I didn't invite him. Etta did."

"Why would he come, even if she invited him? What does he want?"

"Me," I joke. "I thought I'd tell Jack that it's over between us at Etta's wedding and then I'd ride off on a donkey down the Alps with Pete."

"The way he looks at you, he wouldn't mind it."

"That's all in the past."

"Yeah, well, this is the Land That Time Forgot, so you better be careful."

Etta turns in early so she'll be rested for her wedding day. I give her a few moments to get ready for bed before I go in to say good night. She is sitting up in bed reading.

"Am I interrupting?"

"Not at all."

"What are you reading?"

"Shakespeare's *As You Like It* in Italian."

"Why did you pick that one?"

"Stefano gave it to me. It's about these characters who are displaced and find their way by falling in love."

"Sounds interesting."

"You know, all of Shakespeare's plays end in either a funeral or a wedding?"

"I remember that."

"It's almost as if the two most important days in your life are when you're murried and when you're buried." Etta smiles.

"We never did have our big talk about sex, did we?" I ask my daughter.

"Sure we did. In bits and pieces, here and there, over the years. I got the facts, Ma. Don't worry."

"You know, there never is a perfect moment to have that discussion. Believe me, I've been working on *that* one for seven years."

"You did great, Ma."

"I didn't come in here for you to tell me how great I am. I came in here to tell you how wonderful *you* are. It's been a great privilege to be your mother. I was thinking that I always made a big deal out of everything you did wrong, instead of honoring all the things you did right. And now I know what a waste of time it is to focus on the things that really don't matter. It took two children to teach me that. I'm just glad I got the lesson before you checked me into Heritage Hall Nursing Home to live out my days."

Etta throws back her head and laughs. "I won't put you in a home."

"Never promise your mother *that*. I may very well end up there making fudge with the Tuckett sisters."

"You're young, Ma."

"Thank you. I never thought I'd think that was a compliment, but by God, I'll take it."

"Ma, I love Stefano so much."

"I know you do."

"We know we're young, but we feel ready."

"Then it will work, honey. It works when you make it work."

"Would you marry Dad again?"

"Absolutely. We're very different, but somehow we admire our differences instead of letting them annoy us. And the real truth is, he's a great man. They don't make them any finer than your father, so why would I choose anyone else?"

Etta looks at me for a moment as though she wants to ask me something; and I've known this girl since the day she was born, so I know what she wants to know.

"Why did you invite Pete?" I ask her.

"He's such a part of Italy to me. That summer we were here. I remember the trip to his marble quarry and when he took us to Florence on the train."

"You remember all that?"

"Oh yeah. He made you happy again, Ma. After Joe died, you

hardly ever laughed. And when we came over that summer, you started to smile again. And one night, you even danced. That's when I knew you *could* be happy."

"Pete was, he is, a good friend." I look at Etta. "And that's all he was. A friend."

"I figured that, Ma."

"It's true," I tell her. "It was nice of you to ask him to come. Dad likes him too."

"I know! See, even that was meant to happen. Dad made a good friend because you did."

"Is that what the stars tell you?" I ask her.

"I don't need stars to tell me that." Etta looks at me seriously. "Do you have advice for me, Ma?"

"You really want my advice?"

"Sure."

"Well, I would just be patient with Stefano. He grew up very differently from you. He didn't have a mother and father, and that created a void in him that no one can fill. I know this because I went through it. When my mother died, leaving behind a letter that told me that Mario Barbari was my father, not Fred Mulligan, it took me a long time to understand what had happened and what it meant. And Stefano will spend much of his life trying to understand why things happened to him the way they did. And if you're smart, and you are, and if you're like your father, and you are, you'll know how to handle it."

"How did Dad handle it?"

"He let me be sad about it. And he listened. And he never tried to make up for what I didn't have, he just loved me for who I am, knowing that my sadness was part of me."

"I'll remember that."

"Ma, do I have everything?" Etta asks me.

"You did a more thorough job packing than Aunt Iva Lou did when she came to Italy when you were fifteen."

"That good?" Etta smiles.

"That good," I tell her. "You're going to have the best honeymoon. Rimini is perfect."

"Thank you for everything, Ma. For coming over and for your support."

"I have something for you." I give Etta a package wrapped in white paper with a pink satin ribbon.

Etta tears into it. "An empty book?" she says, flipping through the leather-bound journal.

"Your dad and I—"

"It's my own anniversary book! Isn't it, Ma? I always loved that you and Dad wrote to each other every year."

I try not to cry, but I realize now that she noticed everything, including the good stuff. All these years we watched Etta closely, and the whole time she was watching us. Maybe she is ready to write her own story. "I got the one with the extra pages, since you're getting married so young," I joke. "Dad and I went with a slimmer volume, since we got married later in life." Etta and I laugh.

"And one more thing. I don't want you to be scared about having children. We lost Joe, but it was out of our hands. I still don't understand why, but even if I knew why, I wouldn't trade one day of the time we had with him."

"Me either," Etta says quietly.

"If you can, don't make any decisions based upon fear. Try to choose the big things out of love, and I don't think you'll ever go wrong."

Etta and I hold each other for a very long time. Parenthood, the least permanent job in the world, just ended for each of us, and a new story begins tonight. This next chapter ought to be a doozy.

Etta and Stefano's wedding day, September 3, 1998, is the most beautiful day I have ever seen. The cobblestones on Via Scalina, on the way to La Capella di Santa Chiara, glisten. The sky is aquamarine blue without a cloud, and the air is cool enough to wrap yards of silver taffeta over my shoulders like a countess. My husband looks so handsome in his Italian-cut navy blue pin-striped suit with the red handkerchief. We didn't say a word as we got ready this morning. He just kissed me every chance he got.

Zia Meoli and Zio Pietro are sitting in the front row of the chapel. Before the procession begins, I go up the stairs to the tiny choir loft and say a prayer by the stained-glass window of the Blessed Mother that my great-grandfather designed and installed so many years ago. I pray to my mother and to Ave Maria Albricci, who took care of my mother when she was alone with only me inside of her to keep her company. Jack comes up the stairs to tell me it's time for the service to begin.

Don Andrea, the priest who married Jack and me, stands at the altar. The alpine air must be good for him; he seems as robust as the day he married us. Etta has asked her father and me to walk her down the aisle. We are preceded by Federica's daughter, Giuliana, who wears a pink tulle dress and carries a small bouquet of edelweiss and is followed by Chiara, in a simple pale green silk sheath with a small wreath of boxwood.

Giacomina is the matron of honor, and Papa is the best man. Stefano, in a black Edwardian suit with a pale blue tie, never takes his gaze off our daughter as we walk down the aisle. When we reach the altar, I kiss my girl and step away. My husband kisses her and holds her for a very long time. Only I could know what these two mean to each other, because I have seen from the moment she was born that she felt understood and heard by her father, treasured by him. They have always been the best of friends, and it gives me great comfort that she has the very thing I was missing all of my life.

I expect to cry through the ceremony, but I don't. I listen carefully to the instructions that the priest gives my daughter and my son-in-law. He tells them that love is central to a marriage, but forgiveness is the one element that makes a marriage last. Jack takes my hand when he hears this, because he and I know from experience that it is the truth.

"Isn't she beautiful?" my husband whispers to me. I nod. And truly, in all of my life, I have never seen a woman so lovely. Etta's long brown hair is twisted into a low chignon and set in place with tiny clusters of edelweiss. She is tall and slim, almost her husband's height, and as they stand beside each other, I see that she is every bit his equal. Her eyes are the same deep green as her grandma Mac-Chesney's, the Scottish freckles peek through the pressed powder, and her rosebud mouth is set with determination.

Theodore must know what I am thinking. He reaches over the back of the pew and takes my hand. I don't let go. I turn around and smile at him. A couple of rows behind Theodore is Pete Rutledge, who smiles at me. Here, under one roof, are the most important men in my life, who have loved, accepted, and changed me. What sort of fate has brought us all together? What strange karma? Why does it feel that we have all been here before, in this chapel that smells of frankincense and white lilies? What connects us all is in some cases a blood tie, but more often than that, it's some centrifugal force that throws us together for reasons we can never understand. Did my mother have to leave these mountains to go to the hills of Southwest Virginia so I might find Jack MacChesney? And why, after all of that, does my daughter return to the very place where her grandmother was born to find her true love? I almost laugh, but I catch myself. We Vilminore women, we always take the long way home.

I saved up all my tears for the flight home. Jack tries to nap but wakes up intermittently just to see if I've dried up yet—I haven't. Etta and Stefano left for Rimini on their honeymoon, and for a few seconds, I thought I would jump in the car and join them. Jack held me back, or maybe he was resisting the urge himself. He and I have spent so much of our time and most of our conversation on Etta for the past eighteen years. So it seems strange that we hardly spoke about her this week. We didn't stay up and talk through the night before the wedding, we didn't analyze it at breakfast that morning, and we didn't say a word on the way to the church. Of course, this is my husband's way; when something really matters to him, he can't talk about it.

I take a walk up and down the aisles to stretch my legs. When I return, Jack is awake. I slide down into the seat next to him and lie across his chest. He encircles me with his arms, and I rest my hands on his.

"Why are we going home?" he asks me.

"Because we live there," I tell him.

"Our daughter's in Italy. What are we going to do back home?"

Jack is right. Pearl is in Boston, and with Janine in place managing the pharmacies, they don't need me. Spec is gone, and when he died, my anchor died with him. I love the old stone house in Cracker's Neck Holler, but it was made for a family, a family to eat in that kitchen by the fire, to rest in those rooms with the big windows, and to run in the field that faces Stone Mountain. The woods will get lonely with two middle-aged mountaineers passing through once in a while when the mood hits them. The woods should be filled with kids, hanging from trees, fishing in the stream, and eating the wild strawberries from the thicket by the Lonesome Pine tree.

"What do you want to do?" I ask him.

"Are you wide open to any possibility?"

"What does that mean?"

"Can you think with your heart, not your head?"

"I could."

"What are we going to do with the second half of our lives? I say half because I'm being generous." Jack laughs.

"I haven't thought about it."

"I have a little."

"Since when?"

"Since Etta told us she was getting married."

"We can't follow her to Italy," I tell him. The last thing a good mother does is horn in on her newlywed daughter.

"I don't want to follow her, I just want to be closer."

"Do you think the Olive Oil King still wants you?"

"Maybe."

As Jack holds me, I turn my head to look out the window, but there is nothing to see. It's as though a black velvet drape has been drawn on our window, in the dead of night. I know the Atlantic Ocean is under us and somewhere, buried behind these clouds, is the moon. In my husband's arms, these are the only two things I am sure of.

"We have to redream," I say.

"What do you mean?"

"Well, you have to be honest, to start with. You have to admit that one story has ended and another one needs to begin."

"We know one story has ended, Ave. What do you want that you haven't had?"

"That's a hard question for a goal-oriented girl. I always tried hard for what I wanted, and when I got it, I figured I was lucky."

"Do you think I'm part of your future?" Jack asks without an ounce of self-pity. "If you could, would you choose me all over again?"

"Maybe a thousand times."

"Good. Because I choose you every morning."

Jack settles in his seat to go back to sleep. I pull his arms close to me as he sleeps, and I decide to be completely open to his dreams and encourage him to follow his heart. If we wind up in a Tuscan olive grove, that is fine with me.

"Are you on your honeymoon?" a woman with white hair asks me as she passes.

"Yes," I tell her.

"It's always sweeter the second time around."

"First time wasn't so bad either," I say.

"Don't tell *him* that," she whispers, pointing to Jack Mac, and proceeds down the aisle.

I lean back on my husband and do what I always do, which is inhale deeply and exhale until my breathing is in rhythm with his. Of all the decisions I have made in my life, marrying Jack MacChesney was certainly the best.

As we fly through the night sky, it's good to know I did something right. Love may not be enough, but when it's right, it's plenty.

ACKNOWLEDGMENTS

*How lucky I am to have Anthony Trigiani for my father! He has the best comic timing of anyone I have ever met. My dad is a big risk taker, and never seemed to care what the outcome of taking a chance would be, just that it was important to try. That sort of fearlessness is catching, and it made me ask the question, "What's the worst thing that could happen if I try this new thing?" When my father taught me how to drive, he said something at a yellow light that I always remember: "He who hesitates is lost." It never made much sense to me, until I understood the heart of that sentiment: make a decision and move. It works in driving and it works in life.*

*At magnificent Random House, my everlasting thanks to my Editor Queen, Lee Boudreaux, the fabulous Ann Godoff, Prince of Publicity Todd Doughty (someone please find anyone on earth who works harder!), Dan Rembert, Beth Pearson, Ivan Held, Laura Ford, Libby McGuire, Victoria Wong, Allison Heilborn, Ed Brazos, Eileen Becker, Steve Wallace, Sherry Huber, and Stacy Rockwood. At Ballantine: the great team led by the amazing Gina Centrello, Maureen O'Neal, Alli-*

son Dickens, Kim Hovey, Candice Chaplin, Kathleen Spinelli, and Cindy Murray. And thank you to the irreplaceable Lorie Stoopack.

To Suzanne Gluck, the best agent on earth and an even better friend, my love and gratitude. More of the same to WMA's hit parade, including: Emily Nurkin, Karen Gerwin, Jennifer Rudolph Walsh, and Cara Stein. At ICM, more still to my champion Nancy Josephson, Jill Holwager, Ben Smith, Caroline Sparrow, Betsy Robbins, and Margaret Halton. In Movieland, I adore and thank Lou Pitt, John Farrell, Michael Pitt, Jim Powers, and Todd Steiner.

My love and thanks to the fabulous Mary Testa, Tom Dyja, Ruth Pomerance, Rosanne Cash, Bill Persky, Joanna Patton, Phyllis George, June Lawton, Larry Sanitsky, Jeanne Newman, Debra McGuire, John Melfi, Grace Naughton, Dee Emmerson, Gina Casella, Sharon Hall, Beth Thomas, Wendy Luck, Sharon Watroba Burns, Nancy Ringham, Constance Marks, Cynthia Rutledge Olson, Jasmine Guy, Susan Toepfer, Craig Fisse, Joanne Curley Kerner, Max Westler, Pamela Cannon, Dana and Richard Kirshenbaum, Marisa Acocella, Sister Jean Klene, Reg Bain, Fred Syburg, Susan and Sam Franzeskos, Jake and Jean Morrissey, Beata and Steven Baker, Brownie Polly, Aaron Hill and Susan Fales Hill, Kare Jackowski, Rhoda Dresken, Bob Kelty, Christina Avis Krauss and Sonny Grosso, Greg Cantrell, Rachel DeSario, Mary Murphy, Rita Braver, and Irene Taylor. Heaps of gratitude and love to Caroline Rhea, president of the Ave Maria Fan Club, and to the ever-true Elena Nachmanoff and Dianne Festa—my love and thanks and a big dinner that includes liquor. Thank you and love to Michael Patrick King for inflating my life raft and giving me the shove out to sea.

To the Trigiani and Stephenson families, to my Italian relatives, the Spada, Maj, and Bonicelli families, thank you. To the people of Big Stone Gap and their neighbors in the Blue Ridge and Appalachians, my everlasting gratitude for your support and readership.

And to my husband, Tim Stephenson, who shares my life and the fear dance at three A.M., thank you for everything else, so considerable in size and scope it could not fit in the state of Rhode Island.

ABOUT THE AUTHOR

ADRIANA TRIGIANI grew up in Big Stone Gap and now lives with her husband in New York City. In addition to being the bestselling author of *Big Stone Gap* and *Big Cherry Holler*, she is an award-winning playwright, television writer, and documentary filmmaker. She has written the screenplay for the film version of *Big Stone Gap*, which she will also direct.

ABOUT THE TYPE

This book was set in Electra, a typeface designed for Linotype by W. A. Dwiggins, the renowned type designer (1880–1956). Electra is a fluid typeface, avoiding the contrasts of thick and thin strokes that are prevalent in most modern typefaces.